The Fiery Wheel

BY THE SAME AUTHOR

The Fiery Wheel

by
Jean de La Hire

translated, annotated and introduced by
Brian Stableford

A Black Coat Press Book

Visit our website at www.blackcoatpress.com

ISBN 978-1-61227-217-7. First Printing. October 2013. Published by Black Coat Press, an imprint of Hollywood Comics.com, LLC, P.O. Box 17270, Encino, CA 91416.

Introduction

La Roue fulgurante by "Jean de La Hire" (Adolphe d'Espie), here translated as *The Fiery Wheel*, was first published as a *feuilleton* serial in the daily newspaper *Le Matin*, between 10 April and 23 May 1908, and was reprinted in book form later that year by Tallandier. Further editions appeared from various publishers in 1922, 1929, 1938, 1942, 1952 (as *La Soucoupe volante* [The Flying Saucer]), 1973 and 1998. The serial was a radical new departure for both the author and for the newspaper. La Hire became one of *Le Matin*'s leading provider of serials for some time thereafter, and although *La Roue fulgurante* was not the only item of *roman scientifique* [scientific fiction] he supplied to the paper, or even the only one with an interplanetary theme, it remained the most adventurous, and might have been even more adventurous had he not opted—perhaps in response to editorial pressure—to provide it with the kind of ending that he did.

The novel remains a work of considerable historical interest, as the first work of fiction to feature the theme of "alien abduction," all the more so as the abduction is effected by means of a vehicle not dissimilar to the "flying disks" or "flying saucers" that were later to be credited with so many supposedly-real abductions of that sort in the second half of the twentieth century. That coincidence is not the only remarkable thing about it, however, and its timing seems, in retrospect to be highly significant because of the strong thematic links it has with two other novels published in France in 1908: *Aventures merveilleuses de Serge Myrandhal sur la planète Mars: Sur la planète Mars*, by-lined H. (for Henri) Gayar, published on 15 June of that year and *Le Prisonnier de la planète Mars* by Gustave Le Rouge, published on 1 July.

Both of the latter novels were planned as the first parts of series, and Gayar followed up his publication on 15 July with the second volume of the *Aventures merveilleuses de Serge Myrandhal*, *Les Robinsons de la planète Mars*, while Le Rouge's *La Guerre des vampires* appeared the following year.[1] Although it seems inconceivable that any direct imitation was involved, Pierre Versins pointed out in an article appended to a 1976 reprint of *La Guerre des vampires* that an intended third part of Gayar's series did not appear in 1908, and that when Gayar eventually issued a heavily revised version of his enterprise in a single volume as *Les Robinsons de la planète Mars* (1927), by-lined "Cyrius," he removed many of the elements that overlapped with Le Rouge's original novel, evidently intent on reducing the similarity.

The timing does leave open the possibility that both Gayar and Le Rouge had been prompted to embark on their own ventures by La Hire's serial in *Le Matin*, and that they both elected to differentiate their endeavors from his by parallel narrative moves, but Versins also

---

[1] An omnibus translation of the two Le Rouge novels is available from Black Coat Press as *The Vampires of Mars*, ISBN 9781934543306. *Les Aventures merveilleuses de Serge Myrandhal* will be published by Black Coat Press in 2014. Another relevant work of the same period is Arnould Galopin's *Doctor Omega*, Black Coat Press, ISBN 97810974071114.

refers to other precedents that probably had a significant influence on the narrative strategies of all three writers—most significantly Theodore Flournoy's best-selling *Des Indes à la planète Mars* (1900; tr. as *From India to the Planet Mars*), an account by a Genevan psychologist of revelations produced by a medium, "Hélène Smith" (actually Elise Müller) while supposedly entranced, by the method of "automatic writing." Flournoy attributed the revelations in question to the medium's imagination—much to her displeasure—but she regarded them as accounts of actual other lives that she had lived in various locations, including India and Mars.

All three novelists would have been aware of the experiments with automatic writing previously carried out in the vicinity of Paris by the famous French popularizer of astronomy Camille Flammarion, in which some of his collaborators—most notably the playwright Victorien Sardou—had also produced visions of life on other planets, where human beings might be reincarnated. All three of them would also have been familiar with Flammarion's series of philosophical dialogues *Lumen*, first published in the 1860s but updated in several subsequent editions, which describes the supposed revelations of a disembodied soul free to roman the universe, observing and experiencing incarnations of other worlds very different from Earth, and with his similarly best-selling follow-up volume *Uranie* (1889; tr. as *Urania*), which contains an elaborate description of a reincarnation on Mars.

It is, however, very obvious that in *La Roue fulgurante* and its two swift successors, the inspiration of Camille Flammarion is combined with another, equally powerful if not quite as explicit: that of the English writer H. G. Wells. Wells' early scientific romances, pub-

7

lished in England between 1895 and 1901, had been rapidly and extensively translated into French, initially in the popular science magazine *La Science Illustrée*, which had a regular section *feuilleton* section under the rubric *Roman Scientifique*, and then in the upmarket literary periodical *Le Mercure de France*, founded as an organ of the Symbolist Movement, as well as in book form. Both periodicals had serialized translations of *The War of the Worlds*, which became the best-known of Wells' scientific romances in France.

Although the French naturally considered that the one and only true pioneer and paragon of *roman scientifique* was Jules Verne, there could be no doubt that Wells had injected considerable new life and energy into the genre, having never been subjected to the restraining hand of the publisher who had Verne under contract, Pierre-Jules Hetzel, who always wanted him to exercise stern imaginative moderation. Oddly enough, the nascent genre of scientific romance that formed around the nucleus of Wells' work in England was, to a large extent, similarly hampered and channeled by editorial reticence, with the result that the examples provided by his two interplanetary novels, *The War of the Worlds* and *The First Men in the Moon*, were only followed up significantly in fiction aimed at juvenile readers and a handful of vanity publications. That was not the case in America, where interplanetary fiction was popularized by Edgar Rice Burroughs after 1912 and eventually became the core of generic "science fiction," and there was a brief moment—specifically, in 1908—when it seemed possible that French *roman scientifique* would take the same direction, led in fairly spectacular fashion by *La Roue fulgurante*.

In fact, it did not, and the trio of novels that attempted to fuse the influences of Flammarion and Wells into a distinctly French kind of space fiction flattered mainly to deceive. In France as in Britain, the entire genre of speculative fiction—and the interplanetary subgenre in particular—having been tested, was deemed to have insufficient mass appeal, and moved to the margins of the literary marketplace. At least it was tested, however, and very fairly, *Le Matin* being the best showcase it could possibly have had. Nor was the rejection sudden; La Hire tried very hard indeed to establish *roman scientifique* as a standard genre in *Le Matin*'s repertoire, and to establish interplanetary fiction as a central pillar of that genre, but he was only partly successful. The paper's star *feuilletonist*, Gaston Leroux, whose career ran alongside La Hire's, became far more celebrated for his detective stories, but he routinely introduced elements of *roman scientifique* into his thrillers, even though he fought shy of interplanetary fiction, and his work was far more inventive than that of La Hire's immediate predecessor, Michel Zevaco—the dedicatee of *La Roue fulgurante*—who specialized in "*cape et épée*" historical romances of the kind developed half a century earlier by Paul Féval.

La Hire wrote *cape et épée* fiction and crime fiction too, as well as working in other genres on a prolific scale, but he made a swift return to *roman scientifique* in the pages of *Le Matin* with the earthbound *L'Homme qui peut vivre dans l'eau* [The Man Who Could Live Under Water] (1908; reprinted 1910), to which he provided an interplanetary sequel in *Le Mystère des XV* (1911)[2],

---

[2] tr. as *The Nyctalope on Mars,* Black Coat Press, ISBN 9781934543467.

which is also an explicit sequel to Wells' *The War of the Worlds*. That was his last throw of the Wellsian dice for some time, however, and although the hero of *Le Mystère des XV* was reincarnated for a long-running series in 1920[3], when the interruption of the Great War had concluded—shortly after La Hire had published a Wellsian novel, *Joe Rollon, l'autre homme invisible* [Joe Rollon, the Other Invisible Man] (1919 as by Edmond Cazal)—the elements of *roman scientifique* that were initially prominent in the series were gradually de-emphasized relative to its more conventional thriller components as it extended further. As the 1920s wore on, La Hire was gradually marginalized himself, eventually no longer able to address himself routinely to *Le Matin*'s vast readership.

Just as La Hire was not the only author to attempt a fusion of Wellsian and Flammarionesque ideas, so *Le Matin* was not the only mass-market newspaper to experiment with *roman scientifique*. Its chief rival, *Le Journal*, which fostered a more sophisticated image, gave a much higher priority to short fiction than long serials, and that restricted the scope of the more extravagant forms of *roman scientifique* considerably, but it did feature a number of very striking short serials by Edmond Haraucourt between 1906 and 1910, translations of which can be found in the Black Coat Press collection

---

[3] Several further works in the Nyctalope series have been translated and published by Black Coat Press, including *The Nyctalope vs. Lucifer*, ISBN 9781932983982), *Enter the Nyctalope* (ISBN 9781934543993), *The Nyctalope Steps In* (ISBN 9781612270289), *Night of the Nyctalope* (ISBN 9781612271026) the interplanetary romance *Le Roi de la nuit* (included in *Return of the Nyctalope*, ISBN 9781612272115).

Illusions of Immortality.[4] There too, however, the eventual verdict was negative, and such imaginative boldness had been eclipsed even before the social context was dramatically transformed in August 1914 by the outbreak of the Great War. Writers who experimented with *roman scientifique* in book form also found it difficult to follow up their initial experiments, including Maurice Renard, who published *Le Doctor Lerne, sous-dieu* in 1908 [5] and might also have taken a hint from La Hire in writing his far more sophisticated—but conscientiously earthbound—fantasy of alien abduction *Le Péril bleu* (1912).[6]

It is not surprising, in retrospect, that the experiment connected by La Hire and *Le Matin* failed, in spite of the rapid support it obtained from a handful of other writers, including Gayar and Le Rouge—the former of whom only wrote a handful of conspicuously unadventurous novels after abandoning his projected Martian trilogy, while the latter drastically reduced the scope and frequency of the *roman scientifique* component of his subsequent work. Indeed, some of the reasons for that failure are glaringly obvious in the pages of *La Roue fulgurante*, and must have seemed so in immediate retrospect as well as more distant and studied contemplation. The story, borne along by its own zestful impetus, runs head-first into all the problems innate in imaginatively ambitious exercises in futuristic speculation, discovering a series of logical impasses, and provoking a set of narrative problems, all of which were to cast a long shadow

---

[4] Black Coat Press, ISBN 9781612270753.
[5] tr. as *Dr. Lerne*, Black Coat Press, ISBN 9781935558156.
[6] tr. as *The Blue Peril*, Black Coat Press, ISBN 9781935558170.

over the future development of French *roman scientifique*, British scientific romance and American science fiction—and continue to afflict them, in spite of the fact that the American genre eventually contrived to obtain an enduring toehold in the bosom of mass culture.

The temptation to fuse elements of scientific and occult speculation was not entirely due to the influence of Camille Flammarion, although the existence in France of such a high-profile figure equally interested in astronomy and "spiritism," certainly enhanced the attractiveness of the fusion to writers of imaginative fiction. Indeed, the entire "occult revival" of the *fin de siècle* had been based on exactly such a fusion, whose duality was the philosophical core of Madame Blavatsky's Theosophy and the avid activities of the Society for Psychical Research. Given that the fundamental basis of the appeal of such hybrid notions was esthetic rather than rational, it is not surprising that it appealed to litterateurs willing to bite the bullet of testing the limits of imaginative fiction. The coincidence linking *La Roue fulgurante* with the novels by Gayar and Le Rouge is not the only one worth pointing out, and it is worth noting that its publication was intermediate between the British scientific romance *Lieutenant Gullivar Jones—His Vacation* (1905) by Edwin Lester Arnold and the ground-breaking American pulp magazine serial "Under the Moons of Mars" (1912), initially by-lined "Norman Bean," by Edgar Rice Burroughs, reprinted in book form as *A Princess of Mars*. Both of those novels employ a "psychic" means of space travel and both of them describe hectically colorful adventures on other planets in much the same cavalier spirit as *La Roue fulgurante*. In literary terms, La Hire has stronger affinities with Arnold and

Burroughs than with H. G. Wells or Camille Flammari-on, and the same is true of Gayar and Le Rouge.

Again, the coincidence is certainly just that; the strong similarities between the British and American works are probably due to the common influence of Rider Haggard, whose *She* (1887) had provided the first classic hybrid of occult and quasi-scientific speculation, but which was not translated into French until 1920, delaying its influence there considerably. Setting that element aside, however, the elements common to all three interplanetary romances are entirely due to parallel thought process and similar responses to new horizons of literary possibility. The fact that the American experiment proved spectacularly successful, whereas the British and French experiments failed, is probably due to a complex network of social and marketing factors, and certainly has little or nothing to do with relative differences in narrative plausibility or literary sophistication.

The difficulties involved in providing a plausible narrative framework for interplanetary fiction had been illustrated well enough by Jules Verne, whose conscientiousness would not let his voyagers in *De la Terre à la Lune* (1865; tr. as *From the Earth to the Moon*) contrive a landing on the Moon because there was no way for them to come back, and whose farther-ranging travelers in *Hector Servadac* (1877; tr. as *Off on a Comet*) eventually find their entire adventure called into question by an ending that is both enigmatic and paradoxical. La Hire was undoubtedly aware of these awkward precedents—as were Gayar and Le Rouge, and perhaps Arnold and Burroughs—and his own devices are perhaps best regarded as an attempt to get around them without having recourse to the solution that had by then become traditional in England, of inventing an arbitrary "antigravity device," as employed by the pseudonymous Chrystostom Trueman, Percy Greg and others before Wells used it—and was roundly criticized by Verne for doing so—in *The First Men in the Moon*. The device La Hire employs to bring his travelers back from Mercury is certainly no improvement on that arbitrary invention, but the means of getting them there—the *"roue fulgurante"* itself—is certainly a bold and fascinating improvisation.

Because modern UFO-enthusiasts have co-opted chapter 1 of the Biblical book of *Ezekiel* into their lore, it is tempting to think that La Hire might have borrowed his notion from there, but the word *fulgurante* does not occur in French versions of the relevant scriptural text, the description of the peculiar vortices seen by Ezekiel does not match La Hire's description of his interplanetary craft, and the angels associated with Ezekiel's "wheels" bear no resemblance whatsoever to the supposed Saturnians aboard La Hire's, so any influence can only have been remotely suggestive. The aliens in question are fascinating in themselves; although Flammarion's *Lumen* had set a high standard with regard to the imagination of radically alien physiques adapted to radically alien environments, La Hire makes a good stab in *La Roue fulgurante* of rising to that challenge, and although his Mercurians are not nearly as far-fetched, they do have a certain determined peculiarity that saves them from mere triviality. In that matter too he was to be outdone by a far more sophisticated writer, when J.-H. Rosny Aîné produced the Martians features in *Les Navigateurs de l'infini* (1925)[7], but like Maurice Renard, Rosny was probably not unaware of *Le Matin*'s seriali-

---

[7] tr. as "The Navigators of Space" in the eponymous Black Coat Press collection, ISBN 9781935558354.

zation of *La Roue fulgurante*, even if it was not a newspaper he read. The principal problem with La Hire's inventions is that the author could not follow them through, and was eventually content to leave almost everything about his aliens and their technology pusillanimously unelaborated as well as frustratingly unexplained. Renard and Rosny did far better, but it cannot be said that they overcame the difficulties completely.

La Hire's inability to make sense of his own inventions as soon as he tried to examine their logical corollaries is unfortunate, but by no means unusual for its time, and there is a certain wry virtue in the fact that he did not let it put an immediate brake on his inventive spirit, at least until he reached the climax of his story—after which, alas, the reticence he had cultivated during the writing of *La Roue fulgurante* blighted the rest of his career, insofar as his contribution to the development of *roman scientifique* is concerned. All the subsequent "wheels" he invented were considerably less fiery, but no less likely to fall off in transit and leave his plots stranded. He was one of many pioneers of speculative fiction whose imaginative reach far exceeded their logical grasp, but if that is a sin, it is more venial than deadly—at least in the eyes of readers and critics who think the reach more important, or more interesting, than the grasp. *La Roue fulgurante* is not a good book, but it is a brave one, and its flashes of ambition allow it sometimes to rise above the silliness and defy the confusion that eventually bog it down. It is, at any rate, an essential piece in the evolutionary jigsaw of 20th century speculative fiction, without which the picture would be incomplete.

This translation was made from a copy of the 1973 reprint of *La Roue fulgurante* published by J.-C. Lattès.

Brian Stableford

PART ONE
THE SATURNIANS

Chapter One
In which humans see something never seen before

It happened on the eighteenth of June. The first man to see the Fiery Wheel was a captain in the Spanish frontier-guards named José Mendès.

Preceded by his daughter Lolla and his manservant Francisco, who was carrying a heavy suitcase on his shoulder, he was calmly coming down from the fort at Montjuic toward Barcelona. The three of them were going to the railway station del Norte to catch the four-fifty train to Saragossa. The road, steep and picturesque, passes through the gardens of Miramar, overlooks the sea and the coal docks of the merchant port from a height, and then falls abruptly to the bottom of the hill, where it becomes an insanitary street.

It was three o'clock in the morning. The sun had not yet emerged from the eastern sea, but the stars were beginning to pale in the brightening dawn twilight. Captain José Mendès was smoking one of those wretched cheap cigars that the French praise in their ignorance and Spaniards of good taste never touch, and going down the steep slope slowly. He stopped momentary to detach a tenacious bramble that had clung on to the bottom of his trouser-leg. When he resumed walking, Lolla and Francisco were several strides ahead of him. Plump and short-legged, he did not hurry to catch up with them, thinking that they would wait for him at the bottom of the hill.

Suddenly, a peculiar throbbing caused him to raise his head, and what he saw rocked him back on his heels, stiff and motionless. He dropped his cigar and opened his eyes wide in amazement.

Imagine an immense wheel of fulgurant light. It was spinning in the sky with vertiginous rapidity. It hub was a black ball pierced with holes, from which beams of green light were projecting. The dazzling wheel was moving from west to east. According to the estimate subsequently made by the captain, it might have been five hundred meters above the Castillo de Montjuic.

Suddenly, it stopped, veered at right angles and set off in the direction of Montaña Pelada. The captain thought that it must have been over the Gracia quarter when he heard a noise like multiple thunderclaps.

Instinctively, he looked at where his daughter should have been, and could not believe his eyes as he saw Lolla and Francisco lifted from the ground, raised into the sky and drawn into the Fiery Wheel. Immediately, an intense light dazzled him; something struck him forcefully on the forehead, and he felt flat on the ground, where he remained, unconscious.

When he came round, he found himself in a hospital bed. The doors of the ward were wide open and stretchers were continually being brought in laden with wounded people whose moans responded to the lamentations of the orderlies, who seemed more distressed than the injured themselves.

José Mendès felt a sharp pain in his head. He put his right hand to it and touched a thick bandage. Then he remembered.

"Lolla!" he cried. "Lolla!"

No one paid any attention to him.

"Lolla! My ninã! My darling!" His eyes welled with tears, and, turning his head to the right and the left he stammered: "Where is she? Taken away by that terrible fiery thing in the sky!" And he shouted again: "Lolla! Lolla!"

"Silence!" said a passing orderly.

Was the order addressed to him? Perhaps not—but the captain understood that it would be better to shut up, to think, to observe and to wait. He choked back his tears, mastered his distress, and, after a momentary pause, looked at his neighbors. One was breathing hoarsely, his head swathed in bloody bandages. The other, sitting on his bed, met the captain gaze with a smile. He was a pale young man with bizarrely red hair.

"What happened?" the officer asked.

"What—you don't know?"

"No. I saw a fiery wheel in the sky, and as it flew away toward Montaña Pelada the earth shook and I was knocked unconscious..."

"A stone hit you on the head."

"A stone? Yes, perhaps..."

"I was with friend. We were at the corner of the Paseo de Gracia and the Grand-Via-Diagonal. We were coming back from a friend's house, where we'd been drinking and singing since dinner. Suddenly, we saw a wheel of fire heading, as you said, toward the Montaña Pelada. And we heard a terrible roar and...but you won't believe me!"

"Yes, yes! Speak!"

"Well, we saw, a hundred meters away, an entire block of big houses rise up from the ground, violently torn away, and fly up to the wheel like lightning...and disappear into a vast flame..."

"Like my daughter!" cried José Mendès.

"Your daughter was with you?"

"Yes, my daughter Lolla and my valet Francisco. They've been stolen, devoured…oh, it's terrible!"

"Calm down," said the young man, a trifle brusquely. "It's not just Lolla and Francisco who've been stolen last night in Barcelona! At any rate, a big stone hit me in the legs and I fell down unconscious, like you. My injury's not serious, though."

"Houses, you said?" stammered José Mendès.

"Yes, houses sucked up like dead leaves by a passing train…"

The captain felt weak again, and fell back inertly on his pillow.

That same day, at five o'clock in the morning, the prodigy was observed at Christiania in Norway, where the wheel sucked in a courtroom and a convent, leaving two immense holes at least a hundred meters deep.

Finally, at seven o'clock, at Astrakan on the Caspian Sea, at the mouth of the Volga, the infernal wheel lifted up a bridge like a vacuum cleaner lifting up a wisp of straw.

The telegraph and the telephone spread these items of news around the world, so effectively that, the following day, most of the major newspapers in the Old and New Worlds alike reported the incredible facts in precise detail.

On the twenty-first of June in Colombia, in a café resounding with the noise of numerous loud voices, three men were sitting silently side by side on one side of a table insolated in a corner. They were reading a newspaper dated the nineteenth. Two of them were

Americans, Arthur Brad and Jonathan Bild, and the other a Frenchman, Paul de Civrac. As they read the astonishing news, they felt the fear growing within them that was beginning to make the whole world tremble.

For twelve days, having been traveling in the interior, they had not seen a single newspaper. So, after having read one in with the adventure of the Spanish captain José Mendès was related, they spent the day scanning all the public papers on sale in Bogota. They learned nothing new, although an illustrated magazine that had appeared the day before, had a photograph of Lolla Mendès, transmitted by telegraph. The young woman was pretty, with an amusing expression of audacity.

During the nineteenth and the twentieth, the Fiery Wheel had not put in any further appearances or perpetrated any further ravages. Consulted by reporters, astronomers had proffered the opinion that the phenomenon was moving through interplanetary space and probably would not return to the terrestrial atmosphere. The astronomers of Bogota agreed with those of other observatories.

Then, at four o'clock in the afternoon, newspaper-vendors spread through the streets at a run, howling: "Fiery Wheel seen in America, in South Carolina. Half the city destroyed! More than thirty thousand victims!"

The vendors were brandishing sheets of red paper, printed with the latest news received by telegraph twenty minutes earlier. The public were snatching them out of their hands.

Then there was an indescribable terror in the town. The Fiery Wheel would come! What could they do? Where could they hide? Women ran through the streets in groups, clutching children in their arms and wailing. Men committed suicide. Others ran away with valises on their shoulders. Where were they going? A wind of madness was blowing through people's brains.

In the evening, the Stock Market, where telegrams were being posted on the walls that had arrived from New York and all over the world, was invaded. A dispatch from Paris announced that the Wheel had excavated an enormous ditch in Orleans, parallel to the Loire. A village on the outskirts of Berlin had just been annihilated. The port of Hong Kong had been ravaged. The luminous Wheel had snatched up forty-three boats with their crews as it passed. All that, including the American visitation, in four hours.

An obvious question arose: could a single Wheel, even as powerful as the one seen in Barcelona, go from France to Germany, then to China and America, or were there several of the extraordinary bolides scattered around the terrestrial globe?

The terror that was galloping around the surface of the globe was detectable in the laconic dispatches. There was no possible defense against the mysterious calamity. How and with what could it be attacked? So many irritating questions, unanswerable and, in consequence, all engendering horror and panic! What was the luminous wheel, in reality? Why did its hub, black amid the brightness, not turn with the wheel? What did the black ball contain? Inhabitants of a planet? Saturn, perhaps, or Mars? What were they like? What did they want? Were they even aware of the havoc they were causing on Earth? Of the horrible war in which no resistance was possible?

And the crazed terror of humans increased as they sought reasons for courage and composure.

Paul de Civrac, Jonathan Bild and Arthur Brad spent the night of the twenty-first and twenty-second wandering around the city. At three o'clock in the morning they felt hungry. A brightly-lit restaurant, with all its doors open, appeared before them. They went in.

It was deserted: no owner, no waiters. A dinner had been set out on a table, which no one had touched. They sat down.

When the food and wine had refreshed them—they had drunk more than unusual and their ideas were not entirely clear—Jonathan Bild said: "It's stupid. We've been leading an imbecilic life for twenty-four hours."

"True," said Arthur Brad.

"What does other people's terror matter?" Jonathan went on. "If the Martians, or the Saturnians, or the Selenites..."

Paul de Civrac interrupted to say, rather naively: "It must, in fact, be inhabited, the airship..."

"You mean the wheel!"

"Let's call the thing the Fiery Wheel, like everybody else, shall we?" said Jonathan, incisively, "and for the sake of convenience, let's suppose that they're Martians..."

"It would first be necessary to admit," Brad objected, "that the planet Mars is inhabited..."

"It's admitted!" exclaimed Bild.

Paul agreed; Brad smiled.

"Well," Bild resumed, "if the Martians are coming here, what do they want? The best thing is to be rational..."

"I'm with you, Jonathan," said Paul, gravely.

"However," said Brad, "we mustn't abandon ourselves to Muslim fatalism. I've noticed that it's never been reported that the Fiery Wheel has sucked up water. Remember the bridge at Astrakan—only the bridge leapt up, with all its arches. Not a drop of water from the Volga!"

"That's true…that's true…"

"In that case," said Brad, triumphantly, the only safe place is on water!" And the stout man lit a cigarette.

"What are you getting at?" asked Bild, ill-temperedly.

"Yes?" said Civrac, intrigued.

But Arthur Brad's only reply, to begin with, was an enigmatic smile. Then, after taking four drags on his cigarette, he repeated: "Incontestably, the only safety is to be found on water. While the world's trembling, let's go down to the Magdalena and get on a boat as soon as it becomes navigable. At Savanilla, we'll charter a ship and sail the Ocean from port to port until we hear no more mentions of these Saturnians…"

"Martians," Bild corrected.

"Damn it! Martians, Saturnians, Venusians, Selenites—what does it matter? In truth, Jonathan…"

"What about the wheel?" Paul exclaimed, in order to prevent the imminent dispute.

"What if it comes?" Brad resumed, calmly. "As soon as we see it, we jump into the sea. Dive, swim, dive, swim again…and trust me, there's every chance that…"

"Agreed!" said Jonathan, striking the table with his fist.

The three friends seemed quite excited, shaken by a continual desire to laugh.

They got up. As they were leaving, four ragged individuals came into the room and started collecting up the cutlery as they went to break open the cash-register.

"There are looters in Bogota!" said Brad, laughing.

"And firing squads!" said Bild.

Indeed, gunshots rang out, mingled with the howls of a frightened population. There were occasional houses on fire in the streets through which they passed. Civrac thought briefly about the valises they had left at the hotel. They only contained clothes, however; all of the three friends' money was in letters of credit.

A trivial loss, Paul thought. *At least we have free hands—a good way to travel.*

He dropped behind momentarily to light a cigarette, and then ran to catch up with his friends, at the sight of whom he could not help laughing. Jonathan Bild prided himself on being thin, bony and tall; Arthur Brad, by contrast, was short and stout.

They were going across a vast deserted square on the edge of the city when the sky, feebly illuminated by the dawn twilight, suddenly lit up violently.

Paul looked up. "The Fiery Wheel!" he cried.

The terror that ran through his body rendered his mind absolutely lucid. Bild and Brad came to a stop, after moving closer to him, looking up into the sky in bewilderment.

It was indeed the luminous wheel with the black hub described by Captain José Mendès. It was descending, directly above the three men. They stood shoulder to shoulder, trembling.

And suddenly, to his horror, Paul found himself lifted from the ground, into the air, drawn upwards. He perceived, vaguely, that Bild and Brad were rising up with him...

There was a blinding light, and he lost consciousness.

Chapter Two
In which a mysterious individual makes mysterious promises

While these amazing things were happening in Colombia, the entire world was in chaos. In France, especially, where the revolutionary spirit is excited more readily than in other nations, the people were agitated, urged on by leaders for whom anything is an opportunity for political demonstrations. The government understood the necessity of reassuring public opinion.

On the evening of the twenty-first of June, the President of the Council, the Minister of the Interior, called a meeting in his office in the Place Beauvau of some twenty individuals, among whom were all the Ministers; the Military Governor of Paris; Monsieur Torpène, Prefect of Police; the illustrious astronomer Constant Brularion; and Professor Martial of the Academy of Sciences. That assembly of important politicians, military men and scientists was to examine the situation and make a decision that would be ratified the next day by the President of the Republic.

After a few emotional words, conventionally diplomatic in their imprecision, the Minister of the Interior gave the floor to Constant Brularion. The astronomer, by contrast, was succinct and precise.

"I don't know anything; we don't know anything; nobody knows anything. The Fiery Wheel is an unprecedented phenomenon. Of what is the frightful wheel composed? Where does it come from? Where is it going? Will it remain in our atmosphere for long? If so, how long? If not, should we be afraid that it will come back? No answer is possible to these questions, nor to the other questions that people might ask on the subject..."

There was a somewhat embarrassed silence.

"So be it!" said the Minister of War. "But if we can't explain the Fiery Wheel, can we at least fight it!"

"With what?" Brularion replied, unable to help shrugging his shoulders.

"Cannons..."

"Children's toys, General. The Fiery Wheel appears, ravages, disappears. Where will it appear? When? At what height? That's what we'd need to know in advance in order to aim your cannons and fire them." Brularion shrugged again, this time with utter disrespect.

The discussion then became somewhat confused. Thanks to their old parliamentary habits, the ministers had no hesitation about all speaking at the same time, in excited exclamations, ironic interrogations or fine sonorous and cadenced phrases—all devoid of meaning in the circumstances, however.

Monsieur Martial timidly proffered the hypothesis that the Fiery Wheel might by a minuscule planet inhabited by only a few bizarre individuals. Ingenious as it might be, it did not alter the fact that the city of Orléans had had half of its outlying districts very really destroyed by the hypothetical individuals of the minuscule planet...

When their throats were too dry and the ministers finally thought it advisable to shut up, Monsieur Torpène, who had not yet said a word, raised his hand.

"Does the Prefect of Police have something to say?" said the Garde des Sceaux ironically. He did not like Monsieur Torpène.

"Speak, my dear Prefect," said the President of the Council.

"Messieurs," said Torpène, in a grave and tranquil voice, "only one man can give us rational explanations and effective means of action. Only one man might perhaps know what the mystery of the Fiery Wheel signifies, represents and means. The entire world has been repeating his name for months. Monsieur Brularion and Monsieur Martial know him well. The man in is Paris..."

"Dr. Ahmed Bey!" exclaimed the astronomer.

"Ahmed Bey," repeated Professor Martial.

"Yes, Ahmed Bey," said Monsieur Torpène.

"I didn't think of that," murmured the President of the Council. "Perhaps he knows..."

"If the thing is within the limits of human understanding," Torpène went on, enthusiastically, "if it's definable, Ahmed Bey is the one man who can understand and define it. I ask you, gentlemen, and the Council, to authorize me to go immediately to consult Dr. Ahmed Bey and, if possible, to get him to come here and talk to you..."

The President looked at his colleagues, who nodded assent.

"Go, then, my dear Monsieur Torpène, and ask Dr, Ahmed Bey, in the name of the Republic, to come and tell us what he knows, if anything..."

Torpène got to his feet.

Two minutes later, he leapt into a carriage, shouting to the driver: "Ahmed Bey's house!"

But who and what was Ahmed Bey, whose science and renown appeared to be as immense as his power must have been redoubtable?

A mysterious person if ever there was one.

Dr. Ahmed Bey had only been living in Paris for six months. Immediately, he had made himself known as the most powerful medium of his era. Where did he come from? No one knew. It was only evident, from his lifestyle, that he was very rich. He never treated any patients, and the title "doctor," which he put on his card, was accorded to him without anyone knowing what it implied, or whether he was really entitled to it.

He was a man of about forty, tall in stature, slim, muscular, with a thin face devoid of a beard or moustache. His complexion, his lips, the shape of his nose and his entire head were suggestive of Arabic origin. As no one had ever heard him mention his past, however, curiosity was reduced to conjectures, which did not cast any light on the dark mystery surrounding Dr. Ahmed Bey.

His truly prodigious spiritualist séances, which he held on a weekly basis, had soon been attended by all the scientific, literary and political celebrities living in or passing through Paris. As for Monsieur Torpène, the Prefect of Police, he had been admitted into the circle of initiates because he was greatly interested, with a rare depth of intelligence, in psychic and spiritualistic questions.

Dr. Ahmed Bey owned and lived in a magnificent house on the edge of the Parc Monceau. In a matter of minutes the Prefect's carriage arrived at the gate to the exterior courtyard of the house. Two colossal negroes were on watch in the courtyard night and day. They recognized the carriage and the coachman and opened the gate. Monsieur Torpène ran up the perron.

At the sight of him, the manservant on guard beneath the peristyle bowed and said: "The master is walking in the park, Monsieur. It will take me a few minutes to find him. Will Monsieur please wait in the drawing-room..."

The valet opened a door, and flicked an electric switch. Chandeliers lit up in a green and gold room; Monsieur Torpène went in.

Three minutes went by. The valet reappeared. "The Master," he said, "requests that Monsieur join him in the park..."

At that time of night the Parc Monceau was closed, but thanks to a special authorization, Dr. Ahmed Bey could go directly from his house into the park, which he thus had to himself from midnight to seven o'clock in the morning.

Torpène found the doctor in the central pathway that extends from the Boulevard Malesherbes to the Avenue Hoche. He was smoking a cigar and strolling at a slow pace with his hands behind his back. The park's electric lights were out, but the full moon was shining in the sky and the stars were scintillating in the large clearings between the trees.

"*Bonsoir*, my dear Monsieur le Préfet," said the Doctor, extending his hand to Torpène.

"*Bonsoir*, Doctor."

After shaking the hand that was offered to him, Torpène opened his mouth to speak again, eagerly, but the Doctor cut him off.

"Don't waste words! I know why you've come."

"You know?"

"Yes. There's a Ministerial Council meeting in the Place Beauvau. A thousand stupid things are being said about the Fiery Wheel."

"But..."

"Oh, my dear friend, I know you. You haven't risked a word yourself, but when the torrent of futility had run its course, you mentioned me. And here you are, as a delegate of the Council, come to consult me on the subject of the Fiery Wheel..."

"That's right!" stammered Torpène, amazed. "But how did you know?"

There was a momentary silence. Unable to restrain his impatient curiosity, however, the Prefect of Police repeated: "Yes, how did you know that the Ministers were meeting, and that they'd sent me..."

"Bah! Child's play!" Ahmed Bey replied.

"Then, Doctor, you can tell me..."

"Nothing."

"What! But..."

"Nothing!"

The Doctor stopped walking, threw away his cigar, turned abruptly to face Torpène, made a curt gesture, and said: "I don't know anything at all about the Fiery Wheel...but I will know something else, soon, that will surely permit me to elucidate the mystery and avoid our globe suffering further catastrophes. I need a few days— eight, ten, perhaps a fortnight or three weeks. When I know, I'll call you."

The Doctor paused briefly. Then, in a graver voice, he continued: "What you will see then will be so extraordinary, so astounding, so *divine*, that you will even forget the Fiery Wheel, Monsieur le Préfet."

He fell silent again, took another cigar out of his pocket, lit it, and resumed walking and smoking, his hands clasped behind his back. In a placid tone, he said: My dear Monsieur Torpène, officially, I have nothing more to say to you—but if you'll give me the pleasure of conversing with me, I shan't be going to bed for another hour..."

Torpène knew Ahmed Bey, and knew that the Doctor would not say another word about the Fiery Wheel or about the promised mysterious phenomenon. He therefore suppressed his emotion and his curiosity in order to reply, calmly: "Excuse me, Doctor, if I leave you right away, but you can guess how impatient the Ministers and scientists who are waiting for me are..."

"Go, go! And remember what I said to you..."

In the Council, there was considerable annoyance when Ahmed Bey's mysterious response had been revealed by Monsieur Torpène. The Ministers resumed making eloquent and confused speeches, trying to suppress the fear that had gripped them. Martial modified his hypothesis. Brularion shrugged his shoulders every two minutes and Torpène kept quiet.

Finally, the Council agreed on the note to be communicated to the newspapers, which read as follows:

The Ministers and a number of military and scientific experts met last night at the Place Beauvau, under the chairmanship of the Minister of the Interior and President of the Council. Monsieur Torpène, the Prefect of Police, was present at the meeting. After a profound examination of the situation created in France by the mysterious and perpetual threat of the Fiery Wheel, the Council decided to entrust the President of the Council with the drafting of a proclamation, which will be read today by the President of the Republic to the Chambre des Députés and the Sénat, meeting in extraordinary session, and will then be posted in all the communes in France.

That proclamation will precede practical measures that will be ordered and taken incessantly throughout the territory, with the collaboration of the army.

When the communiqué was finished, copies were handed to the reporters who were waiting in an adjacent room, who immediately hastened to their respective newspapers.

Then, congratulating themselves but not without a dull and atrocious anxiety, and not without a certain shame at their absolute impotence, the members of the extraordinary Council went their separate ways. The chronometers marked three forty-seven a.m.

At that exact moment, two-thirds of the way to the antipodes of the Place Beauvau, in Colombia, the Fiery Wheel picked up three human beings named Paul de Civrac, Arthur Brad and Jonathan Bild, like three wisps of straw, in the same fashion that the beautiful Lolla Mendès and the manservant Francisco had been lifted up in Barcelona.

Chapter Three
In which the fiery wheel yields some of its secrets

Paul de Civrac never knew how long his insensibility lasted. When he recovered consciousness, his first action, in advance of any reflection, was to open his eyes—but he closed them again abruptly, dazzled.

He kept his eyelids closed for several minutes then, trying to take account of his situation. It was impossible for him to move his head, his arms or his legs. His entire body was stuck to a flat surface, his legs straight and his arms outstretched. He could feel the back of his neck, his elbows, his hands, his back, his thighs, his calves and his heels indissolubly glued to a soft, cold substance. His left cheek was lashed by a violent and continuous wind. His ears were resounding with an enormous hum. Through his closed eyelids he could see a uniform pink hue, as when one turns non's closed eyes toward the midday sun.

Meanwhile, blood was throbbing in his ears, and he was having great difficulty breathing. It seemed to him that he was short of air. His breathing was abrupt and harsh, but without any sound in his nose or throat.

He opened his mouth and uttered a cry. Two other cries replied, one from his right and the other from above.

"Arthur! Jonathan!" he shouted.

"Paul! Paul!"

Bild and Brad were alive—but he was surprised to hear their voices, and his own, as if they were coming from far away, thinly, as if produced in a rarefied atmosphere. And that continual oppression in his lungs!

Of course! he thought. *We're outside the layer of breathable air that surrounds the Earth. If we continue to draw away, we'll die...*

Then, very gently and gradually, he opened his eyes, in order to accustom himself progressively to the bright light that had dazzled him at first. It required a good quarter of an hour simply to maintain his eyes half-open. He could not see anything in front of him except the immensity of the sky—but it was an extraordinarily luminous sky. He was about to make the attempt to rotate his eyes in their orbits, in order to see as far as possible around him, when he felt himself slowly sinking into the substance to the surface of which he was stuck.

"Paul! Paul!" cried the implausibly thin voices of Bild and Brad simultaneously.

"Arthur! Jonathan!"

He had scarcely finished that desperate appeal when the substance on which he was lying disappeared from beneath him. He fell. Other human bodies collided with his own, and he suddenly found himself sitting in the darkness. Something was bruising his side; with one of his hands, now free, he felt it. It was a human foot enclosed in a large boot.

"Paul!" said a voice to his left.

"Paul!" said another voice, behind him.

"Jonathan! Arthur!" he exclaimed. "Are you there?"

"Yes."

"Yes."

"Injured?"

"No. Are you?"

"Me neither."

"I'm having difficulty breathing."

"Me too."

"Me too! We're in thin air. It hurts the lungs..."

"And our voice? Have you noticed our voices?"

Indeed, they sounded bizarre, tenuous and distant, so that they had to shout in order to hear something quavering and indecisive.

"It's the thinness of the air," Paul repeated.

"Yes, obviously..."

"But for God's sake, where are we?" said the voice of the massive Jonathan Bild, as fragile as that of a little girl.

"Yes, where are we?" Brad added.

"I don't know," Paul replied.

There was a moment's silence. Then Bild said, decisively: "We're inside the hub of the Martian wheel."

"Or Saturnian," said Arthur.

"Have you got any matches? Damn, how dry and jerky my breathing is! Will we end up getting used to it if it lasts?"

"Yes, certainly, after a few hours."

There was another brief silence...two scratching sounds...a light. Paul turned round excitedly, and the bewildered faces of his friends appeared to him. Bild and Brad were each holding a lighted match, but the two little flames were pale and minuscule, and the thin sulfurous wicks were being rapidly consumed.

All three looked at one another, without saying a word. The matches went out simultaneously.

"Wait!" said Paul. "I have my pocket torch."

He took an apparatus from his pocket shaped like a cigar-case. He pressed a button. A little beam of light sprang forth. He got to his feet abruptly—but to his great amazement, the perfectly normal effort he exerted caused him to leap into the air.

"Where are we?" Jonathan Bild repeated.

He stood up at the same time as Arthur Brad, and Paul saw them both leap up a meter above the surface on which they had been sitting. They came down on their feet, and Paul noticed that their feet, like his, sank slightly into the substance on which they were standing, like the feet of a light bird sinking into an eiderdown.

Their hairless faces were pale; Arthur's blue eyes were blinking, and Jonathan's dark ones were sparkling with an extraordinary gleam; their hands were trembling.

Paul took a step toward them, but the movement launched him violently into Arthur Brad's abdomen.

"Ah! What are you doing, Paul!"

"I understand," said Paul. "Don't get annoyed. The air's thin here—the atmosphere is different from the Earth's. Density and weight are different too, do you see? Remember that, according to reliable calculations, a terrestrial kilogram transported to the surface of Mars would only eight 376 grams!"

"A third as much!"

"Yes—well, it's the same thing here. We weigh less than we do on Earth…and as our muscles are exerting the same force…you see?"

"Yes. The muscular force exerted to take a step…"

"Causes us to make a big leap. Exactly! We have to measure our efforts… educate our muscles…"

Paul was proud to observe that he was the calmest of the three. He was conscious that his possession of the electric torch, his self-composure and his scientific knowledge made him the leader of their little group. From now on, he had to think, speak and act like a leader.

He felt extraordinarily overexcited. He had no doubt that the excitement in question, which he could also see on the faces of Bild and Brad, was caused by the ambient air, which was certainly richer in oxygen than the terrestrial atmosphere.

"We'll get used to it..."

It seemed to him, in fact, that his respiration, although still halting and harsh, was less difficult, and hardly painful at all. They were beginning to adapt to the strange environment, in which they might have to live for a long time.

"Right, let's see!" Bild exclaimed. "Can you tell us where we are?"

"Of course," Paul replied, violently. And, measuring his gestures with circumspection, he set about examining their surroundings.

The exploration was brief. They were inside a bizarrely-formed chamber. Imagine a polyhedral box with twenty faces about five meters high; put yourself inside it, standing on one of the triangular faces, and you will have an idea of the appearance their prison presented to them—for it was definitely a prison. No door, no window, no opening of any kind was visible. The walls were smooth; but the most astonishing thing was the substance of which the walls were made. One could not describe it better than by comparing it to an extremely dense fog, dark gray in color—the walls of a dense cloud!

How had they been precipitated into that geometric cell? A mystery.

With the butt of his revolver, Paul rapped on the walls that he could reach. His revolver and his arm sank into them soundlessly.

Suddenly, like a gap opening in clouds, a large opening appeared in front of them, through which a flood of dazzling light came.

Instinctively, without a moment's hesitation, the three friends leapt into that gap together—but they had not taken the new conditions of weight into account. Their unmeasured bound took them a long way, and instead of taking a long step outside the cell, they remained suspended in the air for half a minute, gliding toward a kind of gray dome, into which they were thrown. They penetrated into a dark and suffocating environment, which rejected them immediately, as an elastic mattress would have done. They tumbled into one another pell-mell, bruisingly, but without sustaining any great harm. When they got up again, it was just in time to see the gap that they had just come through close up again.

Paul thought that he was the victim of a fantastic dream; he wiped sweat from his forehead with a cold hand, and then rubbed his eyes. He had his revolver in his hand, though, and the cold of the steel passed from his hand into his whole body. He understood then that he really was awake, living in reality and not in a dream.

He felt that he had the simple, bare and feeble soul of a young child, an obedient and docile soul, but madly curious. He sat down slowly on the bizarre floor that seemed to be made of dense and opaque cloud, and it appeared to him that he was stretching himself out on a soft divan. His hand, moved forcefully, penetrated into the cloudy substance, and he perceived a slight resistance.

Bild and Brad sat down with him.

"What the devil is all this, Paul?" said Bild.

"I don't know. We'll observe…reflect…"

"And we'll end up understanding," said Brad.

The "room" in which they were located represented the interior of an immense polyhedron; the faces were so numerous that it seemed almost round.

It was illuminated by a diffuse green light—coming from where? The light seemed to emanate from the very substance composing the spherical wall of their strange abode...and abode that was otherwise absolutely empty.

"Obviously," said Paul, "we're inside a cloud..." But that presented an association of ideas so crazy that he fell silent.

There was a long silence.

"May I be electrocuted," Jonathan Bild suddenly began, "if..." But he trailed off.

Brad sniggered, and said: "Jonathan, old man, whether you like it or not, this is the start of an unimaginable electrocution. These Saturnians that..."

"Martians!" howled Bild, furiously.

"Come on, Arthur, Jonathan!" said Paul. "Calm, down!" But the ridiculous tenuousness of his voice, which he had tried to strengthen and make energetic and vibrant, took him by surprise again, and he stopped. His two friends seemed slightly mad. He wanted to show them how calm and strong he was, and got up to walk around. This time, he thought about his minimal weight and moved gently, with an extreme prudence. He observed then, with pleasure, that he was breathing with increasing ease, although his breath was still short and unusual.

In spite of the immensity of the room, the declivity of its polygonal walls was very evident. Imagine the interior of a polyhedral sphere, if mathematicians will permit me that unaccustomed alliance of words, which creates the right image. As he walked, he felt his body, incessantly perpendicular to the soft surface in contact with his feet, remain "upright" in the direction of the radii of the circumference, and, walking on determinedly in spite of his bewilderment, he soon found himself above Bild and Brad, head "down," with his feet on the "ceiling." He continued walking, and made a circuit of the room in that fashion, as an ant might do in a hollow cannonball, and came back toward the astonished Bild and Brad from the direction opposite to the one in which he had set out.

After a long moment of silent reflection, he said: "Many other phenomena will doubtless surprise us in the Saturnian world."

"Martian," said Jonathan, obstinately.

"But after all," said Brad, "Why are you so determined that we're in something coming from the planet Mars?"

"Why are you and Paul holding on to the notion that the planet Saturn has something to do with our adventure?"

"Because it was my idea," Brad replied, drily.

"No, it's not that," said Paul, authoritatively. "Personally, I think that the Fiery Wheel, in whose hub we are, in all probability, miraculously enclosed..."

"*Miraculously* is the word!" Bild put in.

"Well, the Fiery Wheel comes from the planet Saturn because it has exactly the same form."

"Yes—Saturn and its ring!" exclaimed Brad.

"That's not proof!" said Bild.

"It's a probability."

"Insufficient!"

"Well, so be it," said Paul, determined to make peace. "We'll find out later if it's Saturn or Mars. The thing is, what can we do?"

"Exactly!" said Arthur and Jonathan.

"Whether it's Martian, Saturnian, Selenite or Jovian…in this place, the laws of attraction, equilibrium and weight, such as we know them on Earth, don't apply. The Saturnian matter—let's use that term provisionally, shall we?—of which this polygonal and spherical wall is made, exercises an attraction of its own upon us, since I can walk down here and up there without falling, my head always pointing in the direction of the center of the room. And when I was up there, I didn't experience any sensation of being upside-down, although, according to terrestrial laws, I really was. Anyway—and this is the most extraordinary thing—instead of coming from the center to the circumference, as in the terrestrial world, this attraction comes from the circumference."

"That is strange!" said Bild.

"I can't see any other explanation," said Brad. "Shall we try, Jonathan?"

They stood up, and had already started walking when a penetrating whistle tore Paul's ears. He had the mysterious sensation of the presence of someone other than them. He put his right hand on Bild's left shoulder, and murmured instinctively: "The Saturnians!"

In front of them, a part of the wall vanished, like thick smoke opening up before a powerful jet of water, and they saw...

An intense column of green light came in through the abruptly-created opening, and then another, and then a third. They were as high as a tall man, and at the summit of each of them a globe of pale, phantasmal white light floated, from which crackling sparks sprang continually: three heads of opaque fire above the slender transparency of three green columns!

While these singular apparitions, now arranged in a line abreast, glided toward them, Paul stepped back, trembling and chilled by fear, and had the vague impression that Brad and Bild were recoiling with him.

The columns stopped, and each of them in turn emitted a spray of sparks, with rhythmic crepitations. Then they glided forward again.

They saw the columns surround them—how can these indescribable things be expressed?—*like a light fog surrounding a tree*, without hiding them, and they perceived that the three globes of pale fire were settling on their heads.

Long sheaves of sparks sprang from the luminous globes, with rapid crackling sounds. Then a long shrill whistle rang out. The globes reappeared before their eyes, at the summit of the transparent green columns, and glided toward the part of the wall from which they had emerged.

While the green columns were disengaging from the three friends, Paul had succeeded in gradually suppressing his instinctive terror. He opened his mouth to speak, but no sound emerged from his throat, which was still taut. He was, at least, able to raise his right arm in an unthinking gesture, but the green columns carrying the luminous globes, gliding slowly and smoothly, disappeared. Immediately, the opaque cloudy wall was as it had been before, smooth and clear, without any disturbance in its continuity.

"Haven't I been dreaming, Paul?" said Jonathan. "Am I not going mad? I saw three columns of green light, three..."

"Me too, three!" said Arthur Brad, in a voice that was hardly perceptible.

"And three balls of white fire..."

"White fire, indeed, which launched crackling sparks..."

"And which placed themselves on our heads, around our legs..."

"Yes, around all three of us—eh, Paul?"

Paul turned to his companions. They were lived, and their eyes were shining strangely in their bloodless faces; their pale lips were trembling.

Paul undoubtedly looked the same, but he was conscious of his absolute presence of mind, and the indisputable possession of his reason. He was not mad, nor was he hallucinating. He had seen it, and they had all seen the same thing, so it was true. The three vertical columns bearing globes of pale fire existed, had been there, and had acted—yes, *acted*—with one accord...

"Jonathan, Arthur, I saw it too. You're not mad. We're in a strange world..."

"Did you notice that the columns and globes of fire didn't emit any heat or radiant light?"

"Yes, indeed…only sparks..."

"But what can they be?" stammered Bild.

"I don't know. Those luminous globes make on think of heads…and the sprinkling sparks..."

"Yes, that's it—sprinkling…like words, or gazes..."

"Ah! Thoughts…or materialized, active intentions…that's it!"

"Of course: thinking being, concentrated, having become a pure fluid..."

"But that's inconceivable!" Brad protested.

The word had just been pronounced when Paul heard a noise to his right that immediately woke in his mind the memory of the rustle of a silk skirt. He turned abruptly, and he saw, at the same time as the wall split open and closed again, a pale and beautiful young woman standing beside a man who was bowing!

This time, he doubted his eyes. He was advancing toward the new apparition when a flash of memory illuminated his mind.

"Ah!" he cried. "Lolla Mendès!"

After the three columns of fire, that was a contrast so striking that he burst out laughing. Behind him he heard the nervous laughter of Bild and Brad—and they repeated, between its spasms: "Ha ha! Lolla! Lolla Mendès!"

It was, indeed, the young Spanish woman who stood before them.

And Paul recognized, then, the face of the young woman that he had seen in Ahmed Bey's crystal cup in Calcutta.

Chapter Four
In which the delights of love and the dolors of hunger arrive in tandem

At the sight of Lolla and Francisco, the three men experienced a real fit of dementia, but it did not last long.

When Paul got tired of laughing, his reason returned, and he made a sudden resolution to accept everything, even the most illogically implausible events, as if it were simple and natural.

In the blink of an eye, he had scanned the young woman and the valet.

Slim and lithe, but not thin, of slightly more than medium height, Lola Mendès was dressed in a red bodice and skirt. Her hands and feet were elegantly slender. Her bare neck, full figure and fine skin were a delicate shade of brown, gracefully supporting an oval face helmeted by admirable black hair, with mat white cheeks, a straight, a proud nose and flared nostrils, and a narrow forehead, beneath which large dark eyes sparkled between marvelously long and dense lashes. Her lips were a vivid red, slightly thick but precisely designed. Energetic and languorous at the same time, Lolla Mendès' beauty was impressive.

Intelligent and bewildered at the same time, the valet Francisco's ugliness was grotesque. Even thinner and taller than Jonathan Bild, the fellow had twisted legs and enormous hands, and as slightly hunchbacked. A few strands of a moustache bristled beneath his donquixotic nose; his cheekbones protruded enormously from his parchment-like complexion, and his bald head was like an ostrich's egg in bright sunlight. Beneath his enormous eyebrows shone exceedingly dark eyes, deeply sunk within their orbits and sparkling with intelligence. He was standing askance, his left fist on his hip, his right holding a yellow melon hat far from his body, but his two feet were set together with military precision beside a traveling valise protected by a gray sheath.

While the valet bowed, the young mistress stared, silent and nonplussed, with an expression of considerable embarrassment. Paul felt a need to speak. He had recovered all his mental vigor and composure, for the presence in the Fiery Wheel of two human beings had brought about a salutary reaction in him—and, he sensed, in Bild and Brad too. Then too, Lolla Mendès' beauty moved him, and gave him an ardent desire to appear valiant.

"Mademoiselle," he said, bowing, "you're probably surprised to hear me pronounce your name, and that of your servant. It's because your adventure was related by Captain Mendès..."

"My father's alive?" cried the young woman, blushing.

"He's alive—at least, the terrestrial newspapers of yesterday, the twenty-first of June, affirmed it. Those newspapers told us everything. We had read them a few hours before being abducted, just as you have been..."

"Well said, Paul," said Jonathan Bild and Arthur Brad, simultaneously.

"Mademoiselle," he continued, "we are now happy to find ourselves in the Fiery Wheel, since you are here. We might perhaps be useful to you..."

"Do things properly, Paul," said Jonathan. "Make the introductions."

47

"Do that, Paul," Brad approved.

Paul moved to his left and drew his tall, thin companion toward him. "Jonathan Bild, officer in the United States navy," he said. He turned to his right, and saw that his short, stout companion had stepped forward. "Arthur Brad, Professor of Natural History at the University of Boston." And indicating himself, bowing deeply, he added: "Paul de Civrac, correspondent of the Académie des Inscriptions et Belle-Lettres de Paris, lieutenant in the Colonial Infantry..." He straightened up and added: "All three of us charged, by the American and French governments in association, with a scientific mission to the excavations at Neiva in Colombia. We were passing through Bogota when we were kidnapped by the Fiery Wheel."

Paul de Civrac was about thirty years old, of medium height; his two friends were a few years older. Although Paul's delicate oval face, his blond moustache, dark hair, brown eyes and the entirety of his aristocratic and muscular were exemplary of a pure-bred Frenchman, his two friends, Jonathan Bild and Arthur Brad—the former very tall and slim, with dark eyes and wavy chestnut-colored hair; the latter small, plump and blue-eyed, with his red hair cropped short—represented the two types of the true American.

The three friends—so dissimilar physically but equal in their intelligence, benevolence and courage—stood up stiffly, with a slight inclination, in front of the young woman.

Since her filial exclamation, the young Spanish woman had not said a word. Her dark eyes, seemingly immense—her face had gone pale again—were gazing with an expression that passed slowly from amazement to confidence. Her valet seemed less emotional. While

Paul was speaking he had dissolved in comical reverences, and as soon as the young man had finished, he was the one who replied, in a corncrake voice rendered even more bizarre by the tenuousness of the atmosphere.

"Be welcome, Señores, to this diabolical machine. Personally, I'm getting used to it, and as long as the provisions last..." He cast a glance at the valise. "One sees things here to make one invoke the name of the benevolent and generous Virgin del Pilar a hundred times a day, but there's no danger, since we're still alive. Unfortunately, the Señorita is desolate, remaining sad and frightened, lamenting..."

He approached Paul and, making a trumpet of his hand around his mouth, the Castilian Scarpin whispered in his ear: "Between us, Señor, I was afraid the Señorita might go mad. This uncommon abduction, you understand...the columns of green light, the balls of fire...but perhaps you've already seen them? Yes? Good—now I'm tranquil...the Señorita...well, since you're here, three gallant caballeros, men of flesh and blood, Christians like her father and myself..."

He stopped dead. The young woman had taken a step forward and put her pretty hand on the domestic's shoulder. She pushed him gently backwards. "Enough, Francisco," she said, in a commanding tone. And addressing Paul, while her beautiful eyes moistened with tears and her admirable throat palpitated, she said: "Excuse my emotion, Monsieur. For as long as I've been here—two days, according to the date you've pronounced—I've felt myself gradually going mad. Now, I have all my presence of mind. I accept your help. You'll explain to me...there are so many strange and frightening things here. But my father is alive, did you say?"

"Yes, Mademoiselle."

Paul reported to her, briefly, what he had read in the newspapers. For fear of seeming insane, he did not tell her that, a year before, he had seen Lolla's face in a crystal cup full of water. He even swore to himself that he would never reveal that magical event—but he remembered Ahmed Bey then, with a shiver of fear and admiration. While he was speaking, he wondered why he had not recognized Lolla on seeing the photograph of the young woman carried off by the Fiery Wheel in the newspapers in Bogota. Perhaps, he thought, the photograph was poor, and lacking in authenticity.

While following these thoughts internally, he was speaking aloud to Lolla Mendès. When he had finished, he fell silent.

"So," she said, "we're in some kind of balloon that's come from the planet Saturn?"

"Yes, Mademoiselle, probably..."

"Unless it comes from the planet Mars," said the incorrigible Bild.

Paul shrugged his shoulders. Putting himself entirely at ease in the exorbitant situation, he acted in that vast and bizarre room as he would have acted in his own study. "Would you care to sit down, Mademoiselle. There are no chairs, but the floor of the room is so soft..."

She sat down in front of him, while Bild and Brad let themselves fall beside them, and Francisco took up a position slightly apart.

The circumstances were so extravagant that, in spite of her trouble and anxiety, Lolla Mendès could not help smiling. Bild and Brad followed suit. Pail did likewise, but the less discreet Francisco exclaimed: "Ha ha! This would be enough to amuse me all my life if..." A glance from his young mistress cut him off.

There was a momentary silence, during which Lolla Mendès observed the three friends while they observed her in their turn.

She spoke first. "Where are we now?"

"In relation to the Earth?"

"Yes."

"Difficult to conjecture," said Brad.

"Impossible," said Bild.

"But Mademoiselle," said Paul, "where were you before you came in here?"

"In another room—round, like this one, but smaller."

"Have you come here before?" asked Bild.

"Yes, twice."

"How?" asked Brad.

"Each time, a hole opened in front of us," Francisco explained, evidently eager to involve himself in the conversation. "We went through. The first time, it was from the little round room into this one; the second time, from this one to a little round room; and then the same again..."

"It was the first time we came into this big room that we saw the columns of fire and the balls with little lightning flashes," Lolla continued. "I nearly died of fright...but I wasn't harmed."

"We've seen them too," said Bild.

"They're probably Saturnians," Brad risked.

Lolla's eyes widened in astonishment.

"Yes," said Paul, in his turn. "We think that the columns are a special luminous matter supporting pure minds...almost-perfect intelligences...brains, if you wish, brains arrived at such perfection that they don't need any organ and present themselves in the form of globes of fire...like certain apparitions observed on Earth by mediums..."

"Souls, then?" stammered Lolla Mendès.

"Yes, souls—that's it!" exclaimed Francisco, enthusiastically. "These Saturnians, or Martians, are souls, pure souls without bodies..."

Paul resumed, more forcefully: "It's for exactly that reason that I believe they're Saturnians rather than Martians. In fact, according to what we know about the planet Saturn, the characteristics of which are contrary to those of Mars, the light specific density of substances and the density of the atmosphere there are such that the Saturnians are necessarily incapable of living on the ground. They can only be aerostatic beings floating in the atmosphere above the thick and heavy clouds that cover their ringed world. And the walls of this room and others are constituted by the assembled cloud, to which the Saturnians can give any form they wish. And that cloud, that vapor, supports us because we're so inconceivably light here that we don't weigh anything relative to the density of the vapors. Think of an ant on an eiderdown!

"What a world! Even our astronomers, rationalistic as they are, affirm that, in view of the physical and physiological conditions of their planet, the Saturnians must have transparent bodies of an incomparable lightness, flying through their sky without wings...without material needs of any sort. Enlarge that still-purely-human conception a little, and the columns of light and the globes of fire justify the timid hypotheses of our astronomers admirably. Pure spirits in the form of light! What a world!"

"And their will, in order to be carried out," said Arthur Brad, "only needs to *be*, to exist...those crackling sparks are its determinations. By their mysterious force they can open the walls of this room at a distance; they can modify forms..."

These possibilities were so exciting that silence fell again.

"But how were we lifted up?" the young woman asked, all of a sudden.

Paul had thought about that. He replied: "The Fiery Wheel must need matter to maintain its radiant activity. Undoubtedly, at moments determined by the Saturnians, it possesses a considerable attractive force. That explains the raising up of houses and land at certain points of its passage. We know that movement, abruptly interrupted, is transformed into heat. It's a physical law. The house, rocks and soil captured by the Wheel catch fire on contact with it, providing it with fuel, and heat..."

"That's ingenious," said Bild.

"It must be right," said Brad.

"Yes, but it doesn't explain why we haven't been annihilated like the houses of the Paseo de Gracia," said Francisco.

"Perhaps the Saturnians calculated and directed the attraction of their machine in such a way that we were drawn to it at an angle, into the black hub of the wheel and not on to the ring of light."

"However," said Bild, hesitantly, "I'm wondering why the Saturnians, since they are Saturnians, need a habitable hub for the Fiery Wheel. If they're pure minds, why can't they travel freely in interplanetary space without this bizarre machine...?"

"Yes," said Brad, "like light, or sound, they could go..."

"Indeed, but doubtless the interplanetary void and atmospheres other than that of their planet of origin aren't appropriate to the existence of the Saturnians..."

"They can die, then?" said Francisco.

"Why not?"

"Get away! Souls don't die!"

"How do we know? In that case, an intelligence, a mind, isn't a soul...in which case, an intelligence, a mind, a Saturnian, can die..."

There as a momentary silence, and Paul de Civrac suddenly exclaimed: "Oh, if we only had Dr. Ahmed Bey with us!"

"Ahmed Bey?" said Jonathan Bild. "Who is this person that's worth the trouble of being missed in the situation we're in?"

"Believe me," said Francisco, "I miss all the people of Earth! If they were here, we could set off to conquer Saturn and all the other worlds..."

"Francisco!" Lolla interjected, severely.

"Who is Ahmed Bey?" asked Brad, calmly.

"A strange scholar I met in Calcutta, during a voyage to India" Paul replied. "Ahmed Bey knows a great many things. It's said, in Calcutta, that he possesses all the terrible secrets of the ancient Brahmins, who were absolute masters of life and death."

"I don't see what use this demigod would be to us here," muttered Bild.

"He'd be able to explain to us clearly what we can only sketch with difficulty in vague conjectures," Paul said.

The skeptical Bild shrugged his shoulders and pulled a face, which testified that he, personally, did not believe in the exorbitant faculties of the said Dr. Ahmed Bey."

Paul dared not insist—but that would not have been his emotion if he could have known that, at that very moment, on Earth, Dr. Ahmed Bey was thinking about him, Paul de Civrac, remembering their meeting in Calcutta, and preparing to go, in the most prodigiously unexpected manner, to the rescue of the prisoners on the Fiery Wheel!

In spite of all the marvels of thought-transmission, however, Paul could not know that, and he did not know it.

He had let himself drift into a reverie, in which he was reviewing the episodes of his terrestrial life with a certain bitterness, when the voice of the young woman, his companion henceforth, suddenly brought him back to the present and its anguishing reality.

"What strangeness!" Lolla murmured. "But how long will it last? Will we return to Earth?"

"A mystery!" pronounced Brad.

"We shall see!" said Bild

"Unless we die of hunger between now and then," the pragmatic Francisco sniggered.

The remark was so judicious that all eyes turned to the valet.

"Well, yes," he said. "These Saturnians, as you call them, if they're pure minds, or souls, would doubtless laugh at a slice of cold ham, a slice of bread and three hard-boiled eggs! Have they asked you if you were hungry? Have they offered you food? No, they haven't, have they? What, then? It's probable that your Saturnians don't understand French, Monsieur de Civrac, nor English, Messieurs Jonathan Bild and Arthur Brad, nor Spanish, Señorita! How will you make them understand, if you even see them again, that we, who aren't pure minds, need to nourish our bodies with something other than white sparks, green light and condensed cloud? *Ay caramba!* There are five of us, and I only have enough food for two days..."

So saying, the rational and comical Francisco seized his valise, set it on his outstretched legs, opened it and took out various packets, which he weighed in his hand, murmuring: "Chicken...ham...bread...tinned sardines...hard-boiled eggs...fish and tomatoes...one more liter of wine and half a bottle of mineral-water... Yes, with careful rationing, there's enough to nourish five people for four meals. Oh, I did very well to disobey the captain and bring provisions...he wanted to eat breakfast and dinner in buffets! The buffets of Saturn...they must be jolly!"

The valet's words were only humorous in appearance. Far from making anyone laugh, they inspired very black thoughts. There was nothing agreeable about the prospect of a long sojourn in the enigmatic hub of the Fiery Wheel, without any possible communication with the beings inhabiting it, and probably without food and water. They saw themselves all condemned, however briefly the present situation was prolonged, to the most horrible of deaths, by hunger and thirst...

Paul took out his watch. It was ten minutes to twelve. It had, therefore, been eight hours since Brad, Bild and he had been abducted by the Wheel.

"Today is the twenty-second of June," he said. "We need to establish a calendar in order that..."

"I have one!" said Brad. He opened his wallet, which was indeed furnished with a calendar.

"There's neither day nor night here," said Bild. "Brad will therefore be responsible for keeping his calendar in line with the hours elapsed..."

"Agreed!"

"Lunch is served, Mademoiselle!" said Francisco.

In front of them, on the opened and inverted valise, the valet had "laid the table."

Lola Mendès served herself with her own fork, knife and glass, Brad, Bild, Paul and Francisco each had ten fingers and a good traveling knife appropriate for all needs, the delicate as well as the rude.

They ate without talking. The meal was rapid, brief and—it must be said—insufficient, but Francisco rationed the food with as much prudence as equity.

"And that's one!" said the valet, closing the valise again. "You still have three meals of the same magnitude. After that..." He clicked his fingers in mid-air, then took tobacco and papers from his pocket and rolled a cigarette, which he lit.

Bild had four cigars. He offered them round and everyone, except for Lola Mendès, was soon surrounded by a cloud of smoke.

While taking slow puffs on his cigar, Paul studied the young woman. She was sitting straight-legged, with her arms folded, her chin lowered over her chest and supported by her left hand. She sighed, and tears soon began to roll down her cheeks. Disturbed, Paul threw away his cigar and drew nearer to her.

"Mademoiselle…"

She shivered, raised her head, wiped away her tears with a swift gesture, and said, in a soft voice: "I was thinking about my father. But I have to be strong. You won't see me cry again."

She forced herself to smile, and their eyes, having met, did not turn away. Paul's were full of encouragement and consolation; Lola's seemed grateful. Spontaneously, Paul offered her his hand. She gave him hers and he felt the sight pressure of her fingers.

"You're not doomed," he said. "I shall save you…"

He was strangely emotional. He would have liked to say more, to express his devotion, but two voices abruptly returned all his composure,

"We'll save you!" they said. They were the voices of Bild and Brad, standing beside Paul, each holding out a hand to the young woman.

With a brisk movement, she stood up and gave her left hand to Brad and her right to Bild. The handshakes were firm and vigorous, but Lolla's eyes did not turn away from Paul's and the young man suddenly felt a surge of joy pass through him and fill him with an invincible courage.

"Now," said Bild." We need to do something…"

"To find out where we are…enter into communication with the Saturnians," added Brad.

Paul gripped his revolver and started rapping on the walls with the butt, sometimes here and sometimes there—but his revolver and his hand, penetrating the dense vapor, rebounded like a spring.

He launched himself head first against the wall, but he felt suffocated as soon as his head was in the vapor—which immediately threw him backwards in any case.

Bild and Brad stayed to either side of Lolla, inactive, and watched, as did Francisco, with a mocking expression.

After a good half hour of exercise, Paul put his revolver back in his belt, saying: "If the Saturnians know what we're doing, they don't want to respond…"

"I think it's necessary to await their caprice," said Lola Mendès.

"Let's wait, then!"

They all sat down again, and smoked cigarettes rolled by Francisco. They talked, coming up with a thousand increasingly crazy conjectures…and the hours went by, bleak and empty. No Saturnian appeared; the silence was so profound that, in order not to hear it, they continually made some noise with their hands or feet when they were not talking.

The same anguishing question was repeated a hundred times: "Where are we?"

At eight o'clock in the evening, Francisco declared, impassively: "Dinner is served, Mademoiselle."

As at midday, they ate rapidly, and very little; they were obliged to drink even less.

"And two!" said the valet, closing his valise.

Lolla Mendès lay down, and while they smoked she went to sleep.

"Santiago de Compostela be praised!" murmured Francisco. "It's the first time the Señorita has been able to sleep since..."

"We ought to get some sleep too," said Brad. And he lay down not far away from Lolla. Bild did likewise, then Civrac, and then Francisco.

Side by side on the strange Saturnian eiderdown, they fell asleep, overwhelmed by the emotions of the extraordinary day.

Meanwhile, having traveled many thousands of leagues since they had emerged from the terrestrial atmosphere, the Fiery Wheel was speeding through interplanetary space like a capricious comet, heading toward the sun.

Chapter Five
In which six revolver shots have terrible and unexpected consequences

The day of the twenty-third of June was bleak and dismal for the prisoners of the enigmatic Fiery Wheel.

They did not see anything; no sound struck their ears. No green column carrying a luminous globe appeared in the vast polyhedral room. It seemed that the Saturnians had satisfied their curiosity fully during their first visit. Where were the mysterious beings, then? What was there beyond that immutable cloudy wall with a thousand regular faces, with no gap in its continuity? How was the soft green light produced?

A mystery!

Lolla Mendès, Paul de Civrac, Jonathan Bild, Arthur Brad and the valet Francisco discussed all those questions but no certainty emerged from their hypotheses.

At midday and seven o'clock they ate two meals—the last!

And again, after the men had diffidently smoked a cigarette, they lay down....

But how can one sleep with the thought that, tomorrow, one will have nothing to eat? How can one rest when the mind is tortured by a hundred insoluble questions and the heart is gripped with the anguish of the frightful mystery? How could they even close one's eyes under that implacable green light filling the hallucinatory spherical room? None of the unhappy heroes of the alarming adventure was able to achieve the comfort of sleep.

"To hell with the Saturnians!" exclaimed Paul, breaking the silence after having turned over a hundred times between Bild's sharp shoulder-blades and Brad's broad shoulders.

"To hell!" muttered Jonathan.

"May the plague choke them!" growled Arthur.

"They have no fear of that!" sniggered Francisco.

"My God, what are we going to do?" moaned Lola Mendès.

No one was hungry or thirsty, even though the final meal had been far from abundant, but the apprehension of imminent hunger and thirst, which would be unslakable, hollowed out their stomachs and dried out their throats.

"We have to get out of here!" Bild exclaimed. "We have to find a way..."

A long whistle resounded and, as before, through an opening suddenly produced in the cloudy wall, three green columns bearing luminous globes came in.

They young woman and the four men remained motionless.

"The Saturnians!" Paul whispered, unconsciously.

The three columns stopped their forward glide simultaneously. A thousand brief sparks erupted from the globes, crackling. Then, even the sparks were no longer manifest. The green hue of the transparent columns weakened somewhat, and the globes became an opaque white, slightly tinted with blue, lighted from within but not radiant.

The Terrans studied the three motionless Saturnians calmly. Long minutes went by.

Suddenly, a voice spoke: "Fire a revolver shot at one of those luminous globes," said Francisco, brutally.

"What?" said Bild, his expression indecisive.

"Yes," the Castilian repeated. "Smash one of the stupid balls—that one there!" And he pointed at the Saturnian in the middle.

"Why?"

"Because the diabolical Saturnians might do something. In any case, it will break the monotony of or present existence."

"But the consequences!" Paul exclaimed. "Think about the consequences? How do we know whether…everything might fall apart?"

"Well," said Francisco, "we'd die of something other than hunger or thirst."

Brad had listened without saying a word. He drew his revolver and examined it.

"Damn!"

"What does it matter?" said Francisco. "Go on—shoot!"

"In truth…" said Bild, and raised his right arm.

"Shall we, Arthur?"

"Let's do it, Jonathan."

Arthur Brad raised his revolver too. Their movements were stiff and somnambulistic, their voices strange—hallucinated voices.

Paul de Civrac looked at them, his mind confused, while Francisco sniggered—but Lolla Mendès launched herself toward the two Americans and put herself between them and the Saturnians.

"No, no!" she cried. "Don't do that! You'll lose us everything. Wait…perhaps things will change soon enough…" She turned to her valet. "Francisco! I forbid you to give bad advice. I forbid it!"

She was extremely excited, her cheeks pink, her gaze shiny.

"Al right, Mistress, all right!" the man muttered. "I'll shut up. But we'll die all the more surely of hunger and..."

"Shut up! Shut up!"

She pushed Bild and Brad back to Paul's side, made them put their revolvers back in their holsters, and sat down beside the Frenchman, who gazed at her with an expression in which there was admiration, and a certain other sentiment.

The Saturnians disappeared the same way they had come.

In absolute silence, the hours passed...

What would have been the night, in terrestrial terms, went by without bringing any change, and then more hours went slowly by, and what would have been day gradually faded into the past.

At eight p.m. on the twenty-fourth of June, Francisco said: "I'm hungry."

"Me too," muttered Bild."

"And I'm thirsty," murmured Brad.

Only Paul and Lola had the strength not to complain. Paul was suffering more by virtue of seeing the young woman suffer than from his own need. He squeezed one of her pretty pale hands in his, and wished that all his vigorous masculine blood might pass into Lolla's veins.

There was another long interval of silence.

"How long can we live without eating or drinking?" Francisco asked, suddenly.

"It depends on the strength and temperament of each of us," Civrac replied.

"In that case," the valet went on, "the Señorita, certainly the weakest of the five of us, will die first?"

No one said a word. In the bleak silence, each of them could hear their own hearts beating. After a slight sigh, Lolla Mendès let her head fall on Civrac's shoulder.

At that moment, the whistle announcing the Saturnians sounded—and, indeed, they reappeared immediately. This time, the green columns supporting white globes were four in number. They stopped three paces away from the group formed by the Terrans.

At first, Paul's attention was attracted by the arrival of the Saturnians. Then he felt an unaccustomed weight on his shoulder. He turned his head and saw Lolla Mendès, pale, her eyes closed and her lips bloodless.

Francisco, Bild and Brad had seen it too. They got up, their features taut, their gaze resolute, facing up to the impassive Saturnians.

"She's fainted," Paul said.

"Well, it's necessary to finish it!" exclaimed Francisco, excitedly. "I'd rather doom us all at a stroke that see the Señorita die in front of me, little by little, without being able to do anything..."

He grabbed Paul's revolver. Bild and Brad drew theirs.

"It's mad!" cried Paul. "Mad!" But he did not feel that he had the strength to intervene.

In unison, Bild, Brad and Francisco each took aim at one of the intolerable luminous balls.

"Fire!"

They fired.

Presumably, the gestures went awry because their fingers were trembling; nothing happened.

"Again! Again!" Francisco screeched.

They pressed the triggers together.

A formidable shock suddenly shook the polyhedral chamber. Bild, Brad and Francisco fell on top of Paul, who had instinctively clutched Lolla Mendès in his arms. Howling, they clutched at Civrac and Lolla, and the human cluster, thrown to the right and the left in a confusion of gleams, flashes and crackles, fell through a large opening in the wall...

The four men, their minds in chaos, had not lost consciousness. They had a sensation of falling through burning air. Then that sensation weakened, and they understood that they were falling more slowly.

Where?

Although closed, their eyes were hurting, assaulted by an intense light...

They were suffocating...

Then, a kind of twilight suddenly succeeded the violent light. The contrast was sharp enough to render Paul de Civrac all his presence of mind. He opened his eyes, and his thoughts succeeded one another, rapidly:

We're in a cloud...not as thick as that of the Fiery Wheel...it's not as hot...we're falling through extremely dense air...so dense that it's slowing our fall...we must be much lighter than in the terrestrial atmosphere...the cloud has passed...

Then, beneath him, at a great depth, he saw a red-brown prairie traversed by a golden yellow river...

He was suffocating atrociously...

He thought he was about to die, before even crashing into the ground far below. He hugged Lola more tightly to his bosom, and had the strength to apply his own lips to the young woman's, in a unique and supreme kiss.

Then, with one last glance, he embraced the spectacle: above him, a dark cloud; on every side, a sort of transparent mist; beneath him, the russet prairie...

He felt Brad's fingernails sink into his arm, while Bild's arm squeezed his ribs and Francisco's hands clung to his left ankle.

There was a blinding light, an unsustainable heat, a supreme suffocation...and he lost consciousness.

And the human cluster of five bodies suddenly came apart, continuing to fall slowly toward the mysterious land, indecisively, tossed around like sheets of paper thrown from the gondola of a balloon...

PART TWO
THE MYSTERIOUS PLANET

Chapter One
*Which serves as an unusual introduction
to what follows*

Jonathan Bild was the first to recover consciousness after the fall. He tried to open his eyes but he was blinded by a violent light, so he closed them again and shielded them with both hands. He remained lying down, without moving, for some time. At first, his bewildered intelligence could not contrive to reconstitute the events in consequence of which he seemed to be hurting all over. He felt an intolerable heat throughout his body, and he was choking.

Gradually, his memory cleared. He remembered the night in Colombia, the Fiery Wheel, Lolla Mendès and her domestic, the revolver shots, the fall...

"Good," he said. "We've fallen on to a world, probably a planet. Why a planet? Bah! We'll find out later. But where are the others? Damned light!"

He had opened his eyes too abruptly again, had had the sensation of a red hot iron passing in front of his pupils. After that, he was more prudent. Gradually, parting his eyelids very slowly, he succeeded in keeping his eyes sufficiently open, although squinting, to be able to see clearly.

He was then able to take account of the fact that he was lying on long red grass, that blades of which were scarcely curbed by his eight; it formed an extremely elastic mattress. The sky that was above his head was composed of enormous dense green clouds, without any gap permitting him to see beyond them.

He raised himself up on his elbow and shouted, as loudly as he could: "Arthur Brad!"

To his great astonishment, a powerful echo repeated: "Arthur Brad!" and immediately a second echo, and then a third, and then twenty others, repeated the three sonorous syllables with decreasing force. The strangest thing was that the echoes came from the sky, as if they had been produced by the bizarre green clouds.

But no human voice succeeded the rumble of the echoes. Arthur Brad did not reply.

Without renewing his appeal, Jonathan Bild tried to get up. He succeeded, but only after considerable effort, for all his limbs seemed weary. His feet and legs, not offering as large a resistant surface as his whole body, sank into the russet grass. His feet came to rest upon genuinely solid ground when the tops of the grass stalks had reached breast-height—and Jonathan Bild was a tall man! When he felt that he was steady on his feet, with his legs apart and his and his hands forming a shade over his eyes, he looked around.

He found himself almost in the middle of a vast field of reddish grass, fairly similar, except for the color, to ripe wheat, but taller, stouter and more flexible. In front of him, the prairie was limited by a broad yellow ribbon—a golden river—beyond which sterile mountains rose up, as black and shiny as slate, whose summits were lost in the clouds.

To the right was a metallic gray forest; to the left, a similar forest, and behind him—for he made a complete rotation—the American saw rounded hills covered in bright red vegetation. There were no animals anywhere: not a single bird, insect, biped or quadruped. And over the motionless solitude, unruffled by any gust of wind, there was a more-than-tropical heat and light, with a death-like silence.

"Funny place!" murmured Bild. "But those damned clouds are the most disconcerting thing of all!"

The clouds were green—bright green—indefinable and undulating, dark in the middle and bright at the edges. They seemed formidably thick and heavy, rolling heavily and slowly toward the slate mountains, against which they collided, rising up, to be incessantly replaced, without any gap, by other clouds surging from beyond the scarlet hills. The intense light—unbearable to fully open eyes and painful even for squinting eyes—which came from the extraordinarily cloudy sky, was also green: a very bright green that did not modify the color of objects.

"How hot it is!" murmured Bild.

It seemed to him that he was in an oven, and that his skull was about to burst as his brain boiled. His entire body was streaming with sweat.

As rapidly as the pain in his limbs permitted, Jonathan got rid of his jacket and trousers; he remained in his jersey and long-johns, with his boots. He did not experience any relief. His mind slightly numbed, he was thinking about the exhausting heat when he heard a voice calling to weakly from his left: "Jonathan Bild!"

Immediately, in the sky, the echoes repeated in a rapid roll: "Jonathan Bild…Nathan Bild!"

"Ah! My old Brad!"

"Jonathan! Jonathan!"

There was such a din of echoes in the clouds that the American understood the necessity of not shouting.

He turned in the direction from which the weak voice had come, and said, quietly: "Is that you, Brad?"

"Yes, Bild, it's me."

"How are you?"

"Broken—bruised all over. But can you see me? Further to the left, Bild. I can't open my eyes, but I can tell from your voice which way you're facing."

With one stride, Jonathan crossed an enormous area of russet grass. He felt extremely light. Suddenly, in front of him, lying full length on a mattress of bent grass, he saw the stout body of Arthur Brad, his apoplectic face steaming with sweat.

The sight of Brad, with his blinking eyes and mouth wide open, was so funny that Bild could not help laughing.

When the aerial echoes of the laughter had died away, Brad said, in a low voice: "Where are we, damn it?"

"Are you injured?" asked Bild, without replying.

"I don't think so?"

"Try to get up, Arthur."

"I feel as if I've been beaten with sticks!"

"Never mind, try! I felt the same as you, bruised all over. As you can see, I'm in one piece. It was the fall that..."

"Yes, the fall! Aiee!" With an effort, in spite of the pain from which all his limbs were suffering, Brad succeeded in standing up. He sank chin-deep. He looked at the red field, the motionless golden river, the slate mountains, the steel-gray forests and the scarlet hills— and then, for a long time, at the thick and heavy green clouds.

"Ludicrous country, eh, Bild?"

"Yes, quite ludicrous."

"But where are the others?"

"Civrac?"

"Yes—Civrac, Lolla Mendès and Francisco."

"I don't know. Let's look for them."

"Let's—but tell me, Bild…I'm stifling…are you as hot as I am?"

"As if I were under a grill."

"Worse than tropical temperature, to be sure, Bild..."

"We must be on a planet closer to the sun than the Earth. And yet those clouds are filtering the heat and light. Otherwise, we'd be roasted like a chicken on a spit."

"In the oven, Bild, in the oven!" rectified the meticulous Arthur Brad.

Bild shrugged his shoulders and took a step forward—but that single pace transported him at least five meters away from Brad, who had remained still.

"Hey, Jonathan—by Jove, you've got seven-league boots on!"

He bounded himself, and that single jump took him further than Bild.

"Arthur," said Jonathan, "we're lighter than on Earth, as we were in the Fiery Wheel."

"Yes, obviously. Let's calculate more carefully."

They came together again by means of prudent steps. As they were looking in the direction of the golden river they saw a human being emerge from the russet grass three paces away from them, leap six meters into the air, and fall back lightly.

"Francisco!"

"The very same—but by Santo Cristo, what does it mean? I jump to loosen my limbs and I fly up into the air like a balloon! *Bonjour*, Señores. Not bad—you too?"

71

"No, not bad," Brad replied.

"Me neither. I woke up some time ago. I heard you talking. Those echoes, eh! What do you think of that? Then you spoke very quietly...and I understood—I'm doing the same, as you see. But come and help the Señorita—she's over there, lying next to Monsieur Civrac. May the Blessed Virgin forgive me! I think I was lying on their legs. We fell from a long way up— *Caramba!* Look! The Señorita's breathing, and Monsieur de Civrac too. I still have my flask, fortunately!"

During this flood of speech, Bild and Brad leaned over Lola and Civrac, who were lying side by side in the russet grass. From one of the vast pockets of his jacket, Francisco had taken a small goatskin flask. He took out the cork and put the neck to Lolla's lips.

"It's *aguardiente*."

"Cognac?" said Brad.

"Yes, and good stuff. It would have resuscitated the dead in the times of Charles Quint. Look!"

Lolla coughed, sneezed and opened fearful eyes, which she closed again immediately, dazzled as they were by the intense light falling from the green clouds.

"Señorita! Señorita! You're alive! We're all alive! San Cristo be blessed!"

And the petulant Francisco turned toward Civrac's body—but he did not calculate his movement, with the result that he pirouetted on his axis four times.

"*Caramba!* That's devilment!"

"No," said Bild. And he explained that, because bodies on this unknown planet were much lighter than on Earth, muscular effort needed to be proportionate to the new weight.

"Understood!" Francisco said—and with meticulous slowness, he turned to Civrac again.

The young Frenchman took longer to recover consciousness than his friends. The top of his head was bloody; he had fallen awkwardly, in such a way that his head has made glancing contact with a big boulder. Francisco washed the wound with saliva and applied his handkerchief to it, slightly dampened with cognac. Then he poured a few drops of cordial between the young man's lips.

Bild and Brad waited anxiously, as did Lolla, who had sat up without difficulty.

Finally, Civrac opened his mouth. "Lolla! Lolla!" he murmured.

He too opened his eyes—but closed them again immediately, dazzled. A long interval of adaptation was necessary. Blinking one eye, and then the other, he gradually got used to the intense light, and when he was finally able to see between narrowed eyelids, he scanned his companions with his gaze, finally resting it on Lolla. Then his eyes cleared, sparkling with intelligence. Revitalized, Civrac smiled.

"Safe and sound," he murmured. "All of us!"

"Yes, all of us," said Brad.

"Try to get up," Bild advised.

"But where are we?"

"We haven't had time to try to find out. Stand up! First you need to convince us that you aren't injured."

"I don't think so," Civrac murmured. "I only feel a slight headache."

"Your head hit a stone," Francisco explained, "but the wound's superficial—it's trivial."

Civrac stood up, without difficulty. He held out his hand to Lolla, who was the last to stand up. And the five Terrans looked around, mutely.

The heat was so intense and the air so heavy that they were choking, suffocated. No sun was visible, however; there was only that terrible pale green light falling from the more intensely-colored clouds. An extraordinary silence reigned over everything, frightening because it was so absolute.

"I'm choking!" said Lola, tugging at the neck of her bodice.

"Me too," said Civrac.

Brad and Francisco had imitated Bild and taken off their jackets, to no avail.

"Let's head for that gray forest over there. Perhaps it won't be so hot under the trees, and we can examine our situation."

"Let's go," said Bild. "But remember how light we are."

Briefly, Civrac explained the phenomenon of the reduced weight to Lolla. Then he took her by the hand, and the five Terrans moved toward one of the forests. Even though it was some three terrestrial kilometers away, they reached it in a few bounds. Every leap kept them suspended in the air for more than a minute; they flew as if they had wings. The sensation of floating made them burst out laughing, so new was it for them, and the aerial echoes multiplied their laughter to infinity.

They felt a strange vitality then, joyful and insouciant, for which they could not quite account. The overexcitement doubtless stemmed from a greater proportion of oxygen contained in the air of the mysterious planet, and yet, by a bizarre contradiction, the air was so dense that it seemed to them to be too heavy, as if too material, to breathe...

At the edge of the forest Civrac stopped and turned to his companions.

"What about the Fiery Wheel?" he said.

At that evocation, they all looked up—but there was nothing there except the eternal green clouds, very high and very dense, gliding ponderously toward the slate mountains.

"We won't see it again," said Bild.

At these words, a depressing impression of solitude gripped the Terrans. They remained silent for a time, their gazes lost in the unaccustomed sky from which they had arrived on that strange planet. Would they ever see the Earth again?

Those terrible thoughts could not overwhelm their courage, however. Paul de Civrac was the first to lower his head and redirect his eyes toward the bizarre soil on which they would be living henceforth.

"Let's go," he said, "and let's not worry about the Fiery Wheel any more, not everything we've known until now. By virtue of an unexpected adventure, we've been thrown into a mysterious world. There's no proof that it'll be hospitable to us. Perhaps that field of red grass is the work of intelligent beings. We'll meet them, and then..."

He fell silent momentarily, and then resumed, forcefully: "Follow me!"

Still holding Lolla Mendès' hand, he plunged into the forest.

It was made up of bizarre trees with rugged trunks that were reminiscent of metallic columns corroded with rust. Silvery foliage spread out in bouquets on stout, high branches, similar to those of terrestrial olive-trees, but which must have been made of a very different substance, for the leaves strewn on the ground were flexible underfoot, like steel blades; they too seemed to be covered in rust.

The trees were very numerous and densely-packed, their foliage forming a continuous dome; beneath that thick vault, air currents circulated between the trunks, producing a relative coolness.

Having walked for some time, followed by his companions, still holding Lolla Mendès by the hand, Paul de Civrac stopped. The Terrans were in the heart of the forest, and there was nothing around them but the infinite bleak succession of trees with rusty trunks.

Chapter Two
In which Terrans and Mercurians come into conflict

In spite of the air currents and the shade, the heat was still so intense in the forest that the faces of the five Terrans were streaming with sweat. They were not suffocating quite as much, though, and their respiration was gradually becoming even, doubtless by virtue of the adaptation of their lungs to the new air.

As if that air were nourishing them, they did not feel any hunger, although they had not eaten for a long time.

"Let's sit down," said Paul. "We won't suffer as much from the heat while we're still. And let's try to examine our situation calmly."

""First of all," said Jonathan Bild, when everyone was seated, "Where are we? On what planet?"

"It's not the Moon," said Arthur Brad.

"Nor Jupiter," Paul affirmed.

"Nor Saturn," said Bild.

"Why?" asked Lolla Mendès.

"Yes, why?" added Francisco.

"Because the climatic and atmospheric conditions of planets are known to us," Paul explained. "What we find here isn't in accord with what we know about Jupiter, Saturn and the Moon."

"We might be on Mars..."

"Or Venus..."

"Or Mercury..."

"Let's not dwell on that question too long," said Paul. "It's of secondary importance to us. The future will doubtless answer it. What we need to know first is whether we can find, hereabouts, what we need to live. The air, although different from Earth's air, is breathable. Since there's air, and clouds, there ought to be water here; will it drinkable?"

"There must be water," said Bild. "That yellow river bordering the red grassland, in the direction of the mountains..."

"Let's go there right away!" said Francisco.

"No," said Paul. "Let's wait for the day to end and for the heat to decline. To judge by the perpendicular direction of the luminous rays coming from the clouds when we were in the grassland, it must be about midday, in the terrestrial sense. Bild, do you still have your chronometer?"

"Yes."

"Is it intact?"

"Intact," Jonathan repeated, after examining his watch.

"Well, wind it up and set it to one o'clock."

In the absolute silence they could hear the friction of the winding mechanism.

"Good," said Paul. "Now, has any of you seen an animal?"

"Not the slightest trace of one," Brad replied. The others shook their heads.

"Perhaps they only come out at night?" Lolla suggested.

"That's possible...or at least at dusk."

"In that case," said Jonathan, "let's not exhaust ourselves with vain words, and get some sleep. By virtue of some unexpected phenomenon, we're not hungry or thirsty for the time being, but the fall has worn us out. Let's sleep—I think we might soon need rested limbs in good condition."

"I'm already asleep, myself," muttered Francisco.

"Go to sleep," said Paul. "I'll keep watch. We don't know what dangers are threatening us."

He made a pillow out of his rolled-up jacket and arranged a kind of bed of flexible metallic leaves. Lolla lay down on it, after an affectionate handshake and a grateful smile. A few minutes later, everyone except Paul was asleep.

Civrac reflected that the overexcitement that had animated his mind a little while before, and those of his companions in adventure, had been succeeded, as soon as they were in the forest, by a perfect calm, and even a slight prostration. They were also breathing more easily. That suggested that the air in the forest was not quite the same as that in the russet prairie. A strange phenomenon!

And of what liquid was the yellow river that he had glimpsed composed?

Was the red grass of the prairie edible?

On the forest floor there were no more plants at all—not the slightest sprig of moss; nothing but the rusty carpet of metallic leaves.

What was this planet, then? Paul started mentally reviewing all the astronomical knowledge that he had acquired on Earth. Curious about everything, and reading a great deal, he had kept up to date with the discoveries and hypotheses published by astronomers and summarized in the monthly bulletin of the Societé Astronomique de France.

By a process of elimination, he arrived at the conclusion that only the planet Mercury responded, for the moment, to the atmospheric and climatic conditions he was able to observe.

Mercury! The smallest of the planets and the closest to the sun—the one that received the most heat and light.

While Paul was thinking along those lines, an irresistible somnolence invaded him. His heavy eyelids gradually closed, and if he had not been leaning against the rugged trunk of a tree he would have fallen backwards, also gripped by sleep. His feeble will struggled, however; he wanted to stay awake, to keep his eyes open—and he scanned the surroundings energetically, with an inexplicably vague gaze...

But dreams were already being slowly woven in his mind. Above all, he saw Lolla, a smiling Lolla, her eyes languid with love, her lips murmurous with kisses...and he also imagined himself saving Lolla from fantastic dangers, carrying her away, gripping her in an embrace that was as amorous as it was protective...

It was then that, in the indefinite quality of the dream, he saw a living being emerge from behind a tree and move toward him: an unexpected and bizarre animal.

It was as tall as a child about twelve years old, black in color and shiny; its round torso supported, without a neck, a rat-like head with a trunk, and was itself supported by a single leg. A unique arm sprouted from the middle of the torso, terminated by three enormous shiny talons.

It came forward, hoping, flexing the knee of its only leg and then straightening the thigh like a spring, carrying the animal forward with a leap of two or three meters.

Above the trunk, which it was waving madly in all directions, an eye opened: a sparkling red eye.

Paul de Civrac watched the little monster coming toward him. He gazed at it stupidly, unconscious of any danger. In the somnolence into which his mind had sunk, the Terran imagined that he was the victim of one of those imprecise dreams that one manufactures and sees before falling completely asleep.

The fantastic being suddenly made two rapid leaps that brought it to the immediate vicinity of the sleepers. With its blazing eye it looked at them one after another, curiously, and then that gaze settled on Paul.

The mobile trunk uttered a shrill whistle, and immediately, from behind the trees where they had been hiding, three other individuals similar to the first emerged, and approached rapidly. Their unique arms were agitating, their trunks whistling, and their red eyes emitting flashes.

And Paul considered the four monsters, unthinkingly....

The first of the monopods[8] suddenly leapt forward, reached out its arm, and its three talons dug into Paul's thigh.

With a cry of alarm, Paul stood up, finally conscious of the reality.

The aerial echoes repeated his cry in rolls of thunder, and the four monsters, bounding away, disappeared into the depths of the forest.

---

[8] La Hire calls the creatures *monopèdes*, fusing Greek and Latin roots in a manner that would make a pedant wince; it is arguably that "uniped" might have been more a appropriate translation than "monopod," because of its symmetry with "biped" and "quadruped," but monopod seems closer to La Hire's term, given that "monoped" is too horrible to contemplate.

"Bild! Brad! Francisco! Wake up!" Paul howled. "Get up! I've seen them! I've seen them!"

He shook his three recumbent companions. They opened their eyes, grumbling.

"What is it?" said Bild. "What have you seen?"

"The...the..."

"Well, what is it?" groaned Brad.

"I've seen...the Mercurians."

"Mercurians? Why Mercurians?"

Bild leapt to his feet, at the same time as Brad and Francisco.

"Where are they?" cried the Spaniard.

"Why Mercurians?" Bild repeated.

"Because," Paul replied, suddenly calm, "I thought about it while you were asleep, and my reflections convinced me that we're on the planet Mercury. Anyway, we'll soon know for sure..."

"How?"

"I'll tell you in a couple of hours."

"But what about the Mercurians?" cried Francisco, searching the forest with his gaze. "The Mercurians!"

"They've gone."

"How many were there?" asked Brad.

"And what were they?" asked Bild.

Civrac described the four monopod monsters briefly.

"Let's pretend to be asleep," suggested Jonathan. "They'll come back. Does anyone not have his revolver?"

"We dropped them at the moment..."

"That's true! Perhaps the Fiery Wheel has been destroyed..."

"I have my knife," said Francisco. He took a long Catalan knife, with a crosspiece at the hilt, from his belt.

"Put that weapon away!" Civrac ordered. "The Mercurians are afraid of us. Besides which, they don't have any hostile intentions. The one that scratched my thigh only wanted to touch me to see what I was. We mustn't open hostilities. Remember that we're only four men against perhaps millions of individuals. Then again, what if these monsters are only animals, not intelligent Mercurians? We need to be patient. Let's only fight to defend our lives."

"You're right, Paul," said Jonathan Bild, gravely.

"Before lying down again," Civrac added, "let's drink a little of Francisco's cognac, in order to vanquish the prostration to which we yielded."

"Good idea!" said Brad.

And the flask passed from hand to hand.

Paul and Francisco lay down to either side of Lola, who was still asleep, in such a way as to defend her from the monopods' touch.

Bild and Brad lay down some distance away, in order that they could get behind a curious Mercurian. They had agreed that they would try to take a prisoner. Francisco's long broad belt would serve to attach the captive to a tree.

An hour went by without any creature appearing. Between their squinting eyelids, the Terrans looked in all directions. To help them stay awake, they spoke to one another occasionally in low voices, and pinched one another's arms. Bild frequently looked at his watch, trying to take note of the figure marking the time.

It was quarter past four when Brad was the first to see a monopod. He signaled the sighting, as agreed, with a long sigh, and the four Terrans strove to remain motionless.

With short hopes, punctuated by prudent pauses, the black Mercurian advanced, arm forward, trunk agitated, eye bright.

When it was no more than six paces away from the recumbent humans, it whistled with its trunk. Immediately, other monopods emerged from behind the trees.

There were four of them, and then ten...and then twelve...and then twenty-two. They gathered together, seemingly consulting one another, their trunks whistling in turn.

Finally, the first monopod detached itself from the group, and with a single bound, jumped in front of Bild and Brad. It bent its knee, extended its arm, and touched Bild's chest gently with its three talons. Then it touched Brad's shoulder in the same fashion. The two Americans did not budge, observing the little black being between their eyelashes.

The Mercurian straightened up, and a long modulated whistle emerged from its trunk. Immediately, four monopods separated from the group and came to join the first with a long leap. Leaving Bild and Brad, the five black beings surrounded Francisco, Lolla and Paul.

They crouched down, and touched Paul and Francisco cautiously with their talons. They whistled with their trunks; their eyes sparkled; the expressionless rat-like heads made rapid movements.

Evidently, the Mercurians were communicating the new impressions caused by the sight and feel of the unknown beings that had come to their planet from some unknown elsewhere.

But as two monopods, directing their arms simultaneously toward Lolla Mendès, appeared to want to take hold of the young woman's head, presumably to examine her hair, Paul and Francisco sat up at the same time, immediately imitated by Brad and Bild.

Howling, the four men leapt upon a monopod, which was knocked down instantaneously, and within a minute, had been tied up with Francisco's red belt, solidly attached, in an upright position, to the trunk of a tree.

At the first cry uttered by the Terrans, all the Mercurians except the prisoner had fled.

"A ludicrous individual," said Brad, planting himself in front of the monopod attached to the tree.

Furiously, the Mercurian's gleaming red eye rolled in its orbit. Its trunk whistled and agitated madly, and its one arm, secured at the elbow with a twist of the belt, struggled in vain to free itself.

Awakened by the racket, Lolla had stood up. Paul brought her up to date with events, and the five Terrans, arranged in a semicircle around the captive, examined it at their leisure.

The monopod's head was shaped like a rat's. The trunk, about thirty centimeters long, prolonged the muzzle. Beneath the trunk, which was equipped with a sucker at the extremity, there was neither a mouth nor a chin. The root of the trunk extended directly to join the body, for the strange being had no neck; he upper body scarcely narrowed to give birth to the head. To either side of the trunk was, not exactly an ear, but an auditory apparatus similar to a fish's gills. Finally, above the trunk, in the middle of the skull, that unique, enormous, bloody eye opened—and the skull immediately turned back, forming the back of the head.

The unique arm emerged forwards from the middle of the torso; it was disproportionately long.

With the aid of his knife whose dimensions he knew precisely, Francisco measured the Mercurian. The entire body, from the foot to the top of the skull measured 1.2 meters. The head alone measured twenty centimeters. The arm, from its point of origin to the tips of the claw, was sixty-five centimeters long. The leg, from the foot to place where the thigh ended and the torso began, was sixty centimeters long.

The captive was rather thin and slender in proportion to its size.

Like its hand, which terminated in three enormous sharp talons composed of a strangely metallic substance, its foot, in the form of a horse's hoof, also had three talons, shorter but thicker, two in front and one behind, like a cockerel's spur.

But the most prodigious thing of all in that extraterrestrial creature was its texture, the substance of its body; on feeling its arm, its thigh, its torso and its skull, the Terrans had the sensation of touching hot ebony-wood. Evidently, the density of that flesh was superior to the density of human flesh; the body was more solidly constructed and framed, and yet it was evident that its specific weight was inferior to the weight of a human body of similar size.

When all these observations had been made, Paul de Civrac said gravely: "We're in a world very different from our own. Later, perhaps, we'll be able to explain it. For the moment, we have to think about staying alive.

"That might not be easy," said Brad.

"We need to establish friendly relations with these indigenes," suggested Bild.

"How do we persuade it that w don't mean it any harm?" asked Lolla.

"I'm going to try!" Paul moved his companions aside and remained on his own in front of the Mercurian. He took three steps back and began a series of bows, amicable gestures and smiles. He put his hands to his mouth to mime eating, and lay down on the ground to simulate sleeping. Then, drawing closer to the monopod, he pointed to the vault of the forest, picked up a stone, threw it up in the air and followed its fall with his extended finger.

By means of that mime he hoped to make it understood that, having fallen from the sky, the only desire the five of them had was to eat and sleep tranquilly.

Then he waited.

The monopod had followed the human's movements with an irritated eye. Its only response as a long whistle.

Then Civrac untied the belt and gradually set the captive free. When the entire belt was unwound, he stood back.

Once free, the monopod started waving its arm and leg, which had presumably gone stiff. Then it looked successively at the four men and—for a long interval—the young woman. Its bloody eye was devoid of expression. Its trunk emitted five brief whistles. Then, suddenly, it flexed its knee extended like a spring, leapt up, bounded over Brad's head, and disappeared in a matter of seconds into the mystery of the forest.

Chapter Three
Which ends with two dissimilar abductions

"*Adios!*" said Francisco, when the monopod had gone.

"Do you think it understood?" asked Lolla.

"I doubt it!" Civrac relied.

"Ludicrous individual!" muttered Bild.

"But why is it made of wood, damn it?"

"Wood, do you think?" said Brad, sardonically.

"Decidedly," said Paul, as if talking to himself, "I'm more and more convinced that we're on the planet Mercury."

"Eh?" said Bild. "A fine conviction—but what is it based on?"

"The intensity of the light and heat. You know that Mercury is the planet nearest to the sun. There are other indications too. Look, our astronomers know, thanks to the comparative observation of the planets, that on Mercury the density of materials is a third greater than on Earth. Hence the hardness of the monopod's flesh, the resistance of the red grass..."

"How is it, then, that we weren't crushed by falling on such hard grass and ground?" objected Bild.

"Exactly!" said Paul. "The atmosphere of Mercury is much denser than Earth's; in addition, our weight has diminished by half. We fell almost as gently as a piece of paper thrown from a tower. All that makes me think that we're on the planet Mercury. And look there, through that gap in the foliage..."

"Well?"

"Notice that beam of light. It's falling perpendicularly, isn't it?"

"Yes."

"What time is it?"

"Half past five," said Bild, after consulting his watch.

"Perfect! Do you remember that at one o'clock, on the red plain, the light was coming down in perpendicular rays from the clouds? Our shadows could only be seen between our parted feet—do you recall?"

"Yes."

"That proves, therefore, that the sun above the clouds hasn't changed its position relative o us. Now, do you know the most recent opinion of the French astronomer Camille Flammarion?"

"No."

"This is it, in summary: Because of the proximity of the planet, the sun has, so to speak, immobilized the globe of Mercury, just as the Earth has done for the Moon, forcing it to present the same face constantly. In consequence, there's eternal daylight in the sunlit hemisphere, and perpetual night in the other hemisphere, which a broad twilight zone between the two."

"I understand!" exclaimed Bild. "We've fallen in the middle of the sunlit hemisphere, and the sun will never set for us. We're immobile beneath it. Well, since we're on Mercury, hurrah for Mercury!"

And Bild brandished his enormous hands in the air, while Lolla admired Paul and Brad and Francisco, somewhat indifferent to what they had just heard, searched the forest with their eyes.

"Whether it's Mercury or not," said Brad, in a dull voice that contrasted with Bild's, "this world doesn't fill me with joy. Shut up a minute and listen."

Everyone pricked pup their ears...

And in all directions of the mysterious forest, there were faint whistling sounds, still distant, but continual and innumerable. Their shrill whine was incessantly drawing nearer.

"We're going to have thousands of those little black monsters on our backs," Bild murmured.

"What shall we do?" asked Lolla, fearfully.

"Wait," said Paul de Civrac, taking her hand. In a lower voice, for her alone, he added: "Don't be afraid, Lolla; I'm here. I'd die rather than..."

"Thank you, Paul," she replied, blushing. And their eyes met, shining with confidence and love—a love as yet unexpressed in words. In spite of the threat of danger, they felt impregnated by a great happiness, an indescribable and profound joy. In that moment, silently, Paul and Lola had given themselves to one another.

The whistles became louder and louder. Soon, they filled the air, and the echoes in the cloud multiplied them a hundredfold.

Suddenly, in the relative gloom of the forest, a red eye shone—then twenty; then a hundred; and then an incalculable number, incessantly increasing. And they heard the sharp rustle of pedal talons on the metallic leaves strewn on the ground.

The circle of little black monsters was tightening incessantly. The first in line were no more than ten paces from the group of Terrans. As far as their sight could reach, the four men and the woman saw flat heads in succession, trunks waving and thousands of red eyes sparkling between the tree-trunks.

"They're going to attack us, Paul," said Bild.

"We have no weapons," said Brad.

"Nor have they," said Francisco.

"They have their claws!"

Terrified, Lolla Mendès clung to Paul, whose arm was around her waist. The young man quivered with joy in hugging Lolla, even though he was thinking about the danger of an attack by the Mercurians.

"What do we do?"

"Let's try to negotiate." And Civrac, with his free arm, began gesturing.

Shrill whistles cut through the air, though; the first rank of Mercurians surged forward, flowed by the innumerable host.

Bild grabbed a monopod by the leg and, using it as a club, started striking out ahead of him. Brad did likewise. By that means, they opened up a passage.

"Follow us!" cried Bild.

"Move backwards!" howled Brad.

Francisco brandished his Catalan knife, stabbing red eyes. Lifting Lola, who had fainted, on to his shoulder, Paul de Civrac defended himself awkwardly with his free arm. And both of them, moving backwards, followed Bild and Brad.

But what could four humans do against that multitude of clawed monsters? Amid a racket of cries and whistles, which reverberated indefinitely in the sky, the Mercurians rushed after Paul and Francisco. Those in front of Bild and Brad moved aside to avoid their blows, but they rejoined those behind them, so effectively that the Frenchman, the Spaniard and Lolla were soon separated from the two Americans.

Suddenly, Francisco's knife, striking a glancing blow against the skull of a monopod, snapped. The blade fell. Instinctively, Francisco tried to bend down to pick it up, but twenty monopods leapt on top of him, grabbed him and immobilized him.

"Help me!" he cried.

"Help!" shouted Civrac, at the same time. He had just slipped and fallen. In the blink of an eye, he too was pinned to the ground by the monsters. He put both arms around Lola and did not put up any more resistance. They could have killed him, though, before snatching the inanimate body of the young woman away from him.

Meanwhile, in response to their companions' cries, Bild and Brad had turned round. They saw that it was impossible to go to the aid of the captives. They were more than a hundred meters away, and the Mercurians were filling that space tumultuously, claws extended. Every fallen monopod was replaced by another. In the meantime, the Mercurians were dragging the captives even further away.

"We'll never catch up with them, Bild!"

"No, Brad, no!"

"The best thing is to get away!"

"We can search for them later."

"Exactly!"

"Grab another monster, Brad—yours is demolished."

"So's yours."

"All right!"

And, throwing away the useless cadavers that had served them thus far as clubs, each of them grabbed a living monopod, and, brandishing it like a flail, began striking out again.

They were covered in wounds, however. The Mercurians' terrible claws had made profound incisions in their arms, thighs and hips, from which blood was flowing.

"Head for the red prairie, Brad!"

"Let's go, Bild!"

And the two men bounded away, striking out and howling, heading for the vast red grassland. They were able to run faster than the monopods now. They hoped, once they were in the open, to escape them more easily than in the forest, where the densely-packed tree-trunks were continual obstacles.

Meanwhile, a hundred monopods carried Francisco, Paul and Lola away. They had tied them up with some kind of fibrous yellow cord. With their joined arms, twelve Mercurians formed a sort of lattice-work stretcher on which the young woman as carried. Twelve others were transporting Francisco in the same fashion and a further twelve Paul de Civrac, who had let go of Lola's body once he understood that the unfeeling brutes would have torn her apart with their claws in order to get her away from him.

Following a broad path with numerous turnings, they went rapidly and silently, without any whistling sounds. Soon, Paul and Francisco, who had maintained their presence of mind, could no longer hear the battle that Bild and Brad were sustaining.

"Where are they taking us, Señor?" asked Francisco.

"Doubtless to one of their cities—for there's no longer any doubt about it; these horrible monsters are intelligent beings."

"And Brad and Bild?"

"Alas…!"

"The Señorita is still unconscious, Señor."

"That's probably better. You can't see any wounds on her, can you?"

"None. What about you?"

"I only have a couple of scratches on my right thigh. You?"

"Nothing, Señor, nothing—a scratch on each arm, hardly worth the trouble of mentioning. But tell me, Señor, these scoundrels don't appear to intend doing us any harm..."

"Not for the moment, no. We'll have to be patient."

"Patient! Santiago de Campostelo protect us! We've fallen into a hellish land."

Suddenly, the two men could no longer see the vault of the trees above them. The sudden light blinded them and they felt the horrible heat of harsh light.

"Señor! The forest's ended..."

Paul turned his head. "We're on the bank of the golden river, Francisco."

The sight of that river was so strange that the two captives forgot their situation in order to feel astonishment and admiration.

At their feet, along a low bank covered with russet grass, an amazing liquid was flowing; it was bright yellow, opaque, and its heavy, blistered waves were rolling along as if in an uneven channel of molten gold.

At that place the river was about a hundred meters wide; its depth was impossible to estimate, since the liquid was not transparent.

"Look, Señor!" shouted Francisco.

While the two men were admiring the river, the Mercurians had arranged themselves in a compact triangle, with the porters and the captives in the middle. One Mercurian was standing on its own at the point of the triangle, orientated in the direction of the current. That Mercurian seemed to be a chief, to judge by its taller stature and a large flexible gold ring circling its trunk. It gave voice to a prolonged whistle and raised its arm. Immediately, the entire phalanx leapt into the river.

It did not sink into the liquid. Carried away like a raft, drawn by the current, it glided along, with the undulations of the waves, traveling at some sixty kilometers an hour.

At the base of the Mercurian triangle, ten monopods were lined up at right angles to the flow; they were kneeling down, plunging their arms entirely into the yellow liquid. Paul, who could see them clearly, noticed that they were modifying the inclination of their arms in accordance with whistles uttered by the chief standing at the point of the triangle.

"Can you see how they're making a rudder, Francisco?" said Paul.

"I can see, Señor." The Spaniard was squinting his bewildered eyes, as much as the intensity of the light permitted.

When they had arrived, diagonally, in the center of the river, the arms of the ten monopods emerged from the liquid, and they moved in a straight line from then on.

In spite of the solicitations issued to their curiosity by the landscape and the extraordinary events, Paul and Francisco did not lose sight of Lola Mendès. She was still unconscious, but just as the forest gave way on one bank to the russet prairie and on the other to the first escarpments of the slate mountains, Paul saw that she was struggling in the arms of her captors. Almost immediately, she opened her eyes.

"Lolla!" he shouted. "Don't be afraid!"

"Paul!"

"Don't be afraid, I beg you, and don't struggle. We're prisoners of the Mercurians. I don't know where they're taking us, but they don't appear to have any evil intentions in our regard."

"What happened? Where's Francisco? Where are Bild and Brad?"

"I'm here, Señorita!" said the Spaniard.

"In a few words, Civrac gave an account of the battle and its outcome; he described the passage over ground and on the river. He had scarcely finished when Francisco shouted: "The Fiery Wheel! The Fiery Wheel!"

"Bild and Brad!" exclaimed Paul de Civrac at the same time.

The Mercurians had seen the aerial phenomenon too, for they began whistling and waving their trunks and arms.

And what happened then was truly the most exorbitant episode in the entire exorbitant adventure.

Bild and Brad were running across the russet prairie, pursued by a host of Mercurians. Above them, at a height that was difficult to estimate, the Fiery Wheel was turning in a direction parallel to that of the golden river.

Suddenly, drowning out the whistles of the monopods, a rumble resounded, reverberated to infinity by the echoes of the eternal green clouds.

The Fiery Wheel increased its glare, and the captives saw Bild and Brad, clinging together, rising up toward the Wheel, drawn in as in Bogota, followed by twenty gesticulating monopods...

The flying bodies disappeared into a fulguration of the Wheel, and the Wheel itself, with a noise like a thousand thunderclaps, abruptly vanished into the clouds.

Meanwhile, rapidly, the golden river drew the three distressed, sweating, blinded captives into the unknown, on the arms of the whistling Mercurians.

PART THREE
THE MERCURIANS

Chapter One
In which horrific scenes conclude with a terrible accident

The rapid glide along the current of the golden river lasted for a long time. The intensity of the torrid heat and the dazzling light had overwhelmed Paul de Civrac, Lola and Francisco. Unconscious, their eyes closed, they remained lying on the arms of their porters, without the strength to exchange their impressions.

From time to time, however, they called out to one another and drew a little courage from the mutual observation that they were alive. None of them knew how many hours that agony in the heat and light lasted; Lolla was the only one who had a watch, but the little chronometer had stopped and the young woman, with her hand tied, could not take it from her belt.

The silence around them was absolute. All they could hear, at long intervals, was the whistling of the monopod with the gold-ringed trunk.

Suddenly, darkness succeeded the daylight, and coolness the torrid temperature. The three Terrans opened their eyes at the same time, and saw that they had entered a subterranean channel. The obscurity was not complete, however. The golden river, on which they were still traveling, radiated a yellow-tinted light. They were moving even more rapidly. The captives saw the black, uneven walls of the tunnel gliding vertiginously rearwards.

Where were they being taken, on this hectic journey?

"How are you, Lolla?" Paul asked—and his voice resounded in the depths of the unfathomable tunnel.

"Much better! This coolness is doing me good. I thought I was going to die in the heat and light outside."

"Santiago de Compostela be blessed!" said Francisco, signaling his contentment by means of his habitual invocation. "But where the devil are we?"

Abruptly, the glide came to a halt, and the prisoners perceived that their porters had leapt on to solid ground. The entire troop of monopods plunged into a lateral tunnel, and the Terrans saw the yellow glow of the golden river fading away behind them. It was now pitch dark.

"Lolla!" Paul shouted.

"I'm here!"

"Francisco!"

"Present, Señor."

"These monsters can see in the dark," Civrac went on, "like nyctalopic animals."[9]

"They're evidently ignorant of the use of candles, lamps and torches," murmured Lolla Mendès.

---

[9] In English, nyctalopia means night-blindess, as its Greek roots clearly imply, not an ability to see in the dark" but dictionaries confirm that the inversion of meaning of its French equivalent, *nyctalopie*, seems to be intrinsic to the French language rather than idiosyncratic to La Hire. There is, however, no other evident way to translate the French *nyctalopique*, so I have allowed the contradiction to remain here, as I have in translations of La Hire's novels featuring his series hero, the Nyctalope.

"And probably of the use of fire. If we're eventually obliged, and able, to seek salvation in flight, how can we get out of these dark caverns? Oh, how I regret now losing my electric torch when I fell out of the Fiery Wheel!"

"I've got a box of matches in my pocket, Señor," said Francisco, laughing.

A distant whistle was heard, to which the chief, who was marching in the lead, replied with a similar whistle. Paul raised his head slightly, and saw a pale light some distance away.

"Patience!" he said, philosophically.

A few moments later, the troop of Mercurians emerged into a prodigiously vast space. It was vaguely illuminated but the radiation of a narrow stream of yellow liquid meandering over the floor. Several times, with a simultaneous leap, the porters jumped over the luminous stream.

Suddenly, they stopped, deposited their captives on the ground one after another, removed their bonds, and moved away from them. Then they all started whistling, in a perfectly rhythmic fashion.

Then, like a flock of nocturnal animals, they dispersed into the immense subterranean cavity and disappeared into cavities, the orifices of which formed disquieting dark holes in the lighted walls.

The three captives found themselves alone, their arms and legs free—but that solitude was of such short duration that they did not even have time to exchange their impressions.

In tight masses, hundreds and hundreds of monopods surged out of the dark holes. They huddled around the captives, who had backed up against the rocky wall, and their semicircle became more and more compact.

Their red eyes were shining like little mobile beacons, their trunks were waving and whistling, and their arms were making jerky gestures. Suddenly, however, without any apparent cause, the most absolute silence and immobility descended upon the innumerable host of black monsters.

Then Paul, Lolla and Francisco saw two monopods leaping over the heads of the multitude, advancing rapidly toward them. With one last bound, the two Mercurians fell to the ground four paces in front of the Terrans. Their trunks were entirely surrounded by flexible gold thread. Undoubtedly, they were the great chiefs of the Mercurian society,

While the great Monopod potentates stood motionless and upright, each of them staring with its unique red eye. Paul took Lolla's hand and said: "Don't be afraid."

"No, Paul, I'm not afraid. Nothing can happen to us that's worse than death."

"And we'd die together, Lolla," Paul said, in a grave voice.

"Thank you," the young woman said, in a whisper.

"Before one of these dirty beasts touches you, Señorita," Francisco growled, "I'll have demolished a good few of them."

"Not a single gesture without my permission, Francisco!" the courageous Spanish woman ordered.

One of the chiefs raised its arm, and let it fall back—and immediately, it uttered a sequence of whistles of varying length, cadenced and separated by pauses. It was speaking—but did it imagine that the prisoners could understand it?

Its companion took over, and whistled for a long time in its turn. Then it seemed to be waiting.

Lowly, Paul straightened up. He wanted to reply, in accordance with his means. Accompanying his words with expressive gestures, he simply said: "We're hungry and thirsty." Then he sat down.

The two chiefs conferred, shaking their rat-like heads, moving their trunks and whistling. Then they turned to the crowd and made a gesture.

The packed ranks of Mercurians parted, and four monopods appeared, moving rapidly, carrying a black mass larger than themselves. They put it down in front of the three Terrans and withdrew.

The circle of the multitude closed again, almost touching the two chiefs. Thousands of red eyes were still staring; evidently, they were waiting to see what the prisoners would do.

Meanwhile, Paul examined the black mass that had been set down in front of him.

"But it's a Mercurian," he said, devoid of claws on its arms and legs, and fatter than the others."

"It looks to me like a fattened Mercurian," said Francisco.

"Do you understand it, Lolla?"

"No."

They reflected momentarily, and then Paul murmured: "I'm afraid I might understand."

The Mercurians' conduct did go unexplained for long.

Confronted by the inaction of their prisoners, the two chiefs conferred again. Then one of them knelt down beside the head of the recumbent monopod—and what the Terrans saw then caused them to cry out in horror.

Into the enormous bulging red eye of the monopod lying on the ground, the kneeling chief plunged the sucker of his trunk, with a single stroke, and while the mass stirred convulsively, from that eye, now punctured—from which a whitish liquid was running that was doubtless Mercurian blood—the chief avidly pumped his nourishment.

"Oh, Paul!" groaned Lolla, hiding her face in her hands.

Paul and Francisco were frozen. In a flash, the Frenchman understood numerous things. The Mercurians ate one another. Presumably, there was nothing living on their ardent soil but themselves. They must reproduce prodigiously, pullulating like terrestrial rats and rabbits, and, in order to live as well as to compensate for the intensive overproduction of their species, the Mercurians ate one another. What were the laws or customs regulating the choice, captivity and fattening of their nutritious victims? It would require a long sojourn on the Mercurian world, the understanding of their language, and the observation of their mores to discover that. But the fact itself was incontestable: the Mercurians ate one another!

And as if the spectacle of the chief pumping the life out of the captive had excited the appetites of the crowd, there was a deafening concert of whistling, and tumultuous eddies. Other monopods, fat and clawless, were brought into the empty space in front of the Terrans, and the multitude of black monsters surged forward. Trunks equipped with suckers punctured eyes swollen with white liquid.

"Paul, Paul!" moaned Lolla.

Fascinated by the spectacle, Paul and Francisco did not have the strength to move a muscle.

Soon, the nourishing monopods doubtless not being very numerous in that location, they saw Mercurians of relatively tall stature knocking down smaller Mercurians, and holding them down...

There was a horrible orgy of feeding, everywhere.

Suddenly, Paul felt a thrill of anguish. A heart-rending cry from Lolla had just struck his ears and broken the perfidious spell of the fascination.

"*Demonios!*" howled Francisco. "They're coming for us..."

Lola disappeared, dragged away by a group of monsters—and claws drew her arms apart, and trunks were directed toward her eyes, widened by terror.

Paul leapt forward, armed with a monopod he had just seized by the ankle. Francisco was already struggling in the middle of the group of abductors.

How could they tear Lolla away from the filthy creatures?

Francisco had lifted the young woman up and had started to run, in enormous bounds, over the tumultuous Mercurians, toward the black hole of a tunnel. Paul followed him, striking out in all directions with monopods that he seized, brandished and then threw away, while the living mass was transformed into a formless viscous sheet.

While running and striking out, he reflected, with a strange acuity of intelligence and an astonishing rapidity of thought.

"Francisco!" he shouted. "We won't be able to see in the tunnel, but they'll be able to see us!"

"I have my matches," the Spaniard replied, breathlessly.

"Take care not to jump too high—you'll smash your skull against the rock."

"Thanks! I'll bear it in mind..."

They reached the tunnel. Francisco and his burden disappeared into the darkness.

"Shout, Francisco! Shout, so that I don't lose you!" And he leapt into the black hole in his turn.

Francisco uttered a cry at every bound. Paul followed him, crying out in his turn and striking out. Suddenly, he perceived that he was thrashing in vain; there were no Mercurians around him. He threw away the shapeless debris of the monopod he was still holding and, solely preoccupied with not losing touch with Francisco, accelerated his pace.

Gradually, he heard the sound of whistling decrease, and they eventually faded away entirely.

"Francisco!" he called.

"Señor!"

"Stop!"

"Why?"

"I can't hear anything. They're not chasing us any longer."

"A halt, then. Here I am, Señor. Don't go any further. Wait while I put the Señorita down and light a match..."

"Paul! Paul!" called Lolla Mendès. The very excess of the danger had prevented her from fainting.

"Lola! Are you hurt?"

"No, not a scratch. Oh, what monsters! You saved me, Francisco."

"Good, good, Señorita! I don't think it's over yet. *Demonios!*"

A match scraped. A little blue flame sprung forth and rose into the air above Francisco's fingertips.

The Frenchman and the Spaniard looked at one another. They were bloodied, and their clothes were in tatters.

"My God!" Lolla exclaimed. "Are you both wounded?"

"No—just superficial scratches. It's nothing—but what about you?"

Lolla had only suffered a slight scratch on her right hand, but the bottom of her skirt had been torn apart.

"Not bad, then," said Francisco. We might get out of this yet. Where are we?"

The match went out, and he struck another.

Swiftly, the three fugitives examined their surroundings. They were in a high, broad tunnel with walls of black slate.

"We have to keep on running," said Paul. "Surprised by our resistance and flight, the crowd of Mercurians is doubtless irresolute, but their chiefs won't take long to resume their authority and give orders. They'll certainly come after us. We have a start—it's necessary to increase it further."

"Let's go," said Lolla, getting to her feet.

"Can you feel the strength of the air-current?"

"Yes."

"From now on, you'll position yourself between Francisco and me, holding each of us by one hand. Our specific weight is so light that you won't have to make any effort. We'll be able to lift you up like a feather while bounding ourselves."

"Let's get going," said Francisco—but then slapped his forehead. "We're stupid! We're going to break our bones against the rock in the dark. We've had astonishing luck to have got this far without coming to grief. We can't go on without light."

Neither Lolla nor Paul had thought about the danger of the darkness in that unknown tunnel. They looked at one another, discouraged, and the young woman's eyes moistened with tears.

"If only Brad and Bild were here," said Francisco. "If there were four of us we could retrace our steps, reach the golden river, and let the current carry us away. It must come out on the other side of the mountain."

"Unless it plunges into an interior gulf," said Paul.

"What shall we do?"

"Listen!" whispered Lola.

They held their breath. They could hear whistling.

"They're coming after us."

"Damn it!" groaned Francisco.

Paul made a gesture of range, and raised his eyes as if to implore the heavens—but immediately, he uttered a faint exclamation.

"We're saved!" he murmured. "Throw away that dead match, Francisco, and strike another."

That was done in the blink of an eye.

"Lift your head," said Paul, excitedly. "Look up. That hole up there, with those rocky spurs. Let's jump. We can grab on to the spurs, get into the hole..."

"Understood!" said Francisco. "The dirty beasts will go past, and we can go back to the golden river. Hop! Permit me, Señorita!"

He held out his right arm, with the match upraised in his hand; he put his left arm around Lolla's waist. "You first, Señor."

Paul leapt up, hung on, remained suspended momentarily, and then swung himself into the hole with a single movement.

"To me!"

Francisco jumped in his turn. The match went out, but the Spaniard had judged the leap well. He bumped into Paul head first and knocked him over; he and Lolla rolled on the floor; the rock stopped them.

"Señor!" breathed Francisco.

"Lolla!" said Paul.

"I'm here, Paul.

"You didn't hit your head?"

"No."

"All's going well!"

"Yes—silence!"

"And let's get further into the hole,"

They huddled in the depths of the excavation, tightly grouped together, and waited.

The whistles became louder. The vaults of the tunnel resonated with the distant footfalls of the host—abrupt, jerky hopping footfalls and the scrape of claws on slate.

"Here they come," whispered Paul.

Although they were ardently curious to see the multitude of Mercurians pass by, the three Terrans obeyed the dictates of prudence. They did not lean over the edge of the hole.

With tumultuous whistles, at a frantic gallop, the ferocious monopods flowed past in a noisy stream four meters below the cavity where the beings they were pursuing, who seemed bizarre to them, had taken refuge. The noisy procession lasted a long time.

While the Mercurians were galloping beneath them, the Terrans reflected sadly. Would they ever see the Earth again? Alas, it seemed impossible. How could they get back there? No means could present itself, even to the craziest imagination. Could the prodigious hazard that had led to their being sucked in by the Fiery Wheel—the same hazard that had carried off Brad and

Bild for a second time—possibly happen again? To hope so would have been insane...

Lolla, Paul and Francisco saw themselves condemned, therefore, to wander in the strange Mercurian world until they died, tracked like hunted beasts by the savage animals that the monopods were. If they had had the good fortune to fall on one of the old and great planets in the solar system instead, perhaps they would have found intelligent beings in the human mold there, knowledgeable, good, civilized and hospitable! But their unfortunate destiny had thrown them on to Mercury, burned by the sun, deserted Mercury, populated only by intelligent and ferocious monsters that seemed to be ignorant of any science, art and civilization.

What could be expected, in fact, of the whistling black horde that was bounding past in the tunnel like a pack of hunting hyenas? Nothing. There was nothing more to do than wait, first to resign themselves and then to struggle, in order to be ready to seize any chance of salvation that presented itself. The things that had happened thus far had been so extraordinary that they might leave scope for the most extravagant hopes.

Meanwhile, the din of the chase diminished and drew away; the whistles and the sound of footfalls gradually faded away in distant tunnels, and silence fell again beneath the tenebrous vaults.

"They've all gone by," said Francisco.

"What shall w do?" murmured Lola.

"Let's go," said Paul. "Let's go back to the golden river and gamble on the current. We'll stay close to the edge so that we'll be able to cling on to the bank if we see the liquid mass falling into a gulf. Whatever the danger is we're heading for, it's no worse than that of staying here. I'm really hungry now..."

"Me too," said Lolla, "and especially thirsty."

"And me," growled Francisco.

"Let's get out! Let's try to get back to the light…even with the accompanying heat, it's preferable to this sepulchral darkness. And who knows, perhaps we'll see the Fiery Wheel again! In our situation, no further incident can increase our distress. Light a match, Francisco. Let's jump down and get our bearings."

"Just a moment, Señor," said the Spaniard. "If you'll permit, I'll carry out a reconnaissance as far as the large grotto, in order to make sure that a troop of the filthy things hasn't stayed behind the one that went past. If that's the case we'd be caught between two fires—if I might use that Terran expression, as Jonathan Bild would say."

Paul smiled at Francisco's irrepressible humor, which could not be defeated by any circumstance, no matter how dangerous. The advice was too good not to be followed. In addition, the young man saw an unexpected means of remaining alone with Lola Mendès— and his voice trembled, not with fear but with emotion, when he replied: "You're right, Francisco. Go—and be careful."

"Does the Señorita agree?" the Spaniard asked.

"Yes, my friend. Go—but I too advise you to be careful…"

"I shall be, Mistress, I shall."

Francisco collected himself, handed Paul a lighted match, and said: "Light my jump, please, Señor!" The he jumped out of the hole.

By the light of the match, Civrac and Lola saw him land gently on his feet, bend his knees, straighten up, light another match, and move off in the direction of the large grotto.

Paul and Lolla were alone.

Emotion made their hearts beat, and if the match that the young man was still holding had not suddenly gone out, they would have seen one another's faces pale and would have glimpsed a disturbance in one another's eyes that would have told them more effectively than words what they were both feeling.

Without seeking, their hands found one another and clasped; without saying a word, their lips touched and melted into a long kiss.

Oh, how far away they were from the terrors of the past, the horrors of the present and the apprehensions of the future! Love carried the two individuals, full of strength and life, far away from the material world. Were they still on the planet Mercury? Had they returned to Earth? No, they were floating, hand in hand, lips united, in the indefinable spaces that love opens magnificently to the hearts of which it takes possession. They were only conscious of one thing: their happiness.

When their lips separated, it was to pronounce the same words in unison.

"Lolla, I love you..."

"I love you, Paul..."

They could not see one another in the darkness, but each of them divined the other's passionate gaze.

"Lolla," said Paul, "when you appeared to me in the Fiery Wheel, it seemed to me that the gap in the wall of cloud through which you passed was the door of heaven, which had just opened. I loved you immediately. What about you?"

"I don't know, Paul. I was weeping, in despair since my incomprehensible abduction...but when my eyes met yours, my pain and my fear went away. Since then, it seems that I'm having a marvelous and very sweet dream, a dream that the flashes of nightmare render even more exquisite. Paul!"

He felt her let herself slide softly into his arms. He hugged her forcefully and murmured: "I love you, Lolla, I love you...oh, how glad I am to love you!" And he covered her face with kisses, seeking the lips that she moved away from him with virginal modesty.

Oh the omnipotence of love! Brought together by a chain of events as terrifying as it was implausible; hurled into perils all the more frightful because they were new and unknown; abandoned on a world of terrible surprises and threats; hunted by filthy creatures, innumerable and ferocious; menaced at every moment, every step and every breath by a death that seemed incessantly more imminent and cruelly various, Paul and Lolla, in one another's arms, only had thoughts of happiness, actions that were caresses, words to stammer their passion, and life in order to love.

The Fiery Wheel, the Saturnians, the planet Mercury, the monopods, the atrocious and bloody scenes, the horrible pursuit, the continual danger, and the death lying in ambush in the darkness were all non-existent so far as Lolla Mendès and Paul de Civrac were concerned. There was nothing, in an indeterminate world, but two living beings: them! Only one thing subsisted in the universe: their love!

And when, vanquished and ecstatic, Lolla finally surrendered her lips to Paul's kisses, the mysterious planet they were inhabiting could have blown apart like a shell exploding in mid-air, and Paul and Lolla would never have known. They would have passed from life to death without their delight being troubled for a thousandth of a second.

"Oh, Paul!" moaned Lolla, "I didn't know what happiness is!"

"Lolla! Lolla!" He could not pronounce any other syllables than those forming her name.

And again, avid for a joy so divine their lips were meeting, when a shout struck them like the brutal stab of a sword-blade. Their embrace loosened, their eyes opened, and, in the depths of the tunnel, feebly illuminated, they saw a man coming toward them.

"Where are we?" Lolla murmured, in a dream-like voice. Immediately, however, she recovered consciousness of herself and everything else, and the exclaimed, at the same time as Paul: "Francisco! It's Francisco!"

"In person, Señor!"

And the Spaniard loomed up before their eyes, lifting a lighted match over his head.

"The way is clear, Señorita. We can escape. Quickly—jump down, both of you, and follow me."

Paul and Lolla exchanged one last squeeze of the hand, gave their souls to one another again in a glance, and jumped together.

A few minutes later, the fugitives arrived in the vast space where the monopods' horrible feast had taken place. They turned away in horror from the flaccid black masses that lay here and there on the ground.

"Let's follow the golden stream," Paul said.

They went out of the cavern by means of a narrow corridor, along which the luminous stream ran, leaving a narrow ledge between itself and the wall.

"Do you have your watch, Lolla?" Paul asked.

"Yes."

"Will you entrust it to me?"

"Here it is."

Civrac turned the resetting wheel, moving the hands so that they indicated twelve o'clock.

"We can't know," he said, "what time it is on Earth, and it's of no importance to us anyway. I'm setting the watch at noon. The instrument will simply serve to map out the hours that go by. That might be useful to us."

He used his cravat to attach the watch securely to his belt.

Meanwhile, they continued walking.

The hands marked quarter past twelve when the Terrans emerged into a kind of crossroads from which several tunnels led away, and where the stream mingled its trickle of yellow liquid with the profound mass of the golden river.

"The Mercurians ride on the liquid," said Paul, "and don't sink into it, as if it were solid ground. Let's try."

He put his foot out and pressed down on the surface of the heavy liquid. He felt a resistance comparable to that of clay, and only sank into it by a few centimeters. The yellow liquid was hot, but the temperature was tolerable.

"Give me your hand, Lolla. Do as I do, Francisco."

Drawing the young woman along, he put both feet on the strange river. Francisco followed Lolla, similarly holding her hand. Immediately, the current dragged them away, and they glided rapidly alongside the rocky walls.

The subterranean channel in which the river flowed was about fifty meters wide, but its height was immeasurable. The yellow radiation that the luminous liquid produced scarcely reached the vault, which was blurred by shadows high above, displaying sharp ridges and overhanging black masses.

"My God, where are we going?" sighed Lolla. Her heart tightened, for a atrocious presentiment had just surged forth in her mind.

They were sliding through space as if carried by a moving walkway. Paul and Francisco kept close to the wall. Ready to slow down and interrupt their progress if it became necessary, by hanging on to rocky outcrops; with that anticipation, each of them had wrapped everything that he had been able to detach from their ragged clothing around their arm and free hand.

Suddenly, they perceived simultaneously that their glide was accelerating and that, about a hundred meters downstream, the river divided into two branches that plunged into two different tunnels.

"I'm scared!" sighed Lolla Mendès, involuntarily.

"Let's stop, Francisco!" Civrac exclaimed.

"*Bueno!*"

And their enveloped hands reached for the wall.

While thinking about impeding their progress, however, they did not see a rocky projection that advanced two meters into the river's course. Paul bumped into it first. The shock knocked him over, caused him to let go of Lolla's hand, and threw him into the middle of the current.

Without pausing for thought, Francisco tried to go to his aid. He too released his mistress' hand and bounded toward Civrac—but they had reached the point where the river divided. The faster current dragged the two men into one tunnel, while Lolla continued into the other, her glide becoming solitary.

"Paul! Paul! Help me! Help!"

The young woman's desperate cry chilled her two defenders with fear.

"Lolla!" shouted Paul, rising to his feet.

"*Demonios!*" Francisco swore—and tried to launch himself upriver, to get back to the fork and take the arm of the river that was carrying the young woman away. It was in vain. With Paul, he was dragged along by the current, with increasing rapidity. A sudden surge of heavy waves tipped the two men over, and they collided as they fell. For an immeasurable interval they rolled in the darkness, groping, grabbing hold of one another, and then being pulled apart by the waves, before finding one another again.

Suddenly, a bright light dazzled them. They had the sensation of coming to an abrupt stop in their vertiginous course—and when they were able to take account of things, they saw that the waves, tumultuous in that location, had thrown them on to a bank covered in scarlet flowers.

"Lolla!" Paul shouted, madly.

Face down, with his head in his hands, Francisco was sobbing. Civrac looked at him stupidly, and only then did he understand the frightful misfortune they had suffered.

Chapter Two
Fully occupied by the vicissitudes
of a fantastic chase

It was as if his entire being had been torn in two. Lolla was lost. At that moment, he saw the full horror of the ardent and mysterious planet—and felt a frisson of terror. So long as the young woman had been with him, so long as he had been able to guide her, protect her and defend her. Paul de Civrac had had been hopeful. For what? He did not know himself. Perhaps he had been hoping for a providential return to Earth, or, at least, a progressive adaptation to the conditions of this new world. With Lolla Mendès, he could have lived there happily...

Now, vague hopes, illusions, confidence in the future—all of it had been scythed down. Lola Mendès had disappeared, dragged away by the river into the depths of the incomprehensible planet...and he would never see her again! If she escaped some gulf, she too would be hurled on to an undiscoverable shore, and would fall prey to the filthy Mercurians!

At that thought, Paul de Civrac surrendered to the craziest despair. He fell on to the burning ground, tore it with his fingernails, bit it...

"Lolla! Lolla!" he screamed.

All that responded to him were Francisco's sobs and the ironic echoes of the eternal green clouds...

But human grief has its limits. Succeeding his fit of insensate despair, a crisis of prostration descended upon the young man. Aided by his bodily fatigue, it plunged him into a death-like sleep.

He woke up unconscious of everything. The implacable light closed his eyes again immediately, and he heard a grave voice saying: "Señor! Señor!"

A painful labor racked his mind. Gradually, he remembered everything....

"Lolla!" he murmured.

"We'll find her again, if it takes every last drop of my blood!"

At these words, forcefully pronounced, Paul blushed at his own weakness. He raised himself up on his elbow and, his eyes gradually becoming accustomed to the intense light of the eternal day, he opened them entirely. He saw Francisco sitting beside him. The Spaniard's ordinarily comical face was so severe and grave that it made a deep impression on him.

"We'll get her back, Señor..."

"We must, Francisco." And a confession, stronger than any reserve, emerged from his lips: "I love her, Francisco...I love her!"

"So much the better, Señor—you'll have all the more courage in searching for her. Me, I saw her born. I've served her father for twenty-three years, and I'd be serving him still if that accursed Fiery Wheel, may Hell crush it...but let's leave the past behind. We need to be strong. And first, you need to eat. Look, do as I'm doing. While you were asleep, I tasted the red flowers. It's not good, but they're nourishing. One might think one were eating iron. Copy me!"

While speaking, the Spaniard was picking red flowers, reminiscent of monstrous poppies and rolling them into balls. He threw them into his mouth and chewed vigorously.

Paul followed the advice. It seemed to him that he was chewing a handful of the ferruginous pills that Earthly physicians prescribed for anemia.

"Is there anything to drink?" he said, when he was sated. "I'm thirsty."

Francisco pointed at the yellow river, which was seething heavily a few paces away.

"I've tried that too," he said. "It's not a drink, though. Have you ever had a drop of the mercury they put in thermometers in your mouth? I've done it more than once, in Barcelona, to amuse the Señorita. Well, the liquid of the golden river gives the same sensation— yellow mercury..."

"What are we going to do?"

"We need to search. Get up"—the action followed the words—"and let's act like men!"

Gradually, under the vivifying influence of the red flowers, Paul recovered all his energy. He got up and clasped his companion's hand. "We're going to find Lolla, Francisco!"

"I hope so, Señor. We're going to make a start. I think we ought to continue going downriver to begin with. The current that dragged Lolla away might join up with it, at a bend in these mountains."

"You're right. But we'll certainly run into Mercurians—we need weapons of some kind."

"I've thought of that. Let's walk as far as that little gray wood over there, on the edge of the river. We'll see whether there's a means to break a couple of trees to make clubs. And I still have some matches. If the trees are made of a substance that will burn, we can sharpen stakes—that would be excellent for ramming into the eyes of the dirty black beasts. Do you still have the Señorita's watch? What time is it?"

118

Paul took the little watch from his belt. He could not look at it without an emotion that brought tears to his eyes.

"Half past eleven," he said.

"When the watch was at twelve we were in the tunnels. We lost the Señorita about half an hour later... Bueno."

Without explaining what conclusions he had drawn from that information, or even whether he had drawn any conclusion at all, Francisco headed toward the wood. Both of them reached it in a few bounds.

The Spaniard picked up a handful of gray leaves from the ground, sought out a shady corner, and struck a match. He put it under the leaves, and they caught fire immediately, burning with a bright white flame.

"*Caramba!*" he exclaimed.

"Those leaves burn like magnesium!" said Paul.

"I don't know about that," Francisco said, "but they burn—that's the main thing."

"But there are no branches on these trees," Paul continued. "Let's set fire to a big heap of leaves around two trunks of a suitable thickness..."

"Yes, Señor."

A few minutes later, two small white fires, maintained with care and rapidity—the masses of leaves burned very swiftly—had communicated their incandescence to two trunks as thick as terrestrial telegraph poles. They burned very rapidly, melting as they did so. When they saw they were breaking, Paul and Francisco sent them crashing to the ground with a push. It only took them half an hour to sharpen one end of each trunk to a point in the flame. Spikes at that end, they were clubs at the other.

The two men carried these weapons over their shoulder without the slightest difficulty. The pikes were three meters long, and the half-ligneous, half-metallic substance of which they were made was compact, dense and hard. They weighed as much as enormous staffs, but on Mercury, the weight of materials was reduced to half of the weight they would have had on Earth, so Paul and Francisco could handle their weapons without difficulty.

"Oh, if only Bild and Brad were here!" said Paul, regretfully.

"God alone knows where they are," said Francisco. "Perhaps we'll never see them again. Perhaps…for everything is so extraordinary in this mad world. For the moment, though, they're not here, and we have to do without them. Your hand, Señor. Let's jump!"

And, holding on to one another firmly, Paul and Francisco jumped into the golden river. It was less bloated there than upriver, so the travel was easier, rapid and without jolts. Imitating the Mercurians, the two men made use of their staffs like rudders and maintained themselves in mid-stream, where the current was faster and smoother.

To their left extended a limitless plain, entirely covered in russet grass and red flowers; those two plants, along with the gray trees, seemed to be the only vegetation in the region, and perhaps the entire sunlit hemisphere of the planet. Here and there, the plain was dotted with little woods.

To their right, falling almost sheerly into the river, high black mountains rose up; their summits were lost in the heavy crumbly mass of the green clouds. The light filtering through the clouds was still as intense, the heat still as torrid, but the two Terrans were gradually getting used to both. The light still made them blink incessantly, though, and the heat had roasted their bodies into one vast area of sunburn, which turned the skin red, then brown. Their adaptation to the strange environment was rapid, and they were soon able to pay no attention to the prickling of their tormented flesh.

While they traveled along the rapid river, a terrible impression of solitude weighed upon them. As far as the eye could see, no other living thing animated the desert of russet grass and red flowers. There was not a single bird or a fly in the air, not a single animal on the ground. Death was sovereign, and the wind, in the upper reaches of the dense atmosphere, always blew the enormous gen clouds toward the desolate mountains. The wind did not descend as far as the ground; it did not give any appearance of life to the rigid stalks of russet grass, the immutable red flowers or the rusty trees bearing their fixed plumes of metallic leaves, by agitating them.

There was silence and immobility, the dryness of the desert and death.

"But where do the Mercurians live?" Francisco said, suddenly, in a voice that revealed his profound anguish.

Paul de Civrac made no reply.

Perhaps the Mercurians lived in the dark entrails of their planet, or perhaps their cities were hidden, sheltered from the eternal and implacable light in narrow valleys, in the shade of the black mountains that loomed up steeply to unknown heights.

The landscape, too, luminous and yet dead, showed no evidence of cultivation, or any sign of intelligent life. The strangeness of the prairie of russet grass, the magnificence of the fields of scarlet flowers, the prodigious phantasmagoria of the green clouds—all those appearances that might have seemed enchanting—were mere desolation, because one sensed that they were futile, too continuously similar...

On the banks of the river, the scenery did not vary: black mountains on one side, russet grass and scarlet flowers on the other, to infinity.

"I'm thirsty!" Paul said. "If we don't find something to slake our thirst soon, we'll die."

"I know," said Francisco.

And silence fell again.

Suddenly, as the river described an abrupt curve, the monotonous prairies disappeared, and the Terrans veered between two high cliffs of slate. Shiny, they reflected light harshly. The encased river flowed in a single mass, without a single wave or sound.

"If the current that carried Lola away emerges from the mountain and joins up with this one," Paul said, "it won't take long for us to meet up with it, for the curve is taking us in that direction—provided that it doesn't veer again!"

As he finished pronouncing these reflections, highly problematic in their accuracy, Francisco squeezed his hand and murmured: "Mercurians!"

Two hundred meters downstream, an inlet was hollowed out in the cliff, forming a beach where a hundred Mercurians were gesticulating.

"We'll strike hard if they attack us," said Paul.

"Yes, Señor.

Already, the two Terrans were arriving level with the beach. They noticed a large hole at the back hollowed out into the mountain, doubtless another tunnel.

"Let's keep to the middle of the stream..."

"Yes..."

They went past the Mercurians rapidly. They expected to see the monopods leap into the river in order to chase them, but the black monsters with red eyes contented themselves with waving their repulsive trunks and clawed arms, and filing their air with a racket of whistling.

Immediately after the little beach, there was an abrupt bend in the river, as if it were doubling back on itself, and the strangest and most frightful spectacle was offered to the Terrans' eyes.

On both sides of the river the mountain drew back slightly, leaving broad banks on which thousands of small slate pyramids rose up. Mercurians were emerging from all the pyramids, hopping and whistling, lining up on the edge of the river. The immense city, which extended to the limit of vision, was in the shade. It was in the shade because the mountain rose up sheerly on either side, overhanging increasingly, the two walls almost touching at a prodigious height. High up, directly above the river, between the crests of the two prodigious cliffs, there was a long narrow band of light and green cloud.

Immediately, Paul and Francisco experienced a horrible choking sensation, even though the ambient temperature had diminished as much as the intensity of the light. They were hypnotized by the spectacle of those two frightful mountains hanging over their heads, when a furious volley of whistles fortunately brought them round.

Everywhere, the innumerable host of Mercurians lined up on the banks was jumping into the river. It was like the invasion of a golden road by black beasts. In front and behind, the monopods launched themselves forward, crowding, and the crowds departing from either side of the river drew together, becoming more tightly packed. They would soon form a single compact multitude, in the middle of which Paul and Francisco would be trapped.

"This time, we're doomed," said the Spaniard, lifting his club, "but they'll know what my life will cost them!"

"Francisco!" Paul shouted. "It's not necessary to fight—it's necessary to escape! Think about Lolla!"

"Escape! How? Where? We have no alternative but to die—and to kill as many as possible before!"

"No, no, Francisco! Do as I say!"

"That's all right be me," the Spaniard replied, calmly. "Give the order!"

As the first ranks of Mercurians were almost within arm's reach, he made a broad windmill movement with his spear, which caused the aggressors to pause.

Paul did likewise.

The continuous whirling kept the monopods at bay, but it was obvious that it could not last, for although the front ranks hesitated before the danger, the crowd behind them kept coming forward, pushing, and the entire multitude soon surged forward irresistibly..

"Francisco," said Paul, without interrupting his windmill motion, "look at the mountain to the right."

"Well?"

"Do you see that gorge opening in the cliff face?"

"Yes."

"It leads upwards."

"So what?"

"Well, I think we could reach the bank in one bound. These monsters won't be expecting that. Let's jump—we have one chance."

"What?"

"To land on the ground and not on the Mercurians' heads. Just there, on the bank, the crowd is spaced out.

Another leap will take us toward the gorge. They'll follow us, but we can run faster than they can."

"God preserve us! Let's jump!"

"Wait...are you ready?"

"Yes."

"Hup!"

Concentrating all their strength in their legs, the two men leapt. They passed over the swarming host that had invaded the river and landed between two pyramids, in the middle of a group of Mercurians, which had instinctively drawn apart.

"Hup!" said Paul.

"Hup!" repeated Francisco.

And they leapt again.

The sonorous valley resounded with horrible whistles. With a furious ardor, the entire immense crowd of monopods had hurled themselves in pursuit of the fugitives.

"They definitely have no weapons," said Francisco, bracing himself for a third leap.

"No, fortunately."

With a lead of more than a hundred meters over the first pursuers, the Terrans reached the entrance to the gorge hollowed out in the vertiginous cliff; it rose up in a steep but practicable slope.

"We can get away!" said Francisco.

"Yes, but what about Lolla?"

"God alone knows where she is now..."

"And if she's still alive..."

Paul fought back the tears of despair that welled up in his eyes, and launched himself into the gorge first.

While they bounded without a pause, they two men could hear the Mercurian host pursuing them, but they were getting further and further ahead of them. The sound of whistling became fainter; then it was no more than a vague murmur. Finally, they could no longer hear it.

By that time, Paul and Francisco had arrived at the far end of the gorge, which opened abruptly on to an immense slate plateau. The Frenchman spotted and overhanging mass under which there was a measure of shade.

"Let's take a rest there," Paul said. "I can't do any more..."

"The fact is that such exertion, in this heat..."

"Oh, I'm so thirsty! How thirsty I am!"

Suffocating, their bodies dehydrated, unable to produce a drop of sweat, Paul and Francisco lay down in the shade.

In front of them, the black plateau extended into the distance, all the way to a second chain of exceedingly high mountains to the flanks of which the eternal green clouds clung as they tore apart.

"What a desolate terrain!" Paul murmured.

"They're coming," Francisco panted. "Listen!"

As if emerging from the bowels of the mountain, whistles and the sounds of falls were audible.

"Let's run again," said Paul, getting to his feet.

"Where?"

"Toward the mountains out there."

And in spite of their horrible lassitude, in their determination to escape and find Lolla again, the two desperate men started running again, taking huge bounds.

Suddenly, Francisco shouted: "Señor!"

"What is it?"

"Look over there to the left. May I lose an arm if it's not rain, falling on the mountain."

At the word "rain," and without thinking that the liquid products of the sky in that strange planet might not be water, Paul felt new blood circulating more strongly in his limbs.

"Yes, yes!" he said, joyfully. "It must be rain..."

There was, in fact, in the distance, something like a curtain of barely-transparent mist: a mist thicker than distant rainstorms are on Earth, slightly tinted green...but which might be rain, might be water...

"Quickly! Quickly! Run that way!"

They were gripped and carried away by frenzy. They bounded like balloons inflated with gas, finding a new lightness with every brief landing.

Suddenly, they felt an indisputable freshness.

"Señor! It's water, Señor!"

And Francisco showed Paul the back of his large brown hand. A large drop of water had just crashed into it. Almost immediately, they were under the downpour. It was falling from an enormous dark green cloud with black depths. Voluptuously, with no other thought than taking in the vivifying liquid, they lay down on their backs, mouths open, receiving drops of water as large as pigeon's eggs over their entire bodies. As the drops hit the ground they made a crackling sound. They drank, slowly but without interruption, and felt with an indescribable joy, the water moistening their burned skin, insinuating itself into all their open pores.

"Ah! Ah!" Paul moaned—and was intoxicated by the formidable deluge.

Their thirst was eventually sated. They sat up.

"Francisco," said Paul, animatedly, "we need to collect the falling water. We need to save it!"

"But how?"

"What about your flask?"

It was suspended around the Spaniard's neck. He took it off, opened it, and presented it to Paul. "Drink! There are still a couple of mouthfuls of cognac left—one each."

When the flask was empty, he held it up in the air in both hands. It did not take long to fill up, because—alas!—it was not very capacious.

Almost immediately, the rain-cloud passed over, carried by the wind of the upper atmosphere. The implacable light and heat replaced its cool shade.

"Look, Señor! Over there!"

With his extended arm, Francisco pointed at a small gap in the slate, where the water had collected. The two men saw the water become tainted in less than a minute, becoming turbulent, then taking on a yellow tint, becoming golden yellow. There was a bizarre seething, and a rapid congelation, like molten gold in a crucible. Paul touched it with his finger; it was hot and resistant.

"Quickly!" he cried. "Look in the flask."

Francisco uncorked it, and they peered into the neck. The little circle of liquid gave every appearance of water, and retained it for three minutes, during which the two men watched. Then the surface of the water blemished slightly.

"Cork it, quickly!"

Francisco drove in the stopper.

"I understand now," said Paul. "The water falling on the ground combines with some element unknown to us and is transformed into that yellow substance, half-liquid and half-solid, which constitutes the rivers of this planet. The heat and the air must also have an influence on the chemical reaction, since the water in the flask began to transform after three minutes of contact with the atmosphere. But because the transformation is much less rapid than that of water on the ground, I think we can keep our modest provision intact for some time. And now..."

But he was interrupted by Francisco, who grabbed his pike, leapt to his feet and shouted: "Here they come again Señor! They're chasing us."

Far in the distance, in the direction of the gorge rising up from the golden river, a dark moving mass appeared, drawing rapidly nearer.

"Run!" said Paul.

And the two men, tracked like hunted animals, but stronger now, and animated by some confidence in the future, recommenced their bounding flight toward the high mountains, which were still a long way off...

Chapter Three
Which reveals stupefying phenomena

They had been running and bounding for nearly an hour when Paul de Civrac uttered a loud cry and sprawled on the ground. Francisco, who had already launched himself into a new leap, doubled back. Leaning over his companion, who was trying to get up again, he said: "Are you hurt, Señor?"

Paul stifled a groan of pain.

"My right foot hit a rocky ledge. I might have sprained the ankle. Take off my boot, Francisco."

Laid bare, the foot only seemed to be slightly bruised on its outer edge, near the ankle. Francisco rubbed it with his broad hands.

"It's nothing. Just twisted nerves, probably."

"I hope so. The pain's already lessening. But can I walk?"

Supported by Francisco, he raised himself up on his left foot, but when he tried to put his right foot down, an intolerable pain drew a moan from him.

"You need to rest it," said Francisco. "Lean on me and hope as far as that cleft over there. We'll be in the shade."

It took them five minutes to cover the hundred meters that separated them from the refuge indicated by Francisco, although, but for the accident, they would have crossed that distance in two bounds, in four seconds.

Once he had laid his companion down in the shade, Francisco moistened the palms of his hands with saliva and patiently began a vigorous massage. Then he sat beside the injured man and said: "Go to sleep! If the Mercurians are still chasing us, they won't get here for a good half-hour. I think you'll be able to walk by then, if not run. We're at the foot of the mountain. As you can see, it isn't steep and we can climb it easily. Once we're up there, I think we'll wear out the determination of those dirty black monsters. In any case, once we're on the far slope, out of sight, we'll be able to hide in some cavern and give them the slip. Sleep—I'll stay awake. Give me the watch."

The hands stood at quarter past four. The two men had, therefore, been walking and running for five hours since they had manufactured their weapons in the little wood on the prairie with the red flowers.

Paul immediately fell into a heavy sleep, populated with nightmares, though which Lolla and the monopods, together with Bild, Brad and the Fiery Wheel, passed in turbulent confusion.

Francisco kept watch. At half past four, he heard a distant and tenuous rumor in the great silence. Ten minutes later, far away, he saw the moving host of Mercurians, very tiny at that distance.

As the plateau over which the monopods were hopping rose in a gentle slope toward the mountain at whose foot the fugitives were stationed, Francisco was overlooking the entire extent.

"Ha ha!" he said. "They're beginning to tire, the dirty monsters! There aren't as many of them. At five o'clock I'll wake the poor young man. As long as Lolla isn't dead! Oh, if I ever give up trying to find her, I'll go back to the city in the valley and massacre as many as possible, so long as a breath of life remains in me..."

The Spaniard continued his monologue until the hands of the chronometer indicated five o'clock.

The host of monopods was still some distance away.

"Señor!" Francisco called, putting his hand on Paul's shoulder. "Señor!"

"Ah! yes...Lolla!"

Poor young fellow, Francisco thought. *He loves the Señorita and he's dreaming about her. Will he ever see her again, alas?* He shrugged his shoulders and said, aloud: "It's me, Señor. The dirty beasts are coming. We have to go."

Paul raised his head swiftly.

"Let's go!" he said, blinking his eyes to reaccustom them to the intense light.

But the condition of his foot had hardly improved. The swelling had increased and darkened, and was very painful to the touch.

"It's more than a twisted nerve," Paul said. "I'll never be able to get my boot back on."

Without making any reply, Francisco hung the useless boot from his belt, tore up the last shreds of his shirt and carefully bound the wounded foot.

"There," he said. "Stand up. Lean on me on one side, on your staff on the other. You'll be able to walk at least as fast as the Mercurians. We only have to maintain the lead that we have."

Paul got up without too much difficulty. Holding on to Francisco's shoulder with one hand, and holding hard to his pike with the other, he started hopping on one leg. He quickly mastered the necessary rhythmic movement, and the two men moved forward rapidly enough.

The mountain was steep and fissured. By means of the ravine that seemed the least difficult, the fugitives began the difficult ascent. From time to time they turned round and looked back at the host of running Mercurians down below.

"They're gaining on us!"

"Alas, yes," Paul groaned, "and my foot is hurting badly. Soon, I won't be able to walk any more. Lolla! What will become of Lolla?"

"A little more courage, Señor. We'll get there!"

Paul stiffened himself against the fatigue and the pain, and strove to move more rapidly. It was in vain. The Mercurians were eating into their lead incessantly. The two fugitives saw them pile into the ravine in a disorderly fashion; their horrible whistling rent the air.

"Courage! Courage!" repeated Francisco.

Already, the gorge was coming up to an abrupt ridge between the two steep cliffs, doubtless to slope downwards thereafter on the other side of the mountain.

"Another five minutes of walking," he said. "Another five minutes, Señor."

But Paul, defeated, let himself collapse. He held a hand out weakly toward his companion and said, in a faint voice: "Save yourself, Francisco, for Lolla's sake. Find her, and tell her that my last thought, as I died, was for her. Go. They're going to catch me and kill me, but you can get away. Hurry. Tell Lolla that I love her and would have given my life for her. But go! Go!"

"By San Cristo!" cried Francisco. "You're losing your mind, Señor! Leave you here! And what would the Señorita say when I told her that I'd abandoned you to the cruelty of those dirty beasts?"

"You can tell her that I ordered you to leave me. Do as you're told. Go!"

Exhausted by pain and physical fatigue, and by the mental torture he had been enduring for so many hours,

Paul de Civrac was on the point of fainting when Francisco, uncorking his flask, made him drink a large gulp of water, slightly scented by rum. Then, growling an invocation to his usual protector, the "*santissimo*," Santiago de Compostela, he took hold of Paul, lifted him up, loaded him on to his shoulders, and without paying any attention to the young man's orders, he started running.

It only took him five minutes to reach the place where the gorge, ceasing to climb, cut a passage through the high cliffs and descended in a steep slope. Accelerating his pace, Francisco began running down the steep and rocky slope.

He made numerous detours, his vigilant eye allowing him to avoid loose boulders, his ears attentive to the sounds of the mountain. But the whistles of the monopods could no longer be heard, and the gorge suddenly opened out on to a narrow plateau—and the spectacle that abruptly emerged was so prodigious, so inconceivable, that Francisco came to a halt and murmured: "*Demonios!* What's this new infernal place?"

He did not hear Paul's voice ordering him to put him down. At a slow pace, he resumed his march and headed for the far end of the rocky platform. Having arrived almost at the ended of a precipice he stopped again. Only then did he hear Paul. Francisco set the wounded man down, gently, on the rock, and embraced the immensity with a broad gesture and simply said: "Look, Señor!"

Paul, his eyes wide open, did not have the strength to speak, so impressive and terrible was the spectacle.

The platform on which they were located was in a kind of green-tinted twilight, which began at the edge of the ravine—which was glittering itself with the dazzling Mercurian daylight.

An enormous void was hollowed out steeply beyond the platform, and the bottom of that precipice was a plain that extended until it was lost in the unknown. The strangeness of the spectacle consisted, above all, in the fact that the precipice, although open to the sky, was dark and gloomy; even darker and gloomier was the plain, which suddenly plunged into night—an immobile and fascinating night, dotted with myriads of stars. From that mysteriously tenebrous immensity came a cold wind: a wintry night-wind.

Paul shivered, as much from horror as cold.

"I wasn't mistaken, Francisco," he stammered. "We really are on the planet Mercury. There, at our feet, and then at the bottom of the precipice, is the twilight zone, which extends as far as the hemisphere of eternal night."

Raising his head, he saw that the clouds, green and luminous behind him, darkened as they passed overhead, descending lower in the atmosphere and going on to lose themselves, like black apocalyptic monsters, in the region of darkness, eternal ice and nameless fears. And there they congealed, in a thick line, beyond which appeared the profundity of nocturnal space, swarming with innumerable stars.

Francisco had sat down beside Paul, and the two men shivered, their eyes staring avidly ahead of them and their teeth chattering. The heat and animation of their race gradually abandoned them; the green light no longer warmed them. On the slope on to which they had come, the temperature, in the shelter from the icy wind, was hotter than that of the equatorial regions of Earth; here, facing the region where the sun never shone, there was a temperature in the final strip of light more glacial than that of the poles.

As sometimes happens during forceful mental disturbances, the physical pain of his injured foot no longer affected Paul de Civrac. Gradually, his customary energy and presence of mind chased away his weakness and the disarray that his inability to escape the monopods had caused him.

He put his hand on Francisco's arm and said: "What are we going to do?"

As if he were waking up from a nightmare, the Spaniard looked at the young man distractedly.

"What are we going to do?" Paul repeated. "Behind us, there are the Mercurians, captivity, perhaps death—but also light, heat, nourishment and the hope of finding Lolla. Ahead of us, there's the absolute desert, the eternal darkness, the snow and ice, and certain death. What are we going to do?

"Señor, I don't..." Francisco stammered. A horrible volley of whistles cut him off.

The two men turned round, and saw the multitude of Mercurians massed on the edge of the gorge, climbing the cliff—and all the swarming monopods were whistling and agitating, crowded in the narrow corridor or hanging on to some spur of rick. But they were all in the full glare of light, or the shadow of the cliff, and none advanced on to the twilit platform.

Mute, the two Terrans gazed at their enemies and wondered what the reason was for their sudden halt, the interruption of such a long pursuit, when it would have been sufficient for a hundred monopods to make ten leaps to capture their prey.

The Mercurians did not come forward. They were agitated, whistling and gesticulating, but whenever one of them, pushed by those behind, set foot involuntarily on the somber plateau, it immediately bounded backwards, and there was a cacophony of shrill whistles and frantic gestures of trunks and arms. The monsters' red eyes seemed swollen, as if wide-eyed with terror. What could they see that was so extraordinary?

"I understand, Francisco!" Paul said, with a surge of vague hope. "The Mercurians are afraid of their planet's unlit zone. Doubtless, for them even more than for us, it's a region of danger and death. Look—they're whistling at us, and threatening us with their furious arms, but they aren't coming forward, even though it would be easy to capture us now. We're out of danger here, Francisco."

"The danger of being captured and having our blood sucked by these vampires, no doubt!" said the Spaniard, calmly. "But they only have to stay there, threatening us and blocking our path, and we'll die of hunger and cold. Look at my lips, Señor. I'm sure they're blue, as I can see yours are…and we're both shivering. No matter what the cost, we have to return to the light and the heat."

"Yes, we must. For Lolla, above all."

And the two men searched for a mean of escape. After long minutes of reflection, during which the monopods stopped whistling, Paul murmured: "I can't think of anything."

"Me neither."

This time, the situation appeared to both of them to be utterly hopeless.

Thirty paces away, in the gorge and on the edges of the back rocks, all the monopods were sitting down, in the fashion that Mercurians sat—which is to say, with the knee bent and the base of their spine resting on the hind talon of their foot.

"It's a blockade," said Francisco.

"They're expecting us to surrender, for, even if we succumb to cold and hunger, without moving, they certainly won't come to fetch us from here. It's obvious that the relative dusk that reigns on this plateau causes them an insurmountable terror.

"We could surrender, after all," said Francisco. "The dirty beats are quite intelligent. They understood you, in the grotto, when you explained to the two chiefs by means of gestures that we were hungry. You could try to make them understand that we won't do any harm to anyone if no one touches us..."

"That's difficult to express in sign language."

"Try anyway, Señor. It's the only means we have, in sum, of saving ourselves and getting Lolla back. Is your foot still hurting?"

Paul stood up and tested his injured foot. Every time his heel touched the ground he felt a dull pain, but he was eventually able to walk, leaning on his staff.

"Oh, well," he said, "I'll try to talk to them."

Francisco got up too. Mechanically, the two men turned toward the immensity of tenebrous space, and exclamations were stifled in their throats, while a volley of whistles stirred up echoes in the sky, and all the Mercurians stood up tumultuously.

Down below, to the right, in the eternal darkness, a fulgurant light had just appeared, and, as if springing from a prodigious invisible lighthouse, it advanced, in a broad, rotating electric beam, directly toward the crepuscular platform.

Chapter Four
In which Bild and Brad provide prodigious evidence of their existence

Stupefied, Paul and Francisco saw the beam approaching the platform, reach it and inundate it with light. They were dazzled by it, but it was already passing by, throwing panic into the crowd of monopods, although they could not perceive it themselves, since they were in the full glare of Mercurian daylight.

The projection passed over, quit the plateau and continued its movement to the left. Some distance away, it halted momentarily, and then came back toward the plateau, more slowly, moving up and down, retreating and then advancing again. Paul and Francisco followed it anxiously with their eyes, and thought about the searchlights of a terrestrial ironclad, searching a harbor by night.

An insensate hope caused their hearts to beat faster.

"What can that be, Señor?" Francisco murmured.

"I don't know. A natural phenomenon? And yet, it seems to me that it's being maneuvered by an intelligence. My God! My God!"

Meanwhile, the beam came back. It touched the edge of the plateau. It slid over the smooth surface of the twilit rock—and when it had enveloped the two motionless men with its cone of light, it stopped.

With an intense surprise, Paul and Francisco saw that prodigious ray, which came from the distant mysterious darkness, narrow down until it only had a diameter of about 1.5 meters, positioned directly in front of them.

The beam shifted, and modifying its form, in order to design, almost at their feet, on the black slate of the plateau, an elongated diamond of white light.

And they were staring at that diamond with their hypnotized eyes when they emitted a hoarse exclamation in unison.

"Francisco!"

"Señor!"

"Am I going mad?" Paul stammered. "Can I see...?"

"Me too—yes...I can see letters..."

"Letters, Francisco! Black letters on that diamond of light. And they're forming words—words!"

"Yes, yes, Señor...and look...more, more letters..."

The diamond grew larger. Yet more letters formed...yet more words...

Fascinated, the two men knelt down in front of the marvelous diamond, and they waited, their hearts beating rapidly, their hands trembling. Their startled gazes could not settle on a single point of the geometric figure; it leapt from one word to another. Suddenly, the diamond, which was still expanding, was immobilized, and below the lines of black words that stood out from the light, four dark letters were designed at a stroke.

"Bild!" cried Paul.

For more letters immediately appeared.

"Brad!" howled Francisco.

And the two men, in a fit of delirious joy, fell into one another's arms, laughing and weeping, while the motionless crowd of Mercurians massed at the entrance to the gorge considered the spectacle with thousand of expressionless red eyes.

When Paul and Francisco had given free rein to their disorderly joy, they recovered their reason, and Paul said: "We're mad, Francisco. We have to read..."

"Read, Señor...I can't, everything's dancing in front of my eyes."

Paul leaned forward, and read aloud the prodigious message that stood out in black against the white background of the luminous diamond:

"Are on planet Venus, where Fiery Wheel and Saturnians have been destroyed. Intelligence of Venusians prodigious. Divine perfection in their science. Have discovered you with their telescopes as soon as have been in hemisphere of Mercurian night. We are sending you this message by one of their astonishing projectors of solar light. We don't yet know how to rejoin you; for the moment, Venusians cannot emerge from the atmosphere of their planet. But in forty-eight terrestrial hours we'll send messages to Earth. Another projection is *en route* and will reach you 35 minutes after this one. Bild and Brad."

Paul had scarcely finished reading when the whole thing was effaced before his eyes. The light disappeared, and he could no longer see anything but the uniform black rock.

"Francisco!" he cried, in anguish. I can't see any more! Were we dreaming?"

"But Señor, the thirty-five minutes must have passed...exactly! Here's the second projection."

Indeed, a flash of light sprang forth from the distant darkness, and another luminous diamond expanded on the rock. In this one too, letters and words were inscribed in black...

Paul and Francisco read aloud simultaneously:

"We're sending messages to Earth; for our part, we hope to come soon and get you away from the inhospitable surface of Mercury, for thirty Venusian scientists are working to resolve the problem of sending us to you. All that remains is for them to overcome a little difficulty stemming from our weight. As we can see everything happening around you, we understand that the greatest danger for you is dying of hunger. You have no other alternatives than these: either you die, or you feed on the monopods that are blocking your path. Don't hesitate, and burn the dead monopods to keep warm. You need to stay alive until we can come to rescue you. But where is Lolla Mendès? Prisoner or dead? Expect a third projection."

Only five minutes went by before the second projection vanished. Almost immediately, the third appeared.

Calmer now, and resolved above all to conserve their strength and their lives, and to recover Lolla, Paul and Francisco read the black message on the diamond of light together:

"This third message will be the last of this first series. We'll only be able to send you more in 96 hours, when the Venusians have made a sufficient new provision of solar radiation. To remain constantly facing you, we're on a Venusian apparatus that remains motionless above Venus as it rotates in space. We'll only leave it to send a message to Earth. At the very least, don't lose sight of the plateau where you are, for if you go back to the sunlit zone of Mercury, we'll no longer be able to see you. Kill Mercurians! But where is Lolla Mendès? We refuse to believe that she's dead. Courage! Courage! Live, and wait for us. Bild, Br..."

The projection vanished before Brad's name could be written in its entirety.

As if those diamonds of light had warmed up their bodies while they were shining, the Terrans felt a mortal chill invading their limbs as soon as the projection had vanished.

"We'll be frozen where we stand!" exclaimed Francisco. "We have to be able to move. Quickly—the Mercurians!"

He seized his pike and bounded toward the crowd of monopods, now silent. With blows of the club he broke the arms and legs of a dozen of the monsters, while the others recoiled in panic, trampling one another.

Paul had walked slowly after Francisco. He dragged two injured monopods behind a ridge of rock, which, while being in the twilight zone, formed a screen against the icy wind blowing from the eternal darkness. Francisco soon rejoined him, dragging two other Mercurians behind him, which he had grasped with one hand. As they were about to obey the ferocious instructions of Bild and Brad, however, the two men shivered in disgust, and even in pity...

The Mercurians were very different from human beings, and yet Paul and Francisco sensed that an intelligence lived behind that unique eye and in the flattened skull—a little of the divine spark that established the demarcation between beings whose reason is expressed in a language, and animals whose actions only reveal instincts.

"Francisco," said Paul, "with other symbols and under another name, these Mercurians might perhaps worship the same ideal as us."

"They're certainly savages!" said Francisco.

"What do we know? They consider us to be malevolent and dangerous creatures, and yet our greatest desire would be to live in peace in their cities..."

"That's possible, Señor, but I can't forget that they devour one another and that they threw themselves on the Señorita without the slightest provocation in order to..." Francisco made a gesture of horror and went on: "Nor can I forget that we don't have any alternative. Either we drink the blood of these cadavers and burn them, or we die of hunger and cold. If we die, the Señorita is lost forever. I'm not hesitating..."

And abruptly, with a light thrust of his pike, Francisco punctured the vitreous eye of one of the monopods lying dead in front of him. A thick white liquid spurted from the wound. The Spaniard bent down and, applying his lips to the hole streaming with Mercurian blood, he drank.

Paul de Civrac had turned away, nausea making his gorge rise—but he heard Francisco's voice say, gravely: "Señor! We've received life in order to conserve it until it pleases it to leave us. If it had been necessary, we'd have died a long time ago. Think of the extraordinary dangers we've run. Now we have to save the Señorita and return to the Earth for which we've been created. Drink, Señor, from the only source of life there is in this infernal world.

Then Paul seized his pike, punctured the eye of a Mercurian, and set about drinking the nourishing liquid. In spite of his disgust, which was much more intellectual than physical, he did not lose his analytical habits, and he noticed, while drinking in long draughts, that the Mercurian blood, which was very thick, had a sugary taste and an unfamiliar but agreeable perfume. And there was something akin to a regeneration of his entire body, a marvelously rapid return of strength.

In the meantime, Francisco had lit a match. He applied it to the cadaver that was now empty of blood, and with a slight crackling, the body burned slowly, giving off jets of white flame, from which a benevolent heat radiated.

No Earthly fire resembled that strange conflagration. There was matter therein for much reflection. No longer suffering from hunger, however, their minds seething with hope, their hearts vibrant with as-yet-imprecise resolutions, the two men seated beside the slowly burning cadaver warmed themselves voluptuously, with no more intellectual curiosity, for the moment, than they would have had before a fire of dry wood.

They thought about Lolla, a tenacious presentiment making them think that she was still alive...oh, they would find her, since they could stave off death now! They thought about Bild and Brad, about possible...probable...certain rescue—and they warmed themselves, their eyes fixed on the hissing flames but their gazes lost within themselves.

Soon, another thought, even more tyrannical than the previous ones, invaded Paul de Civrac's mind. Where did that unexpected memory spring from? By virtue of what phenomenon of thought-transmission did Paul suddenly recalled his meeting in Calcutta with the mysterious Ahmed Bey?

He saw the emaciated face of the enigmatic scientist again; he heard the hermetic words again in which Ahmed Bey had predicted his love for Lolla Mendès.

"Francisco!" Paul exclaimed.

"Señor?"

"Do you know what I'm thinking?"

"But, Señor, it must be about our dear Señorita..."

"Yes," said Paul, "she is indeed at the back of my mind; but what's particularly preoccupying my mind at this moment is the idea of Dr. Ahmed Bey—you know, the marvelous scientist I met in Calcutta..."

Francisco looked at Civrac in surprise, made a scornful grimace and, shrugging his shoulders irreverently, presented his hands once again to the flames of the burning monopod.

Twenty paces away, at the very limit of the crepuscular zone, in the dazzle of the eternal green light coming through the clouds from the invisible sun, the crowd of petrified Mercurians silently considered the natural phenomenon, with which they were probably unfamiliar, of fire.

PART FOUR
REINCARNATED SOULS

Chapter One
Which revisits an individual even more astonishing than the Fiery Wheel

The panic caused all over the Earth by the two passages of the Fiery Wheel had only just calmed down, and people had recovered confidence in the tranquility of their astronomical heavens, when new marvel burst forth like a thunderbolt, if not as dangerous, at least as startling and unexpected as the first.

It was the morning of the eleventh day after the appearance of the Fiery Wheel over Colombia and its definitive disappearance. The four million readers of the *Universel*, the great world daily produced in six languages and printed simultaneously in all the capitals of the Old and New World, found themselves, on opening their newspaper, confronted by a sensational first page. The enormous headline occupied a quarter of it, and was thus conceived:

A MESSAGE PROJECTED FROM
THE PLANET VENUS

There followed, in large print, the following lines:

Last night, at eleven thirty-five, Monsieur Constant Brularion, the director of the astronomical observatory

147

of the Bois de Verrières,[10] *saw on an immense circular projection outlined on the flat extent of an uncultivated field.*

For several nights, Monsieur Brularion, who was observing the planet Venus, had noticed with astonishment that a luminous ray projected from that planet, more intense than its ordinary light, was rapidly drawing nearer to the Earth.

Last night, at eleven thirty-four, the extremity of the prodigious beam struck the Earth, on the abovementioned field.

Amazed by the phenomenon, Monsieur Brularion emerged from his observatory and, having arrived before the luminous circle, observed that letters of the alphabet, a trifle fluid but clearly legible, were standing out in black from the lighted surface, which measured four meters in diameter.

---

[10] There is no observatory at Verrières, a suburb south of Paris, but just as "Constant Brularion" is an obvious substitute for Camille Flammarion, the observatory featured in the novel is an analogue of the one that Flammarion was gifted at Juvisy-sur-Orge, which subsequently became the property of the Societé Astronomique de France. The notion of an interplanetary projection of this kind had first been employed by Louis-Sébastien Mercier in one of the stories in *Songes et visions philosophiques* (1768), "Nouvelles de la lune" (tr. as "News from the Moon" in the Black Coat Press eponymous collrectoion, ISBN 9781932983890), which Flammarion had read and described in his book *Les Mondes imaginaires et les mondes réels* [Real and Imaginary Worlds] (1864), and which anticipated *Lumen* in several key respects. La Hire was certainly familiar with Flammarion's book, and even gave the astronomer a starring role in *The Nyctalope on Mars*.

Aided by three of his colleagues, the savant astron-omer took several photographs of the projection.

Monsieur Brularion, who is, as our readers know, our astronomical reporter, immediately sent a photo-graph to our Parisian editor, who immediately tele-graphed and cabled our editors worldwide. Here is the exact facsimile; our readers can easily complete the text by adding the words of secondary importance that are missing.

No doubt can remain; this is a message from the planet Venus.

It is evident that such an event, which we record with emotion, is rich in consequences. It justifies in a striking manner Monsieur Brularion's theories regard-ing the plurality of habitable worlds.

Our readers will find tomorrow, in the same place, and article by our collaborator of genius on the subject of the Message.

We will finally remark that the Universel *alone is making this prodigious event known to the world today.*

The facsimile of the projection was framed by these lines, all the way to the bottom of the page.

It read:

Four men and a woman, abducted from Barcelona and Bogota by the Fiery Wheel, marooned on the planet Mercury. Two undersigned, retaken by the Wheel, now on planet Venus, sending message to Earth by marvelous apparatus storing and projecting solar light. Woman and other two men remain on Mercury, threatened by death. Will strive to rejoin them, rescue them. Numerous conditions make this message visible fifty-eight minutes on Earth, near French astronomical observatory, which

Venusian telescopes permit distinguish. Same conditions will enable Venus to send second message in direction of Earth in eight years, three months, eight days, eleven hours, thirty-four minutes. Arthur Brad, Jonathan Bild, citizens free America, temporarily City of Scientists, Venus.

The excitement caused on Earth was indescribable. At ten o'clock in the morning, all the important newspapers in the entire world published a second edition reproducing the front page of the *Universel*. Cables and telegraphic wires made their own contribution.

Rapid investigations were carried out, and the next day, all the printed newspapers recalled the abduction of Señorita Lola Mendès and the valet Francisco in Barcelona, as well as the disappearance in Colombia, thus far inexplicable but now explained, of the geological mission composed of Messieurs Paul de Civrac, Arthur Brad and Jonathan Bild.

Monsieur Brularion's article was read by the entire human race, or at least the fraction of it able to read. In any case, it did not reveal anything new, but concluded the existence of life on all the planets and, naturally, the habitability, for human beings, of Mercury and Venus. It asked questions that were to remain unanswered for a long time, since the Venusian message would not be renewed for a little more than eight years.

What was the Fiery Wheel and what had become of it?

What was the threat of death faced by Paul de Civrac, Lola Mendès and Francisco, left behind on Mercury?

How did the Venusian projector work—and also the telescopes that permitted the annihilation of the distance of sixteen million leagues that separated Venus and Earth at the moment when the message was received?

And Monsieur Brularion terminated thus:

Now, above all, we are struck with regret that human science is not yet capable of constructing a machine that would permit us to go to the aid of our brethren, prisoners on the planet Mercury, and to make truly extraordinary discoveries with them.

At eight o'clock in the morning on the day when the *Universel* published that article, the illustrious Dr. Ahmed Bey was eating breakfast on his own in the dining room of his luxurious house on the edge of the Parc Monceau. It was a frugal breakfast, composed simply of a minuscule cup of Turkish coffee. Behind the Master, immobile and upright, stood a servant whose costume and visage testified to a Hindu origin, and in front of Ahmed Bey, a copy of the *Universel* was unfolded, supported by a carafe. While emptying his cup of coffee in little sips, the doctor was reading.

When he reached the conclusion of Monsieur Brularion's article, he set the empty cup down on a saucer and rubbed his hands, while silent laughter wrinkled his emaciated cheeks. Then, turning to the impassive Hindu, he pronounced a few words. The valet went out. Two minutes later, a young man came into the dining room and bowed to Ahmed Bey.

"Monsieur Marlin," said the doctor, "go in person to invite to supper, on my behalf, for midnight, the individuals whose names I shall list for you. Tell them that I deem their presence to be indispensable…indispensable, you hear?"

"Very good, Master."

151

"Write."

And on an ivory tablet that he held in his hand, the young man wrote in pencil while the doctor dictated:

"The astronomer Constant Brularion, Dr. Payen, Abbé Normat, Professor Martial and Monsieur Torpène, the Prefect of Police. Have you got that?"

"Yes, Master."

"Make the visits this morning. This afternoon you'll make sure that the laboratory is set up as for my spiritist séances. And telephone my notary right away to tell him to come to lunch with me. Go!"

The secretary withdrew, but his master called him back. "I forgot. On the invitation addressed to Monsieur Torpène, add this sentence, word for word: 'Dr. Ahmed Bey had found what he mentioned to you in the Parc Monceau on the night of the twenty-first and twenty-second of June.'"

And, sending his secretary away with a gesture, the doctor rose to his feet, folded up the newspaper, smiled silently once again, and left the dining room in his turn, by a different door than the one that the Hindu and Monsieur Marlin had used.

Ahmed Bey spent the day in his laboratory, occupied in mysterious tasks to which no human being was witness. He only interrupted that work for an hour, at midday, in order to eat lunch with Maître Suroit, his notary, to whom he gave meticulous orders regarding the placement of funds.

In the evening, he dined at eight o'clock, very frugally. Then he retired to his laboratory again, after having ordered the Hindu to have the visitors wait in the drawing room until there were five of them, and then to introduce them all together into the dining room, where a cold supper would be served.

Dr. Ahmed Bey's laboratory occupied the entire width of the basement of the house. It was an immense room whose high ceiling was supported by marble columns. It was surrounded by a series of divans, above which numerous shelves fixed to the wall supported four or five thousand books. In the middle stood an enormous and rather intimidating electric machine, surrounded by other smaller machines and porcelain tubs half-full of variously colored liquids.

In front of the electric machine there were two white marble tables, reminiscent of the dissecting slabs in an amphitheater.

Thirty electric chandeliers, each with four lamps, illuminated the vast room brightly. Ten radiators, meticulously graduated, and ten cold air vents also scrupulously graduated, could produce a tropical heat or a Siberian chill. The hot and cold air were produced by machines located in a further basement, maintained in continuous activity night and day by Hindu mechanics.

That day, the temperature of the laboratory was a mere twelve degrees above zero.

At three minutes to midnight, a bell rang. The doctor, who was lying on a divan meditating, got to his feet, went into a cloakroom adjacent to the laboratory entrance, and replaced the long smock he was wearing with a frock-coat. Then he went to the dining room where he guests were waiting for him.

After the customary greetings and salutations, Ahmed Bey placed Constant Brularion opposite him and sat down between Monsieur Torpène and Abbé Normat, a knowledgeable physiologist. Dr. Payen of the Académie de Médecine and the chemist, Professor Martial of the Académie des Sciences, sat to either side of Brularion.

"Messieurs," said Ahmed Bey, while the maître d'hôtel supervised the distribution of the hors-d'oeuvre, of which very small quantities were served, "Thank you for having responded to my invitation at such short notice. You won't regret it. It isn't a spiritist séance that I've invited you to tonight, but a prodigious spectacle that you can't possible expect. And as you'll require all your mental and physical strength, in order to remain calm, I advise you to eat in accordance with your appetite. You'll excuse me for only giving you water to drink, but it's important that your minds are absolutely lucid and composed, and I've often observed that a single small glass of wine diminishes the faculties— slightly, but definitely—even of the best-tempered of men. For myself, I shan't eat, for what I'm going to do requires that my stomach be completely empty. This morning, I breakfasted with cenobitic frugality, and only absorbed liquids of prompt, facile and complete absorption. Don't let my fast influence you, however. Honor the cuisine of my masterful Indian chef."

The five guests complied, but in spite of the placidity of Ahmed Bey, who did not show the slightest emotion, they ate rapidly; their curiosity had been whetted more that their appetite by their host's words.

At fifty minutes past twelve, the waiters served sorbets and fruits. They were barely tasted. When one o'clock chimed on the wall-clock, Ahmed rose to his feet, and his five guests immediately imitated him.

Apart from the speech made by Ahmed Bey at the commencement, not a word had been pronounced during the meal. Everyone knew that the mysterious doctor's strict habit was never to give explanations in advance of his experiments.

"Would you care to follow me to the laboratory, Messieurs," he said, opening a door.

Having traversed a corridor and gone down the thirty marble steps of a broad staircase, the six men went into the laboratory, brightly lit by all the electric chandeliers.

"Please sit down, Messieurs, and listen to me."

The five guests sat down on a divan and Ahmed Bey sat in front of them on a simple wooden stool. He took a newspaper out of his pocket, unfolded it, and read aloud: "Now, above all, we are struck with regret that human science is not yet capable of constructing a machine that would permit us to go to the aid of our brethren, prisoners on the planet Mercury, and to make truly extraordinary discoveries with them."

The doctor folded the paper again and said to Brularion: "That's the conclusion of your article, published this morning."

The astronomer nodded his head.

"Well, my dear astronomer," Ahmed Bey continued, smiling—and his dark eyes flashed in the depths of the immense orbits in which they were hidden—"do not have that regret—or, rather, have that regret no longer."

"What do you mean?" asked Brularion, amazed.

"I mean that although modern science has not discovered, and is not close to discovering, an engine capable of transporting you to another planet..." Ahmed Bey paused in his speech, stood up, and continued majestically: "Ancient science had found the means of suppressing space and distance for the human will. That means permitted a Brahmin, hundreds of centuries ago, to quit the Earth in order to travel through interplanetary space, and beyond the stars..."

"And that means…?" said Abbé Normat, while the other four guests waited.

"Has been lost," Ahmed Bey replied.

"In that case..."

"I have rediscovered it."

That statement fell into the five scientists' anguished silence. They were aware of the mysterious profundity of Ahmed Bey's science, his serious character and the rigorous method of his search for the truth. They could not doubt his affirmation, and were animated by a violent emotion.

"Messieurs," said Ahmed Bey, without departing from his tranquility, you all know what the priests of the temple of Sakoulna in ancient India meant by the disincarnation and reincarnation of souls."

"Yes," replied the voices of the five scientists, in unison.

"With a few words, constituting a formula of incantation revealed by Brahma himself, the thrice holy Brahmins were able to separate their soul from their bodies, subsequently govern that soul, cause it to travel at their whim, and return it to its original body or reincarnate it in another. By modifying the formula of incantation, by as little as a single syllable, a Brahmin was able to command his own souls, and, leaving his human shell on Earth, go in spirit into the infinity of the astronomical havens. Did you know that, Messieurs?"

"Yes," replied Abbé Normat, gravely. "But for my part, I scarcely believed it I scarcely believed half of it. A man capable of disincarnating a soul and reincarnating it is the absolute master of life and death. Such power only belongs to God."

"It belongs to me!" pronounced Ahmed Bey, majestically.

A moment of solemn silence followed these terrible words. Then Torpène, shivering as if he had just emerged from a dream, said: "Well, Monsieur…?"

Ahmed Bey smiled, and slowly said: "Seventeen years ago, I discovered beneath the Great Pyramid a tanned ox-hide conserved by unknown processes and covered with inscriptions in Hermetic Sanskrit. After a year of work, I succeeded in deciphering the inscription. It taught me what I have told you, and what I have subsequently revealed to the scholarly world, without identifying myself. But it also taught me the means by which I might perhaps succeed in discovering the marvelous secret of the disincarnation and reincarnation of souls. Reading it made a profound impression on me. Two years later, my father having died and left me an immense fortune, I left for India. I found the temple of Sakoulna. I had myself initiated into the mysteries of Brahma, Vishnu, Siva and Ganesha. I studied the sacred books that dated from the origins of human intelligence and collected the information that fell from the desiccated lips of Brahmins, Stylites and holy penitents—all with the sole aim of discovering whether the Hermetic inscription might have deceived me. When I was convinced of its veracity, I finally set forth on the supreme research. Alone, I climbed the Tibetan plateau; alone, I wandered in the jungles inhabited by the sovereign serpents and tigers, and where palm trees grow in the ruins of temples…"

Ahmed Bey's voice had become strangely grave and melancholy—what memories his mind must have been recalling!—and he fell silent, lowering his head.

For a few minutes, the scientists respected that emotional reverie—but Ahmed Bey had not finished, and they waited expectantly.

"Go on!" Abbé Normat exclaimed, suddenly, quivering with impatience.

"Ah! Have I not revealed everything?" the Doctor murmured, in a faint voice. Immediately, however, he added, in a clear and vibrant tone: "I possess the secret of the Hermetic inscription!"

None of the five listeners doubted the verity of that extraordinary statement. They rose to their feet, prey to an invincible agitation.

"But if it's true," said Constant Brularion, "that neither time or space really exists for the soul as we know it; if it's true that the disincarnate soul retains all the intellectual and moral soul of the individual that it animated, you can therefore disincarnate your own soul and go to Mercury yourself."

"All that is true," said Ahmed Bey, simply, "and I shall indeed depart for the planet Mercury."

"When?"

"Right away."

That astounding affirmation was followed by a heavy silence—but one tremulous voice eventually said: "How?"

"You shall see," Ahmed Bey replied, smiling. "Please sit down again. When it is all over, you will only have to withdraw. My faithful steward Ra-Cobrah, whom you have sometimes seen here, has the orders necessary for my mortal envelope to be conserved intact to await my return. I only ask you to swear to me, on your honor, the most profound secrecy. Nothing that I have said to you, and none of what you are about to see, must be revealed! Monsieur Torpène, especially, must keep silence—remember that you came to interrogate me! Swear, Messieurs!"

"So sworn," said the five men, in chorus, raising their right hands.

"Perfect!"

The Doctor struck a gong with his closed fist. Immediately, a door opened and a richly-dressed Hindu appeared on the threshold. It was Ra-Cobrah. Ahmed Bey said a few words to him in a language unknown to the five guests, and Ra-Cobrah disappeared. The thaumaturge immediately went into the dressing-room. When he came back, he was wearing a long linen robe without sleeves or a collar; his arms and feet were bare, and he undoubtedly had nothing on his body except that druidic garment.

He went to a apparatus made of copper and turned two small wheels. The temperature of the laboratory swiftly rose by fifty degrees, as indicated by the thermometers. At the same time a door opened and nine servants, visibly Oriental, entered rapidly, forming a strange cortege. One of them was carrying five linen tunics, which he gave to the guests. The latter quickly took off their heavy garments and put on the thin tunics—for without that precaution, which they had taken several times previously in the course of Ahmed Bey's experiments, they would have suffocated.

Four more servants carried in the body of a white man, and another four brought the body of a negro; they laid them down on the two marble slabs.

"Messieurs," said Ahmed Bey, "the white man is a cadaver; it was sent to me two hours ago from the hospital. The man died at midday. As for the negro, he is only asleep. He's a slave, of whom I am the master, the absolute and unrestricted possessor. Before disincarnating my own soul and setting forth for Mercury without the encumbrance of my terrestrial appearance, the body that

159

is presently alive and active before you, I want to demonstrate my power to you. Come closer, and observe that the white man is dead and the negro alive..."

Followed by his friends, Brularion rose first. It was easy for the five scientists to determine that the white man was no more than a cadaver, while the negro was in a hypnotic trance.

"It's true," said Torpène.

Then, before the five spectators lined up beside the marble tables, Ahmed Bey extended his arm to the nearest column and turned an ivory button. All the chandeliers except one went out. That one, directly above the slabs, emitted a dim radiance, like a night-light. The contours of the laboratory were lost in an intimidating obscurity, in which a coppery reflection or a crystal gleam shone in places, like the eye of some monster.

Ahmed Bey commenced magnetic passes. As his hands accomplished the traditional gestures, his lips murmured ancient incantations and his widened eyes flashed. His entire face was transfigured.

With an indescribable emotion, the five scientists soon saw the body of the negro shiver convulsively, while a red-tinted foam moistened his lips. Suddenly, the black body sat up, then fell back along the marble, and a little spark emerged from his open mouth, which hovered in mid-air, bobbing hesitantly.

Ahmed Bey made a broad gesture, uttering a terrible cry, and the spark flew like lightning toward the mouth of the white cadaver, between the lips of which it disappeared.

Turning away from the black man, Ahmed Bey resumed making passes over the head of the white man—and they saw the naked body, which had been a mere cadaver a little while before, shiver, twitch and open his eyes: strange, frightened eyes, still full of the mysteries of the beyond.

Ahmed Bey modified his passes; the resuscitated man closed his eyes again and went to sleep. The thaumaturge took a step toward the column, stretched out his right arm, which made a rapid movement, and the chandeliers spread their bright light once again.

After a few minutes of heavy silence, Ahmed Bey, who had become progressively calmer, smiled, and said in his normal voice: "Now, Messieurs, would you care to observe that the white man is alive, and that the black man is dead. I have caused the latter's soul to pass into the former's body.

In spite of the emotion, and the fear, that was troubling their intelligence, the five scientists were easily able to observe that the former cadaver was, indeed, alive and that the former living man was no more than a cadaver.

Ahmed Bey struck the gong with his closed fist. The eight servants reappeared. At a sign from Ra-Cobrah, who accompanied them, they lifted up the black man and the white man and went out at a run.

"It's terribly marvelous!" murmured Brularion, whose forehead was streaming with cold sweat.

"But what are they going to do with the dead man and the resuscitated man?" asked Abbé Normat.

"The dead man," Ahmed Bey replied, calmly, "will be dissolved in three minutes in a liquid of my own composition; no fragment will remain of him larger than the head of a pin. As for the white man who has been resuscitated, he'll take his place among my domestics.

"But you've given him the soul of a negro!" exclaimed Dr. Payen.

"Of course!"

"That soul will find itself singularly out of place in that white body."

"Not very much. The man I killed was a domestic here; having become white, he'll continue his functions. As for the change in the color and form of his body, Ra-Cobrah will explain it to him by the miraculous intervention of manitous. In a matter of a few days, the soul of the black man will find itself quite at ease in his new white envelope."

"But you've killed a man!" said the Prefect of Police, endeavoring to smile.

"A crime!" said Martial, with a forced laugh.

"No," the thaumaturge replied. "Given that, if I've killed one human body, I've resuscitated another."

"In fact," said the Abbé, "it's merely a substitution."

The five friends sat down on the divan again.

"Now, Messieurs," said Ahmed Bey, whose expression had become grave again, "Permit me to shake you by the hand, and wish me *bon voyage*. In five minutes, deprived of my heavy terrestrial envelope, I shall be flying through interplanetary space, a pure soul."

These prodigious words did not astonish the five listeners. What they had just seen had hardened them. They shook the hand that their host held out to them, and the astronomer expressed their common thought in saying: "We hope that our journey will be brief and that you'll return from it. Try to clarify the mystery of the Fiery Wheel."

"I shall return," said Ahmed Bey "As for the duration of the voyage, I don't know that. I shall go via Venus, in order to disincarnate the souls of Messieurs Bild and Brad and take them with me. All three of us will travel to Mercury, where it will be necessary for us to search for Lolla Mendès, Paul de Civrac and Francisco. We shall be reincarnated, probably in Mercurian bodies. Everything depends, therefore, on the time required by that search."

"And how long will it take to go from here to Venus, and then to Mercury?" asked Dr. Payen.

"A flash of lightning," Ahmed Bey replied. "The pure soul travels as rapidly as thought. Your thought only takes a second to transport itself to the most distant star. Now, Messieurs, I ask you for the most absolute silence, and I permit myself to remind you of your promise."

Having pronounced these words in a grave and imperious voice, Ahmed Bey extinguished the chandeliers again, only leaving the central lamp dimly lit.

Immediately, he lay down on one of the marble slabs. He closed his eyes. Incomprehensible words emerged from his lips. They saw him go pale, quivering with tremors that gradually diminished in strength, and then remain immobile. A pink foam appeared between his lips. A convulsion shook him, his mouth opened— and a white spark emerged, which danced momentarily before the eyes of the five petrified scientists, rose rapidly toward the ceiling, and suddenly disappeared.

A few minutes of tragic silence went by.

The five friends gazed at the body of Ahmed Bey, rigid and motionless on the slab.

Then a door opened, and Ra-Cobrah advanced toward his mater's body. As he passed close to a column he turned an electric switch and the chandeliers illuminated the laboratory brightly once again.

"Messieurs," Ra-Cobrah said, "the Master's soul has departed. Please allow me to give his body the prescribed care..."

The first to recover his composure, Dr. Payen, got up and went over to Ahmed Bey's body. He touched it, felt for a pulse, placed a small pocket mirror over the lips, applied and stethoscope to the location of the heart and listened...

"My friends," he said, in a tremulous voice, turning to his four companions, "it's inconceivable: Ahmed Bey's body, lying here, is a corpse. We have seen...now we have only to wait..."

After putting on their normal clothing, saluted by Ra-Cobrah, the five scientists left the laboratory. Preceded by a Hindu servant, who took back the five linen tunics, they went back up the stairs, traversed a long corridor and a vast antechamber, went through the garden and a gate, and found themselves confronted by their five carriages, lined up at the edge of the sidewalk. They separated, after shaking hands, without a word, their minds in turmoil.

It was four o'clock in the morning, and the first glimmers of dawn were climbing the side of the Panthéon.

Chapter Two
In which an individual as interesting as Ahmed Bey is found

In the desolate regions of the planet Mercury, on the crepuscular plateau on the edge of the immensity of darkness, Paul and Francisco were continuing their struggle against death.

Ten Mercurians they had killed furnished blood and fire for fifty-six hours. The blood appeased their hunger and thirst; the fire diminished the mortal cold falling from the somber sky and coming from the infinity of darkness.

As the penultimate monopod was burning, Francisco said: "You stay here, Señor, while I go hunting. Sixty hours have gone by since the last message; we won't receive another for thirty-six hours. We need to ensure that we don't freeze to death before then. Not one of these monsters has stayed in the gorge, as you can see. When they saw that we were drinking their blood and burning their bodies, they ran away. They must have gone back down to the valley. I'll go after them. In the meantime, you can burn the last one—that will keep you warm until I come back. I'm agile, I won't be running any risk. You wouldn't be any use to me, with your foot still hurting. It's better for you to stay here. In three or four hours I'll come back, and bring half a dozen of these monopods, as you call them. And perhaps I'll also bring back news of Lolla!"

"It's all right—go!" said Paul. He was absorbed by thoughts so sad that, without the hope of finding and rescuing Lolla as soon as his foot was completely healed, he would have let himself die. The arrival of Bild and Brad seemed to him to be very problematic; he dared not believe, in spite of the phenomenon of the projections, that the Venusians would find a way to allow Bild and Brad to travel from Venus to Mercury. In any case, all the strange adventures that he had lived through since his abduction from Bogota seemed so exorbitant that he still believed himself to be the victim of an interminable nightmare, and his energy was gradually declining.

Already, Francisco—who was more inclined to action than thought—had grabbed his pike and set off toward the mountain gorge.

Before leaping on to the luminous slope of the mountain, he turned toward Paul, waved his weapon and shouted: "See you soon, Paul!" And while the aerial echoes reverberated his cry with rolls of thunder, he jumped. Skillfully, he aimed for a spot twenty or thirty meters ahead, calculating his leap carefully, and set off. He scarcely touched the ground; his muscular and elastic legs flexed and straightened again, and he went down the mountain with vertiginous rapidity. Once again he had the sensation of the blinding light and the stifling heat; he was suffocating slightly—but he knew that the malaise would be temporary and did not pay much attention to it.

Without stopping, he traversed the broad plateau where Paul had been injured. There was not a single Mercurian to be seen.

They must have gone back to their city on the river bank, he said to himself.

He headed for a depression that seemed to him to be the place where the gorge that led to the water's edge opened on to the plateau. When he arrived there, however, he leapt back violently and uttered an exclamation. A steep precipice opened up before his eyes, at the very bottom of which the river was shining. It was like an enormous crevasse, whose two edges, about a hundred meters apart, overhung the abyss.

"*Demonios!*" Francisco swore. "I nearly jumped into that!"

Immediately, however, he remembered that he had fallen from much higher when quitting the Fiery Wheel; he reflected on his own lightness, the density of the air and all the scientific matters that Paul had explained to him, and started to laugh at his instinctive fear.

"Bah!" he said, gaily, "I keep forgetting that I'm not on Earth. I don't have to start searching for the path by which we came up. I can jump down…I'll land in the river; it'll make a mattress. Since I didn't come to any harm falling from the Fiery Wheel, there's every reason to suppose that jumping from the top of the cliff to the bottom of the valley poses no danger—and I'll get there more rapidly. Then again, on seeing me arrive in that manner, the Mercurians will be so bewildered that I'll be able to grab half a dozen of them without a fight. Escaping from the others won't be as easy, of course…but perhaps they won't dare to chase me. Come on—*hup!*"

And he jumped, looking down.

It seemed to him that the river was rising up to meet him, and he started to laugh. Immediately, however, he uttered an oath. He had jumped too far from the edge of the cliff, and he was not going to fall in the river but on the bank, in the midst of the pyramidal houses.

He scarcely had time to take account of that unforeseen accident. *If I hit the rock or a house*, he thought, *I'll break my ankles, at least…*

At that moment, he landed, not on his feet but on his back. He felt a violent shock, but he retained all his presence of mind.

"Good," he murmured. "I haven't broken anything, although the impact was hard...."

He was about to get to his feet when he saw mono-pods surging forward from all directions. He brandished his pike—but before the weapon had come down, twenty claws had seized his legs, his arms and his entire body. He struggled, but it was in vain. A rough cord wound around him, immobilizing his limbs, circling his torso and his neck. Half-strangled, he felt himself lifted up and carried away, in the midst of a riot of furious whistles.

Suddenly, he found himself on the ground, alone, in darkness. A square of light at ground level disappeared; a door had just closed. Francisco was a prisoner in one of the pyramidal houses of the Mercurian city.

To begin with, he was gripped by such a fit of rage that he writhed in his bonds, trying hopelessly to bite through them, and hurling all the curses available to a Spaniard at his enemies. That crisis of impotent wrath gradually calmed down, however, and Francisco stopped shouting and swearing—which permitted him to hear, with astonishment, his name pronounced in a low voice...

"*Santa Virgen!*" he said. "Who's calling me?"

"Francisco, it's..."

"Señorita!"

"Don't shout like that! Don't shout!"

"Señorita, Señorita!" exclaimed the poor man—and tears welled up in his eyes when, in the gloom of his prison, he saw the face of Lolla Mendès lean over him.

"Señorita, it's you! You! I'm not dreaming?"

"No, Francisco, you're not dreaming. I've been shut in here for a long time. But what about Paul? Where is he?"

"What? Oh, Señorita, untie me..."

"My hands and feet are bound too. Answer me—what's become of Monsieur de Civrac?"

"Safe and sound, Señorita, safe and sound on the mountain. And he's waiting for me! Oh, if he knew that you were here! He'd come running! He'd let himself be captured in order to be with you..."

"You think so?" said Lolla. Her tremulous voice betrayed her emotion.

"Señorita," Francisco replied, "he thinks of nothing but you. But tell me, how do you come to be here?"

Briefly, Lolla Mendès told him that the golden river had taken her into a cavern. She had been seized by Mercurians and put under the safeguard of a chief. They had come back upriver, and she had been imprisoned in this dungeon. Twice a day, they brought her a sort of white cream in a yellow metal bowl; she drank it with her eyes closed—in order to live! She hoped that Paul and Francisco were looking for her and would save her. No monopod had touched her. Sometimes, the chief, recognizable by the flexible golden ring circling his trunk, came into the hut, closing the door behind him, crouched down in the shadows, whistled, gesticulated, and went away again.

When Lolla had finished speaking, Francisco told her about the adventures he had gone through with Paul. When he reached the episode of Bild and Brad's projections, Lolla could hardly believe her ears. Francisco had to repeat the story three times. Weeping with joy, Lolla exclaimed: "But what about Monsieur de Civrac's injury?"

"Nothing! In a matter of hours, the foot will have healed completely. But what is Monsieur de Civrac going to do now? When I don't come back, will he set out to look for me? Or will he stay on the plateau to wait for the projections? If he does, he'll suffer badly from cold and hunger!"

"My God, my God, what can we do?" Lolla moaned, twisted her beautiful arms, joined at the wrist by thick bonds.

"*Caramba!* If I could just get free! Señorita, have you tried to tear the cords that bind you with your teeth?"

"Yes, but my teeth are too weak. I can't even fray the diabolical ropes."

"I have an idea, Señorita. It seems to me that the cords are made from woven stalks of the russet grass. My teeth are solid, but the monsters have trussed me up so tightly that I can't move my head. Put out your arms. Put your bonds next to my teeth. There! Don't move."

Vigorously, Francisco set about biting the cords binding Lola's hands with his incisors. Soon, one fiber snapped, then another, and then a whole sheaf. Francisco redoubled his efforts—and suddenly, the bonds fell away.

Lolla uttered a cry of joy as she raised her liberated hands.

"Oh, if I had my matches!" Francisco said. "I left them with Monsieur de Civrac. Quickly, Señorita, look around for a stone or a piece of slate—something hard. Hurry! Those black bandits will doubtless be back before long..."

Lolla had soon located a splinter of slate on the floor of the hut.

"Bravo! Scrape the cord around my neck...yes, that one...scrape hard, Señorita. Don't be afraid of scratching me—I've got hard skin..."

When Francisco sensed that the cord had been partly frayed, he tensed his muscles prodigiously, and the worn cord snapped. The Spaniard was able to move his head...and from then on, the task proceeded rapidly. With his teeth, Francisco freed his hands. His strong fingers removed the cords binding Lola's legs, and then those that were wound around his body and legs.

The two prisoners stood up together.

"I don't have a weapon!" Francisco groaned. "Oh, my pike, my pike! How useful it would be now. It's impossible to flee without a weapon to open the way for us. Is there nothing in this cabin? Have you seen anything, Señorita?"

Francisco made a rapid tour of their prison. It was square at the base, the four triangular walls shrinking as they rose up and coming together at a height of two meters. The sides of the square floor were three meters long. There was no furniture and there were no utensils of any kind. There were a few fragments of slate on the smooth floor, about the size of a five-franc coin.

"What about the door?" Lolla asked. "What is it made of?"

"A block of slate," Francisco replied. "I've already thought of that—it's too awkward to manipulate. Since there's nothing else, though..."

The Spaniard was about to look to see how the door was attached when the block of slate fell inwards. The light from outside invaded the hut, and the prisoners were able to see a vast crowd of monopods tightly packed all the way to the river bank. On the threshold, upright and motionless, stood the Mercurian with the shiny gold-ringed trunk.

By means of gestures and whistles it manifested an excitement presumably caused by seeing its prisoners' arms and legs free. As the Mercurians were now aware of the dangerous strength of the extraordinary beings of unknown origin, however, none of the monopods advanced, and even the chief looked back frequently to see whether retreat would be possible in case of an attack.

Bracing himself, with his fists forward, almost crouching on his heels, in order to be able to see what was happening outside through the low door, Francisco reflected. Lolla was standing behind him, ready to obey as soon as he gave an order—for in this situation, the mistress left the domestic the prerogative of making a decision.

Could they flee through that crowd? Impossible without a weapon—all the more impossible because the opening of the doorway was only about a meter high, and Francisco and Lolla would have to duck down to get through it. Once outside, before they could brace themselves for a further leap, they would be grabbed by claws and knocked down, perhaps injured.

Francisco was taking account of all that when he noticed a pronounced disturbance in the crowd of monopods. Arms were gesticulating, whistles resounding.

"What are they going to do?" Francisco growled.

At that moment, however, the prisoners saw, to their astonishment, the slate hut rose up into the air and fall on to its side, and they were grabbed from behind. Twenty monopods leapt on them, knocked them down and immediately carried them into another pyramidal house.

Francisco realized that the huts were simply resting on the ground, without foundations. The Mercurians had lifted up the one in which they were enclosed, and others had attacked them from the rear in order to capture them, taking advantage of the surprise occasioned by the movement of the house.

Chapter Three
Which seems phantasmagorical,
and yet is scientifically real

After four hours of solitude, Paul de Civrac was astonished that Francisco had not returned. The penultimate monopod had been entirely consumed. The young man struck a match and set fire to the feet of the last Mercurian that remained to him. He was not suffering from hunger, for the blood of the monopods was satisfying nourishment, and he was scarcely feeling the cold, sitting against the rock that sheltered him from the wind and in front of the Mercurian, burning with cheerful spitting flames that provided light and heat, but Francisco's prolonged absence worried him.

Another four hours passed, and Francisco did not reappear.

I'll go down as far as the large plateau, Paul said to himself. *My foot's almost better; if I pay careful attention to the terrain, I can still walk quickly enough. The Venusian projection won't shine for another forty-eight hours, so I have plenty of time.*

He waited, however, until the monopod was completely consumed. When the last sputtering flame has gone out, he got up, picked up his pike, and set off for the entrance of the gorge.

He did not notice that just as he got to his feet, two white sparks had raced across the infinite darkness, and that, while he crossed the twilit platform, he was followed by the two minuscule sparks, which were floating in mid-air, horizontally aligned, at shoulder height.

He walked on. In measured bounds, he went down the steep slope of the gorge into the full Mercurian daylight. Now, if he had turned round, he would not have been able to see the two sparks, which had become invisible in the intense light.

More fortunate than Francisco, having traversed the immense plateau that extended half way down the mountain, he arrived at the entrance to the steep path that descended through the black cliff all the way to the golden river.

He was about to go into it when he spotted five Mercurians in a cave hollowed out in the side of the path. He stopped, indecisively—but the monopods immediately bounded toward him, trunks whistling and claws extended.

Fearing for his life, or at least for his liberty, Paul de Civrac raised his pike and brought it down violently on each of the nearest monopods. The blows yielded the same sound as the impact of a sledgehammer on green wood. Two monsters fell, struck down. The other three fled precipitately down the enclosed path.

The war will definitely be unending, Paul said to himself.

As he had just come from a dark and cold region, however, he was inordinately affected by the ambient heat and light. "I need a rest!" he murmured.

And having thrown the two Mercurian corpses—one of which had the gold-circled trunk symbolic of high command—into the cavern. Paul went in and sat down next to them.

Then he saw two white speaks dancing before his eyes. They settled into immobility, in a horizontal line, a meter above the cadavers.

"Why, what's this! Some new phenomenon of this strange country?"

He reached out toward the two sparks, like a child trying to catch flies on the wing, but the motionless sparks seemed to pass through the flesh of his hand.

"I'm damned if I understand any of this!" he whispered. "Doubtless some electrical phenomenon, unless..."

He fell silent, intrigued.

The two sparks descended slowly toward the trunks of the Mercurian cadavers. Paul followed them with his eyes. He saw them flutter momentarily in front of the sucker of each of the trunks—and suddenly, both sparks disappeared.

Immediately, however, the Mercurian cadavers appeared to revive. Each one agitated its arm and its leg, opened its eye—and stood up, with an abrupt movement.

"Hey!" Paul cried, his hair bristling on his head and his eyes widening with fright. "What...!" Seizing his pike, he backed away.

But the two resuscitated Mercurians fell to their knees, inclined their black torsos, and humbly laid their trunks on the ground, as if to implore the Terran not to get angry.

Before Paul was able to recover from his prodigious astonishment, the monopod with the ringed trunk stood up, and with calm gestures and very gentle movements, without the young man feeling the scrape of claws, the Mercurian had removed the diamond-encrusted gold ring that Paul de Civrac wore on the ring-finger of his left hand.

Holding the diamond between its talons, the monopod headed for the smooth wall of the cave, and in front of Paul de Civrac—who wondered whether he might have gone mad, and whether what he was seeing was really happening—the amazing resuscitated individual raised its arm and methodically scratched the slate wall with one of the points of the diamond…

And the scratches outlined letters, which formed words…

As the Mercurian wrote, Paul de Civrac read:

I am Dr. Ahmed Bey, who has come from Earth. The other resuscitated Mercurian is Brad, whom I went to seek out on Venus. All this is done by means of the disincarnation of the soul, of which I know the formula and the secret. Bild insisted stubbornly on refusing disincarnation; he wanted to remain on Venus, declaring that he would return to Earth in the flesh. We left him there. We can't speak to you, because the Mercurians have no throat, no tongue, no teeth, no palate and no other organ that would permit us to articulate human words, but we can hear you, since the Mercurians have ears. We have our terrestrial souls with Mercurians bodies and organs. Speak, then. I'll reply in writing. Where is Francisco? Where is Lolla?

Prepared for the marvelous as Paul de Civrac was, this new adventure was truly too exorbitant and prodigious not to cause his reason to lurch momentarily. He passed his hand over his eyes, got to his feet, moved closer to the engraved slate wall, and read the singular inscription all the way through. Then he looked at the two Mercurians. They were standing before him, gently waving their trunks, and the two red eyes were shining, not ferociously or stupidly, as Paul had always seen them shining before, but with a gleam of human intelligence!

"Come on, let's see!" said Paul, aloud. "I'm not mad! I've killed two monopods; I've seen two sparks go into their trunks; the monopods have come back to life; one of them gently removed my diamond ring and started writing words...."

While Paul was speaking, the monopod with the diamond had moved to the slate wall again, and it resumed writing:

No, you're not mad. We're Ahmed Bey and Brad!

"Ahmed Bey, who I met in Calcutta!" Paul exclaimed. "Is it possible? Am I not the victim of a hallucination? Ahmed Bey here, in this form! And with Brad! But it's crazy! However...here are the lines, written there...I can see them, I can touch them—they exist! I'm in possession of my reason. I'm not hallucinating..."

He stammered these words, his eyes wide, his hands trembling, standing stiffly in front of the two Mercurians so fantastically resuscitated.

Suddenly, the young man had an idea.

"Brad!" he shouted. "Take the watch that's in my belt!"

Immediately, the second monopod leapt forward, put out its arm and took hold of Lolla's watch by the ring with its claw.

"What time is it?"

The monopod Brad looked at the watch, and after gesturing with its arm, it emitted eight spaced whistles.

Paul took back the watch and glanced at it; it was showing eight o'clock.

"Good!" exclaimed Paul. "Now take this box and strike a match."

A few moments later the monopod Brad held up a lighted match.

The demonstration was sufficient. With a sudden surge of crazy joy, Paul de Civrac opened his arms wide.

Brad threw himself into them, and the young man felt the caress of his trunk on his neck.

Several minutes went by in silence and emotion. Then, suddenly sensing that all his presence of mind and composure had returned, Paul de Civrac spoke.

"I'll leave it until later," he said to the monopod Ahmed, "to ask you for enlightenment regarding this inconceivable adventure and Bild's ridiculous stubbornness. And I thank you, my dear doctor, for having replied, perhaps without being aware of it, to the appeal that I cried out to you in the Fiery Wheel. It was a presentiment, then! I'd also like to know what the Fiery Wheel and its inhabitants were, if you've discovered that—but time is too precious now. We have to act, to find Lolla and Francisco. Listen!"

And he described the various phenomena of the Mercurian land, recounted the loss of Lolla Mendès, the flight from the monopods, the fortunate incident of the projections, the twelve monopods killed, drained of their blood and burned, and Francisco's departure to go hunting. He concluded: "I've set out myself to search for him. What should we do now?"

Ahmed Bey reflected. With an entirely human gesture, he supported the extremity of his trunk on the talons of his arm and closed his eye. Brad watched him. Suddenly, he shook his head and walked to the wall. Raising his arm, the claws still clutching the diamond, he traced words on the slate:

Civrac, you'll be our submissive prisoner. Keep your pike, though; it might be useful. Brad, you imitate all my movements and whistles. Let me take the lead. We'll find Lola and Francisco, dead or alive. Civrac, guide us to the Mercurian city, and then act like a voluntary prisoner.

"Understood!" said Paul.

As a sign of acquiescence Brad dipped his drunk several times.

And they set out to descend the abrupt ravine that led to the golden river and the Mercurian city.

During the journey, Paul's mind posed a thousand questions, insoluble for the time being, because the explanations that Ahmed Bey could have given to made the disincarnation and reincarnation of souls comprehensible were scarcely convenient to develop in writing with a diamond as a pen and slate rock as tablets. It would have been even less easy for Brad to furnish revelations on the subject of the catastrophe of the Fiery Wheel on the world of Venus and descriptions of the world itself. Paul de Civrac therefore resigned himself to not knowing. Besides which, the fate of Lolla Mendès was paramount in his thoughts, and after that, Francisco's.

During his sojourn on the twilit platform, his body being forcibly inactive, his mind and heart had been nourished by the idea and the image of the young woman. And, as can happen in circumstances exempt from banality, his sentiments had immediately attained their complete development. He loved Lolla Mendès as if he had lived through years of cloudless happiness with her—and yet, the two young people had scarcely been able to exchange a few words of love, a few caresses and a few kisses, in the midst of terrible events.

Suddenly, Paul was distracted from his thoughts by the appearance, at a bend in the ravine, of the Mercurian city. He stopped and, pointing at the valley open at his feet, with the golden river in the middle and the pyramidal huts on both banks, all in the shade of the overhanging cliffs, he said: "That's it!"

The two false Mercurians had stopped with him. Then, at a gesture from Ahmed Bey, which was understood as soon as it was made, Brad took hold of Paul's left arm, leaving his right arm free, carrying the pike. Ahmed Bey placed himself in front of the pair, and they resumed walking.

The new arrivals had been seen by the Mercurians in the city, however. A concert of violent whistles filled the air. A host of monopods soon surrounded Ahmed Bey, Brad and their pretended prisoner.

Ahmed Bey marched at random into the midst of the huts. He too emitted whistles then, but as he did not know the Mercurian language, he could not space them out, cadence them and pitch them in such a way as to form meaningful sentences. He whistled in brief, equal blasts to the rhythm of his march. Having arrived in the middle of an empty space between the huts, he stopped, immobilized his companion and his prisoner with a gesture, and raised his arm in a dignified fashion.

Then a monopod with a gold-circled trunk emerged from the crowd, stood in front of Ahmed Bey, in whom it doubtless recognized a high-ranking Mercurian, and apparently launched into a speech, for its whistles went on for several minutes without interruption.

Ahmed Bey was embarrassed. He did not know how to respond. He therefore maintained a prudent silence, and an attitude he believed to be dignified. It must have been, in fact, in the Mercurian sense, for the monopod orator did not persist. It turned around and started walking. Ahmed Bey followed it without hesitation. Brad and Paul followed close behind, escorted a short distance away by the whistling and gesticulating host of black monsters.

Having arrived at the door of a hut, the chief stopped and stood aide. Deliberately, Ahmed Bey stopped too and made a curt gesture to his acolytes, pointing at the door. Brad put on a show of forcing Paul to bend down and all three disappeared into the hut, accompanied by the monopod chief.

There were a few moments of silence and immobility. Paul's eyes adjusted to the relative gloom of the hut—but when he could see his surroundings clearly he stepped to the side, bent down, and stood up again, raising his left hand, in which he was holding a scrap of cloth. In a voice vibrant with indescribable emotion he proclaimed: "Brad! Lolla's been here—this is a piece of her bodice." And two tears brimmed in his eyes.

The hut to which the chief had led the individual it believed to be its colleague was the one to which Francisco and Lola had been brought after their second capture. What had become of them since?

PART FIVE
IN COMPLETE MYSTERY

Chapter One
In which even Ahmed Bey knows no more

The discovery of the scrap of red cloth that had been part of Lolla Mendès' costume plunged Paul de Civrac, Ahmed Bey and Brad into profound reflection. The Mercurian chief who had come in with them had closed the door of the hut and, crouched against it, was gazing with its unique eye at the two monopods, whom it could not imagine being vivified by human souls, and their prisoner. Evidently, it did not understand their conduct or their silence, but, as is appropriate in the presence of a superior, the subaltern chief also kept quiet and waited, without its eye manifesting anything but the most absolute stupidity.

Sitting in front of Ahmed Bey and Brad, who had remained standing, Paul could not take his eyes off the scrap of red fabric that he was holding in his hand. He felt a claw touch his arm gently, however, and looked up to see Ahmed Bey. The monopod Doctor leaned over and, in the fine black dust accumulated on the ground, he traced words that Paul read as they appeared:

We need to stay here for at least forty-eight hours. That's the time it will take me...

At that point, the Doctor stopped writing, having run out of space. He rubbed out the words, smoothed over the black and began again:

...to learn the Mercurian words that will permit me to ask where Lolla and Francisco...

He erased them again, and continued in the same place:

...have been taken. I can't see any other means. Is that agreed?

"Yes," Paul replied.

The Doctor resumed writing:

Stay calm, sleep, eat what is brought to you. Brad will keep watch on you, and let me do what I need to do.

"Agreed!" said Paul. "But in the meantime, Lolla might be killed!"

The Doctor did not reply. He looked at Brad, who had also read what he had written, and gestured his support with his trunk.

The Mercurian had watched all these actions and movements with an amazement that was manifest in its widened eye, and the agitation of its trunk and arm. Suddenly, however, Ahmed Bey uttered an imperious whistle and the Mercurian froze. The Doctor marched to the door, easily tipped over the slate plate masking it and, making a summoning gesture to the true Mercurian, went out.

The docile Mercurian got up, and followed him. What turmoil there must have been in its head! It had seen its superior making gestures that no Mercurian had ever made. And the superior did not speak. Doubtless, it did not deign to explain.

Followed by the obedient monopod, Ahmed Bey marched through the Mercurian city. As he passed by, the host of little black monsters parted silently. Sometimes, whistles vibrated. However attentively the Doctor listened, compared and reasoned, however, he could not extract the slightest meaning from the sounds that he heard.

After strolling for three hours, during which he crossed the golden river several times and had made a tour of the entire Mercurian city, he went back to the hut where Paul was enclosed under Brad's guard.

The observations that Ahmed Bey had made could be summarized as follows:

The city was composed of between five and six thousand huts, set up in no particular order, uniformly pyramidal and all completely empty.

The Mercurian indigenes had no knowledge of science or art, save for that of constructing the huts with plaques of slate stuck together with a sort of green clay; they had no trades and no agriculture; they lived in the most absolute inaction. Their only industry was the fabrication of bowls in yellow metal, but although Ahmed Bey saw several of these bowls in the huts, he did not know where they came from.

The monopod indigenes were the only anima life on the planet; no snakes crawled on the ground, nor did any biped or quadruped walk there; there were no insects or birds in the air.

The Mercurians' sole apparent nourishment and beverage was the blood of other Mercurians. During his walk, in fact, knowing already from Paul's account that the monopods were mercurophages, he had seen black monsters sucking the blood of other, fatter monsters, each with a mutilated arm and leg, through the eye. He had passed in front of a row of huts where he had seen the nutritious Mercurians lying on the ground, nourished themselves by other Mercurians, which presented the eyes of smaller, formless monopods—doubtless infants—to their trunks.

How were those infants produced? What laws regulated the choice of newborns that would live and those that would serve to nourish the monopods used as food? The Doctor could not determine that. Doubtless he would have learned it eventually, if the tragic events that followed shortly afterwards had not prevented him from completing his observations. From what he could see, however, he concluded that the reproduction of the species took place, on Mercury, in conditions of extraordinary multiplicity, facility and rapidity—and that Nature had thus provided for the unique need of the living.

He also discovered how the Mercurians died a natural death. Several times, in fact, he saw a nearby monopod turn abruptly on its foot, whistle and fall. They the wide open eye swelled up and suddenly burst. The Mercurian nearest to the one that had fallen then introduced the tip of its trunk into the burst eye, drank the white blood, and went away, satisfied. And the dead one remained where it was, without any other paying any attention to it.

The Doctor came across cadavers that life had abandoned for some time. He touched them; some were as hard as iron, others as flaccid as an empty bladder. The Doctor never found out what stages of decomposition the cadavers passed through, or even if they did decompose.

As for the internal structure of the Mercurian body, Ahmed Bey intended to study it by dissecting a cadaver when he had time to do so and could find a trenchant instrument appropriate to the task.

Throughout his stroll, the Doctor was meekly followed by the monopod chief that had been the first to welcome him. From the attitude of numerous indigenes he encountered, Ahmed Bey understood that he had introduced himself into the body of a very powerful and highly honored Mercurian, perhaps the sovereign of the Mercurian country, or at least of that city.

He was blessing that good luck, which permitted him, under the pretext of dignity, not to communicate with his subjects by means of comprehensible whistles, when he got back to the hut where Paul was enclosed. He could distinguish it from the others because Paul's footprints were still visible in the dust in front of the entrance.

Still followed by his satellite, he went in, and with a gesture that was immediately understood and obeyed, ordered that the block of slate serving as a door should be replaced. As before, the subaltern chief squatted down inside, against the slate slab.

"Any news?" asked Paul, with visible anxiety.

The Doctor replied by writing in the sand: *I no longer hope to learn the language in a short time. We have to try something else. I have an idea. Give me the scrap of cloth.*

When he had the red rag in his claw, he turned to the chief. The other stood up. Ahmed Bey showed it the scrap, emitting an imperious whistle.

The Mercurian remained stupidly motionless, however. Ahmed Bey waved the piece of red cloth in front of its eye, but the expressionless eye remained empty of any thought.

"It doesn't understand," said Paul.

Then the Doctor, still holding the piece of fabric in his claw, opened the door and went out, indicated by a gesture that he wanted to be followed. The chief obeyed, and Brad and Paul also came out of the hut. The Doctor raised the scarlet scrap in the air and extended his am successively toward the four points of the horizon.

Whistles rose up from the host of monopods, but the chief did not budge and its eye, like the eyes of all the other monsters, remained stupid.

"They don't understand," Paul repeated—and he looked at the compact crowd of monopods, his expression both furious and desperate, at the heavy golden river, still the same, at the two slopes of the black cliffs that rose up to either side, only leaving a thin strip between them through which dazzling pale green light passed, descending from the eternal dark green clouds that could be seen moving through the atmosphere...

And the spectacle of that implacable nature in which nothing lived except those little black monsters, cruel, horrible, implausible and repugnant, filled him with a sensation of fearful anguish.

"Brad!" he exclaimed. "Let's get out of here—anywhere at all! Let's search this frightful planet in every direction. Let's search for Lolla until I die of despair!"

But Ahmed Bey seized him by the arm and dragged him into the hut. In the dust, he wrote: *Courage! We'll find them. Pick up your pike. Let's go—but be a man!*

For a few minutes, Paul remained wearily motionless in front of the inscription. When he raised his head, he saw the red Mercurian eyes of Ahmed Bey and Brad looking at him, with an entirely human expression of amity and encouragement. A soul—a veritable soul—animated each of them! And he remembered the prodigy of disincarnation and reincarnation. He was ashamed of his weakness then and, straightening up, he seized his pike with a firm hand and said resolutely: "Let's go!"

Outside, Ahmed Bey, agitating his gold-ringed trunk, had only to start walking for the entire crowd of monopods to part in front of him. Having arrived at the edge of the river, he turned round. The chief was still there, a faithful satellite. He gripped it with his claw and made it stand next to Paul and Brad. Then, spotting two other Mercurians, the trunks of which were only ornamented with a single thin gold ring, he summoned them with a gesture and stood them beside their superior. Then, abruptly, he pointed to the river and jumped on to the heavy elastic waves. Brad, Paul and the three ringed Mercurians imitated him. The crowd of monopods wanted to launch themselves too, but Ahmed Bey stopped them with a terrible whistle and a curt gesture of his extended arm.

The crowd stopped dead on the shore, and the golden river soon carried the little part-human and part-Mercurian company away, and out of the tumultuous city.

Chapter Two
Which concludes with a leap into the unknown

Paul de Civrac looked at the watch that was still suspended from his belt. It had stopped. He wound it up and set the hands to twelve o'clock.

By that means he was able to take account of the fact that an entire half-hour went by before the moment when the river, finally emerging from the overhanging cliffs, broadened out its heavy gilded waves between two vast plains of russet grass. Paul estimated the rapidity of the golden river in mid-stream at fifty kilometers an hour in the enclosed valley; taking account of the position of the city, almost in the middle of the valley, the latter was therefore approximately fifty kilometers long.

Once they were in the plain, the rapidity of the river diminished gradually, until the current was no longer travelling at about twenty-five kilometers an hour. So, without the shade of the cliffs and the relative freshness produced by the extreme velocity of their glide, the torrid heat made itself felt cruelly, not for Ahmed Bey or Brad, whose Mercurian bodies were adapted to such an environment, for Paul, whose sojourn in the twilight zone had dishabituated him to the high temperature of the luminous plain. He was obliged to resume squinting in order to adapt his eyes to the blinding glare falling from the eternal green clouds.

Behind those clouds, which never opened a gap on the infinity of the heavens, the sun was shining, and with what glare! Without the clouds to filter its radiance of light and heat, the entire planet would have caught fire and burst like a prodigious firework.

The journey through the immense russet plain lasted for six and a quarter hours. In the fifth hour the travelers saw mountains profiled in the distance, as yet indecisively. At the same time, the velocity of the river accelerated, until it reached approximately a hundred kilometers an hour. The banks were flashing by like fields and ravines on both sides of a terrestrial automobile driven at top speed.

Anxiously, Paul said to Ahmed Bey: "Where the devil are we? Surely, to acquire such speed, the river must precipitate itself up ahead from the top of some cliff in a frightful cataract…?"

Ahmed Bey could only respond with a futile whistle, but with a gesture he indicated the three true monopods. They were perfectly tranquil.

"I understand," said Paul. "You mean that as long as those monsters conserve their placidity, no danger can be threatening us. You're right…"

As he said it, the three Mercurians emitted a shrill whistle and, as one, lay down prone on the river, heads forward, and used their arms as a rudder to maintain themselves in the center of the current. The Terrans noticed, in fact, that they had been tending to draw apart from one another because of the turbulent eddies in the stream.

"Let's imitate them!" Paul said.

The three monopods had arranged themselves in Indian file, with the trunk of the second wound around the foot of the first and the trunk of the third wound around the foot of the second. Paul lay down behind the third monopod and hung on to its foot with both hands. Ahmed Bey and Brad lined up behind Paul; on the golden river the six creatures must have resembled a bizarre serpent, black at both ends and white in the middle...

The mountains were getting closer by the minute, and the velocity of the current was still increasing. In order to be able to breathe, Paul had to put his head between his extended arms, and his lips and nose sometimes brushed the hot opaque surface of the golden river.

At one point, where the river, forming a lake, was somewhat calmer, he was able to raise his head and say: "As long as this vertiginous race to the abyss is taking us closer to Lolla and Francisco!"

Ahmed Bey and Brad replied with a long whistle.

But the mountains were no more than two or three kilometers away now. A vast excavation opened up in their abrupt base. The voyagers were suddenly engulfed, and there was almost complete darkness around them, into which the mysterious phosphorescence of the river spread the pale clarity of a night-light.

The vaults of the subterranean channel were lost in absolute night.

A few minutes after they had gone into the mountain, the silence—the oppressive Mercurian silence—was strangely troubled. Without any of the Terrans being able to tell where it came from, they heard a kind of rhythmic rumble, which rose and fell in pitch like the profound voices of the wind in a pine forest,

Suddenly, the three Mercurians started whistling, and their whistles, exceedingly shrill, seemed to be expressing fear. Paul sensed that the monopod to which he was hanging on was attempting to detach its foot. He raised his head and saw that the two Mercurians in the lead had separated from the chain and were gliding toward the left-hand wall of the channel. Within a second, they had disappeared into the hole, into which an arm of the river flowed.

"My friends!" Paul Shouted. "The first two monsters have left us! The one I'm holding on to is trying to shake me off too! It's struggling...but I'm not letting go..."

A louder rumble, coming from the unknown, cut off his speech. Immediately afterwards, he perceived that the monopod whose foot he was clutching had stopped struggling, doubtless resigned.

"Some grave danger is threatening us!" he shouted. "My prisoner is no longer trying to escape. It understands that we've passed the place where it would have been able to take the road to salvation. What's going to happen?"

Brad ad Ahmed Bey responded with their habitual whistling, but they clung harder to one another.

The inexplicable rhythmic rumbling was now ringing hollow, frighteningly close by. The Mercurian in the lead was no longer giving any sign of life.

Paul felt horribly alone, exposed to a danger as unknown as it was inevitable. Brad and Ahmed Bey were no help, since they could not talk.

The unfortunate young man did not lose his composure, however; he observed that the velocity of the current was increasing by the minute; the rocky walls, shiny in their phosphorescence, were racing past on both sides with lightning rapidity.

Similar now to claps of distant thunder, the rumbling filled him with a sensation of inexpressible dread.

Suddenly, there was a scream, a prolonged howl, lugubrious enough to chill the blood in the veins—an unusual scream coming from the depths of the abyss—and there were violent fulgurations everywhere...

And in an intense agony of terror that overwhelmed him, Paul saw that the monopod and he were hanging over the edge of a fiery precipice: an unfathomable precipice from which the frightful howling was rising.

He felt himself oscillating, swinging back and forth above the gulf…and, dragged over the edge, he fell.

One last glimmer of thought made him understand that he was still hanging on to the monopod, and that his two companions were falling with him…

And the four bodies plunged into the abyss, while the infernal howl rang out for a third time.

Chapter Three
Which is the tragic counterpart to the preceding one

Five kilometers upstream of the fall that had engulfed Paul, Ahmed Bey, Brad and one other monopod, the golden river divided into two, and a part of the liquid mass plunged into a corridor narrower than the main tunnel. It was by that route that the Mercurians in the lead had escaped. The current became much less rapid therein, until it had no more velocity than that of a horse at a gentle trot.

Two hours before Paul and his companions passed by, a large company of Mercurians, arranged in a triangle with its point orientated in the direction of the current, had arrived at the bifurcation, had turned aside with the aid of arms forming a rudder, and had gone into the smaller corridor. In the middle of the troop, standing up and holding one another by the hand, Lolla Mendès and Francisco had been kept in view. They were not secured by any bonds, but they were still prisoners, for the tightly-packed ranks of the monopods were insurmountable. Besides which, where could they flee in that narrow ad low-ceilinged subterranean channel?

By virtue of a regrettable fatality, Lolla and Francisco had been taken out of the second hut where they had been enclosed and drawn on to the current of the river scarcely an hour before the arrival of Paul and his two companions in the Mercurian city. If Paul de Civrac, Ahmed Bey and Brad, understanding the whistles of the Mercurians in the lead, had veered into the minor arm of the river instead of letting themselves be dragged into the abyss, they would doubtless have caught up with Lolla and Francisco at some point, but destiny had decided otherwise, and while Paul and his companions were plunging into the mysterious abyss, the young woman and her domestic, prisoners of the monopods, were arriving in a second Mercurian city.

This one was built in a kind of funnel open to the sky, which the little river encountered in its slowed course. At first glance, that funnel, with high smooth walls, did not appear to have any other exits than the tunnels upstream and downstream of the river. Before they were shut away in a hut again, however, doubtless to wait for their fate to be decided. Lola and Francisco noticed that the sides of the funnel were holed with excavations not far from the bottom, and that roughly-carved steps led up and down the cliffs to each of those holes. They must, therefore, be the orifices of subterranean tunnels traversing the mountain, perhaps leading to the plains.

When the door of the hut closed again, Lolla and Francisco found themselves alone.

"We need to get away from here, Francisco," Lolla said, "get our bearings, if possible, and head for the plateau where you left Paul. Even if he's set off to search for you, he'll go back there in the hope that you'll return yourself. We need to get away. If we stay, sooner or later these monsters will puncture our eyes and drink our blood. I don't want to die like that. I'd rather be killed trying to escape. We'll have to try, even if it proves impossible."

"I think the same, Señorita," Francisco replied, "but I'm unarmed. Let's wait until one of these monopods, as Monsieur de Civrac calls them, comes to visit us. I'll catch it by the foot and use it as a club…and with the grace of God…"

"I recognize," Lola said, "that we have very little chance of escape. But if I'm caught, you must leave me and go help Paul to wait for the marvelous arrival of Bild and Brad."

Francisco made no reply, but he made it understood with a single glance that, if Lolla perished, he would bury himself beneath a veritable hecatomb of Mercurians in order to avenge her.

The two captives did not have long to wait. They had been silent for a few minutes when the door-slab fell away and a Mercurian appeared in the square of light. Before it could come in, however, Francisco, slipping into the doorway himself, had grabbed it by the foot and picked it up.

"Come on, Señorita!"

Already, however, Lolla was outside the hut, standing up beside him. He offered her his free hand, and, taking advantage of the stupor of the few monopods that were there, they started bounding toward the nearest wall together. Immediately, a volley of whistles told them that they were being pursued.

They had a start, though. They reached the foot of the cliff and were getting ready to climb up by means of the rudimentary steps when Lolla saw a thin trickle of yellow liquid going into a hole some distance to their left. Breathlessly, she said: "Come on, Francisco—let's not go up; let's keep our lead. There's an easier tunnel…"

"Ah! Yes, Señorita, that's lucky. The others are dark, but this one will be lit by the stream. At least we'll be able to see there to direct our flight."

They resumed running and bounding again, and before the monopods were able to bock their way they had plunged into the tunnel. It was narrow and not very light, but easy to follow because of the radiation produced by the stream. Its course was meandering and they jumped over it several times. Behind them they could hear the furious whistling of the monopods, and they ran, encouraged by the certainty that the whistling sounds were gradually diminishing in intensity—proof that the fugitives were still putting more distance between themselves and their pursuers.

"The stream's getting broader, Señorita," said Francis suddenly, without pausing, "and traveling in a straight line. It's running in the direction we're going— let's stay still on its surface. It will carry us faster than we can run..."

"You're right, Francisco. The courageous young woman jumped into the middle of the stream, which was about two meters wide at that point. Francisco jumped at the same time.

The current was, in fact, quite rapid, and the flight of the two fugitives as accelerated without causing them any fatigue. They could only hear the whistling of the Mercurian faintly. Soon, having gone round and abrupt bend in the stream, they could no longer hear them at all.

Their attention was abruptly solicited by other sounds, however. There was a dull and rhythmic rumbling rising and falling in pitch, like the profound voices of the wind in a pine forest.

At the same time, by virtue of the increasing rapidity with which the uneven side walls of the tunnel were receding rearwards, they took account of the fact that the current was becoming stronger in disquieting proportions.

"That rumbling's frightening me, Francisco," said Lolla, "and something tells me that we're being drawn toward a gulf. We have to get to solid ground quickly. Look! There's a ledge between the rock and the stream. It's wide enough to walk along. Let's jump on to it quickly, before the current become too strong..."

"Let's jump, Señorita. Give me your hand."

"Hold on."

"Ready...*hup!*"

Their leap had been cleverly calculated, for their muscles knew by now how to adapt their efforts to Mercurian weight. They touched down on the ledge at a good spot, although their acquired momentum pulled them on and they nearly fell back into the shiny yellow waves. They braced themselves, stiffening their muscles and hung on to projections in the rock, bringing themselves to a stop. Their hands were slightly grazed, but the state of their nervous excitement was such that they were hardly aware of it.

"Let's go," said Lolla.

Animated by the hope of finding Paul de Civrac and waiting with him for the intervention of Bild sand Brad, the young woman now had as much strength, courage and presence of mind as Francisco. She had resumed her rank as mistress; she was in command.

The ledge along which they were moving, with Francisco behind Lolla, overhung the stream; in places it was several meters broad, but in others it shrank so as only to leave just enough room for their feet. The fugitives hung on to projections in the side wall then and, helping one another and favored by their light specific weight, they got past the bad patches adroitly. Beneath them, soundlessly, the seething stream was moving with vertiginous rapidity, rendered sensible to the Terrans' gaze by the intermittent blistering of the heavy waves.

The cadenced rumbling had become progressively louder, now having the intensity of distant thunder.

"What might that be, Francisco?"

"I don't know, Señorita."

"Perhaps the stream falling into an abyss."

"Perhaps."

Dominating the thunderous rumor, however, a prolonged crazed, shrill howl emerged from the invisible depths of the tunnel.

"Francisco!" Lolla exclaimed. She had stopped, with a sweat of anguish on her pale forehead, and she put a trembling hand on Francisco's shoulder, while the other clutched at a ridge on the wall. "Did you hear that?" she stammered.

"Yes, Señorita," the man replied, in a low voice.

They remained silent and still for a few moments, struggling against the nameless terror that was invading them.

The heart-rending scream rang out for a second time, like the desperate appeal of the siren of a ship in mortal danger in a nocturnal tempest.

"We need to go and see," said Lola, in a voice that was tremulous and resolute at the same time. "We can't stay here. Let's go."

"But Señorita..."

"Let's go. My heart is telling me that Monsieur de Civrac is there, in the mystery. Come on!"

"I'll follow you, Mistress!"

They had just resumed marching when they heard shrill noises behind them, still very distant.

"Listen!"

Pausing again, they pricked up their ears. There was no doubt about it: the shrill sounds were Mercurian whistles.

"You see," said Lola. "They're still chasing us. Behind us, there's captivity and death. Ahead of us, there's the mystery—but perhaps Paul too. Let's go!"

The valiant young woman launched herself forwards, immediately followed by Francisco.

Suddenly, however, she uttered an exclamation and grabbed hold of a rock to stop her dead—and she remained suspended over a gulf that opened beneath her feet. Francisco had been able to stop sooner, and only had to reach out his arm to pull Lolla back from her dangerous suspension and reestablish her on the ledge.

The young woman allowed her emotion to calm down, and then, with Francisco, she looked down.

What an extraordinary and terrifying spectacle! At their feet, the ledge stopped dead, abruptly interrupted above an indescribable abyss, from which the cadences rumbling was rising, and, at intervals, the tragic howling. Beneath them, to their right, the stream was sliced at right angles and fell in a silent and unified mass, into the apocalyptic gulf. And finally, lower down and in front of them, falling on the other side of the abyss, they could also see a broad golden river. The two silent cascades of molten gold were emitting a faint yellow radiance, and when they looked into the gulf itself they could not see anything but an opaque cloud of that yellow light at a great depths, diffuse and incomprehensible, produced by the Mercurian "watercourses."

Lolla and Francisco were considering the spectacle fearfully when louder whistles reminded them of all the danger they were running.

"They're getting closer, Francisco," said Lolla.

"I have an idea, Señorita."

The Spaniard lay face down on the ledge, with his head protruding over the gulf. He examined the walls carefully.

When he got to his feet again, he said: "Señorita, you won't be afraid?"

"No."

"Well then, we'll go down there. It's obvious that these yellow liquid masses have an exit at the bottom of the gulf. Even if death awaits us down there, it's even more certain that death is lying in wait for us here, and getting closer. Do you want to go down?"

"Let's go down!" said Lolla, in a resolute tone.

"Climb on to my shoulders, horseback-fashion. Put your legs around my torso, and hang on to the ledges in the rock with your hands, as I'm doing. That way, we won't be separated. Either I'll save you, or I'll perish with you..."

"Without replying, Lolla climbed on to Francisco's shoulders as he crouched down. When her felt his young mistress' legs and feet solidly braced against his sides, he stood up again and, kneeling on the edge of the abyss, began to descend backwards along the vertiginous wall. Fortunately, it had a great many ledges, holes and minuscule platforms. He only placed his feet with extreme caution; like Lolla, he clung on to rocky projections with both hands.

Suddenly, they heard furious whistles on the ledge up above. Lolla looked up. Gesticulating Mercurians were leaning over the abyss—but none of them dared take the perilous path that the fugitives had chosen.

"They won't pursue us any further," she said.

"No—that's one peril less."

While the whistling continued up above, the terrible cadenced rumbling and the incomprehensible intermittent howling rose from below.

Lolla and Francisco soon fund themselves in the luminous mist. Above and below, to the left and the right, they could not see anything except the vague infinity of that mist, similar to the luminosity of the sun rising in the light morning mists on Earth. In front of them was the rugged black rock...

They continued going down. Gradually the noise of whistling decreased and faded away, but the rumbling became increasingly loud and the howls of agony became unbearable in their stridency.

How much time did the perilous descent take? Neither Lolla nor Francisco could have said. Perhaps twenty minutes, perhaps hours...

Finally, Francisco spoke. "We're on a broad plateau Señorita. Get down."

The young woman jumped down from Francisco's shoulders.

They were, indeed, on a plateau, the limits of which they could not see because of the luminous fog. Cautiously, they advanced, their backs turned to the wall they had descended. To their left, the waterfall of the stream fell into a pool, and then the liquid mass ran away rapidly in a channel. They followed the channel.

First, it led them to a kind of golden lake into which the water of the stream flowed. To their right, they saw the enormous mass of the golden river falling vertically, noiselessly, like oil running into oil. It was from the other shore of the lake, in front of them, that the rumbling and howling was coming.

"Let's follow the edge," said Lolla.

They started walking to the right. Soon, they found themselves underneath the cascade of the great reviver. In a single sheet, the liquid gold formed an immense arch above them, striped with brighter scintillations.

Abruptly, they stopped dead, with an enormous surge of emotion. A few paces in front of them, a human body was lying, with two monopods kneeling beside him.

"Paul!" cried Lolla, in heart-rending fashion.

Freeing herself from Francisco's hand, she launched herself forward and fell upon Paul's body.

"He's dead!" she moaned. "He's dead!" And she hugged the recumbent body, delirious with despair.

Overwhelmed herself by surprise, emotion and grief, she collapsed in a faint.

Francisco was already kneeling beside his mistress when he felt something touch his shoulder. He looked round and saw a standing monopod that was making signs with its claw. At first, he did not understand. Then, as his composure gradually returned, he realized that the monopod was pointing at Paul de Civrac and making gestures of negation.

"He's not dead?" he said.

The gesture of negation became more insistent.

Francisco applied his ear to Paul's chest. The heart was beating.

"Santiago be praised!" he exclaimed. "Señorita, he's alive! He's alive!"

He still had his flask in his belt, containing water scented with a residue of cognac. He uncorked it and poured a few drops between Lolla's lips and then between Civrac's.

Two minutes went by. Lolla remained immobile, as if dead, but Paul stirred, and soon opened his eyes.

"Where am I?" he murmured.

"Señor!" exclaimed Francisco. "Señor!

At the sound of that familiar voice. Paul sat up, with a start. His wild eyes recognized Francisco, and saw Lolla lying full length, as if lifeless. The surge of emotion was so powerful that he fell back, with an immense sigh.

That new weakness was of short duration, however. The young man opened his eyes again, got up painfully, walked over to Lolla, gazed at the young woman for some time, and then placed his hand over her heart.

"She's alive," he said. "Found...finally...found..." A violent emotion strangled the words in his throat. He made an effort of will, though, and went on, more calmly: "She'll come round of her own accord. How do you come to be here, Francisco?"

Swiftly, in a few words, Francisco recounted the fats. "But what about you, Señor?"

Turning to the two Mercurians that were standing a few paces away, Paul said, gravely: "Francisco, this is Dr. Ahmed Bey, who has come from Earth, and this is our friend Arthur Brad."

"Señor!" stammered the Spaniard. He thought that Paul de Civrac had lost his mind.

The young man divined his thought. "You think I'm mad," he said, with a smile. "You're mistaken. Listen, Francisco!"

Meticulously, he told the Spaniard everything that had happened to him since they had been separated. He explained the disincarnation and reincarnation of souls as best he could.

Francisco was stupefied. He was about to reply when Dr. Ahmed Bey advanced and, before the eyes of the two men, began to trace characters on the ground with the diamond that he was still carrying in his claw.

It's necessary for Francisco to allow himself to be disincarnated temporarily and take my place in this Mercurian body. Then I'll be able to talk, and be better able to act in the interests of us all.

"By the Virgen del Pilar!" Francisco exclaimed. "All this is devilry!"

But Paul spoke. He demonstrated to Francisco that the mystical operation presented no danger. Endowed with Francisco's body and human speech, Ahmed Bey would be more easily able to reach an understanding with him, Paul, as to what to do for the best.

"He'll wake Lolla up," Civrac concluded, "and he'll save us."

"So be it!" said Francisco. "What do I have to do?"

"Lie down on the ground and wait."

"There!" And the Spaniard lay down.

But Ahmed Bey wrote on the rock, before Paul's eyes:

Explain to him the transformation that will take place in his exterior being when he's reincarnated in the body I'm occupying.

Immediately, Paul explained to Francisco that he would not be able to speak, but only to whistle. He would be just like Brad...

"*Bueno!*" said the brave Spaniard. "Then I'll whistle..."

Ahmed Bey placed himself in front of the patient and commenced his magnetic passes. He whistled in a strange manner, doubtless because he was mentally pronouncing the formula of the incantation. Suddenly, Francisco's body started, and a little foam emerged from his lips. Immediately, the Doctor lay down next to him, and at the same time, a spark emerged from Francisco's mouth and another from the Doctor's trunk. The two sparks danced momentarily, and then exchanged places with lightning rapidity; Francisco's went into the Doctor's trunk, while Ahmed Bey's vanished into the Spaniard's mouth.

Two minutes later, the former body of Francisco got up, vivified by the soul of Ahmed Bey, while the Mercurian body, which had previously enveloped the Doctor's soul, now animated by Francisco's, leapt into the air and went to take up a position beside Brad.

The transmission of the two souls was complete.

Chapter Four
Which clarifies a few mysteries and puts Paul de Civrac in a terrible dilemma

Francisco's soul was doubtless ill at ease to begin within the Mercurian body; the monopod that had become a Spaniard—or, rather, the Spaniard who was now a monopod—stated gesticulating with his leg, his arms and his trunk, whistling and rolling his unique eye in the most comical fashion. Brad's impassive attitude made him understand, however, that an energetic soul ought not to be astonished by anything, and Francisco eventually became tranquil.

As for Ahmed Bey's soul, it obviously thought itself better accommodated in Francisco's body; it could speak in human language.

"How do you feel, Monsieur?" the Doctor immediately asked of Paul.

"Quite well!" said Civrac, shaking the hand that the Doctor offered him. "The fall stunned me, but thanks to my low specific weight and the elasticity of the liquid in this lake, I haven't broken any bones."

"Then let's think about Mademoiselle, whose faint seems to me to have gone on too long."

And the Doctor, in Francisco's appearance, went over to Lolla. Paul had already preceded him. As for Brad and Francisco, they stood a short distance away. A little further away, the body of the Mercurian that had been dragged into the cataract of the golden river against its will was visible, presumably dead.

The rhythmic rumbling was still resounding in the vast cavern, dominated at intervals by the frightful howling. Their minds were entirely preoccupied, however, with Lolla's condition and they scarcely paid any attention to those formidable noises, which were to be explained in singular fashion in due course.

Lying on the ground in the mysterious clarity produced by the cascades and the lake, Lolla Mendès presented a cadaverously pale face. At the sight of that paleness, Paul shivered.

"Doctor!" he exclaimed. "She isn't dead?"

Ahmed Bey had knelt down beside the young woman. Parting the edges of her bodice, he applied his right ear to Lolla's chaste breast. Without replying to Paul, he listened for some time.

When he raised his head again, he murmured: "That's strange." And his eyes expressed an immense surprise. He picked up the young woman's hands one by one and examined them minutely. Then he scrutinized the immobile white face, the features of which were contracted like those of a corpse.

"That's strange," he repeated.

"Doctor, I implore you!" Paul begged.

Ahmed Bey lifted the head slightly and, gazing at Civrac, whose pallor and fearful eyes testified clearly enough to his state of mind, he murmured: "Monsieur, as I predicted in Calcutta, you love this young woman?"

"I'd give my life for her!" Paul exclaimed, with juvenile enthusiasm.

"That won't save her, Monsieur," the Doctor replied, coldly. "But I beg you to summon up all your courage and presence of mind."

"She's dead!" cried Paul, in a heart-rending tone.

"No!" said the Doctor, curtly. After a pause, he continued, more gravely: "We're confronted by an extraordinary case, the like of which I've only seen once before in my terrestrial life, in India... The young woman is alive, although she presents all the symptoms of death except one. Her body will remain flexible and won't decompose, but her heart is no longer beating, and her lungs are no longer functioning. She's in one of the rarest states of catalepsy. When will she wake up? Will she ever wake up, in fact, before passing from the state of catalepsy into death? If we were in my laboratory in Paris, I could bring her round, with appropriate cordials and a magneto-electric treatment. But here...here, I don't know..."

"Oh, Doctor, Doctor! Save her!" Paul fell to his knees beside the inert body of poor Lolla.

While the Doctor was speaking Brad and Francisco had moved closer. Now they too were begging Ahmed Bey, with gestures and whistles.

"Calm and silence, please!" the Doctor said. "Listen to me, Monsieur de Civrac. I'm going to try the only treatment that is within my scope here—which is to say, to disincarnate Mademoiselle's soul." He paused momentarily, and then added: "Have you thought about how we're going to get back to Earth?"

"No, I confess that I haven't?" Paul stammered.

"It will be quite simple. We're five human beings, with various appearances, which aren't our own—except for you, Monsieur de Civrac, who have preserved your own body thus far. Well, it will only require an effort of will on my part for our five souls to be simultaneously disincarnated and fly to Earth. Personally, I'll find my own body on arriving at my house on the edge of the Parc Monceau, but you four, Mademoiselle included, will have to incorporate yourselves in the available bodies, of which we'd choose the most adequate."

The Doctor paused again, then resumed: "But above all, I have to make sure that Mademoiselle's soul is in my power and understands me, in order for it to be possible for me to obtain its obedience and take it to Earth with ours. Now, in the cataleptic state that Mademoiselle is in, her soul, although present, is asleep, confused with her entire being. She can hear me vaguely, since she's alive, but will she be able to understand me, in order to be able to obey me? That's what we have to find out. Brad, bring the body of the Mercurian we killed over here."

Brad went to fetch the monopod's cadaver, and, in response to a gesture from Ahmed Bey, laid it down beside Lolla.

The Doctor stood up, and went to place himself, upright, directly in front of Lolla's feet. He murmured magical incantations over her, making the ancient gestures in the air that operated the capture and disincarnation of souls.

Anxiously, with a cold sweat on his forehead and his eyes, blurred by tears, fixed on Lolla's face, Paul de Civrac waited. Facing him, Brad and Francisco watched, silent and motionless.

Long minutes went by. Ahmed Bey's voice became strangely sonorous and majestic, accompanied by the cadenced rumbling of the abyss, and punctuated from time to time by the howls of agony.

The Doctor's voice rose in more highly-pitched modulations, and then fell silent after a trenchant screech.

But Lolla Mendès' face remained as pale and motionless as that of a marble statue.

Ahmed Bey let his arms fall, lowered his head and murmured: "It's impossible!"

A sob replied to him. Paul de Civrac wept, his head hidden in his trembling hands.

Suddenly, unexpectedly and terrifyingly, tumultuous whistles resounded. The four Terrans turned round; in the distance, on the far side of the plateau, a host of Mercurians was running toward them.

"We have to run," said the Doctor. "We have to get away from them. All is not lost for Lolla."

"My God!" Paul sighed.

"No, no! I'll save her, I promise you. I'll find a way. It will be terrible—but it's the only practicable one. In the meantime, let's escape. Urgently! Follow me, all of you!"

Incarnated in the body of the Spaniard, the Doctor possessed all his vigor. He picked up Lolla Mendès, loaded her on to his shoulders, and with a single bound, leapt into the middle of the lake. Paul, Brad and Francisco launched themselves after him.

They fell into great turbulence. At first they spun vertiginously, but they succeeded in holding on to one another. Then a current gripped them, and drew them away. Within a minute, the immense cavern and the cascades disappeared. They were speeding along a subterranean channel.

They perceived that their glide was taking them closer to the source of the terrible rhythmic rumbling and the frightful shrill screams. Those frightful sounds were soon mingled with furious whistling—and it was as if the din of an apocalyptic battle were resounding in the mystery of immense invisible grottoes.

Suddenly, however, the current drew the Terrans around a sharp bend, and they saw a spectacle that froze them in horror, congealed the blood in their veins and caused their limbs to tremble.

"A new world!" cried Ahmed Bey. "A new Mercurian world! Look! Look!"

"They're fighting!" Paul howled, above the infernal racket.

"We're doomed!"

The current was shoving them toward a shore on which, on the floor of a grotto so vast as to be unimaginable, extending as far as the eye could see, thousands of black Mercurians were rushing to assault a kind of fortress looming up in the distance, on the very edge of the golden river.

That fortress was made of a substance as shiny as new gold and carved into facets like a diamond. Its summit was crowned by strange, incomprehensible machinery. Very tall, with complicated frameworks, they each had a base in a kind of funnel with a broad opening, aimed at the groups of besieging monopods. Nothing came out of those funnels except, at regular intervals, the shrill screams that resembled the agonized scream of thousand of human beings in agony.

At each scream, however, a kind of tempestuous wind blew around the fort, and immediately, a group of monopods would light up, catch fire, melt and explode in a spray of sparks.

As for the rhythmic rumbling, louder now than claps of terrestrial thunder, it was coming from inside the fortress, presumably produced by the automatic maneuvering of the extraordinary machines.

What were those horrible engines of death? What were they projecting? Whatever they were emitting from the monstrous funnels was invisible, as invisible as the wind—and yet, in the distance, at every invisible and noisy volley, the monopods in the line of fire were struck, set ablaze and annihilated.

Was it an electricity of another species than that known on Earth? Or was it merely an inconceivable and powerful displacement of air, driven like a projectile? And why, without anything seeming to touch them, were the monopod assailants exploding like masses of gunpowder struck by a spark?

Mysteries! Unfathomable mysteries!

"Look! Look!" cried Paul. "There are beings at the summit of the fortress!"

"Mercurians!"

"Those are yellow!"

"And larger!"

"They have two eyes!

"And no trunk, no mouth!"

"If they see us, we're doomed!"

"They've seen us! They've seen us! They're directing their screaming machine at us!"

Paul de Civrac and Ahmed Bey had exchanged these cries and exclamations while the vertiginous current of the golden river was still drawing them closer to the shore, toward the inexplicable fortress.

For one minute of supreme anguish, they watched one of the titanic battles engaged by the inhabitants of planets in the mystery of their elements, unknown to Terrans. Evidently, the yellow Mercurians, who were launching an invisible force from the height of the diamond-bright fortress, by means of an incomprehensible black machine, which was annihilating legions of black Mercurians, were a different species, more intelligent and more knowledgeable, physiologically different from the one with which the Terrans had previously had to deal.

What was the reason for this titanic subterranean battle, this conflagration of Mercurian species? Paul, Ahmed Bey and their companions were never to discover that.

In any case, amid the frightful racket of shrill howls and mortal blasts, the rhythmic rumble of the apocalyptic machines, and the crazed storms of furious and desperate whistles uttered by the monopod assailants who were continually being vanquished, the horrified fugitives were only thinking about their inevitable imminent death.

They anticipated that the blasts would be aimed in their direction, and that they would be annihilated in a matter of seconds by the formidable engine of war. How could they not be mad at that nightmarish moment?

"Lolla! Lolla!" cried Paul, sobbing and heartbroken—and, paying no heed to the inevitability of death, the young man embraced Lolla, whom Ahmed Bey was supporting in his muscular arms.

Francisco and Brad, in their Mercurian bodies, could only express themselves by means of inarticulate whistles. They huddled close to Ahmed Bey, trembling.

And those men, so courageous, who had braved the most terrible of deaths a hundred times over, were finally vanquished by the horror of that unimaginable end, in the terrifying surroundings, in the midst of the nightmarish battle being fought by mysterious monsters...

Only Ahmed Bey, presumably thanks to his knowledge of matters of the beyond, maintained an apparent calm, even though his soul was shivering—not for himself, but for Paul de Civrac and Lolla, in whose destiny he was now more interested than his own.

"Courage!" he shouted. "Courage!"

But none of his companions heard him. Eyes widened by fright, they saw, as they were passing directly in front of the fortress that seemed to be built with enormous blocks of gilded crystal, some kind of mirror at the top of the edifice gradually turning its blinding face toward them...and as the mirror turned, an invisible howling blast was turning, turning...

Ineluctably, it was advancing toward them; it would reach them, scything through them and annihilating them as it passed...

"Lolla! Lolla!" Paul moaned, gluing his lips to the white lips of the inanimate young woman—and then, vanquished by grief, he fell in a faint.

Ahmed Bey saw him fall.

"Lie down! Lie down!" he howled.

He dropped Lolla Mendès beside Civrac's body, which was being drawn away by the current. With a single movement he knocked Brad and Francisco down, and extended himself with them. Offering the entire surface of their bodies to the current, instead of merely the soles of their feet, the Terrans were dragged away with even greater rapidity...and they flew like arrows beneath the blast, which passed above them, its shrill screech multiplied a hundredfold in horrifying intensity.

It was then that the entire phantasmagoria of flames and reflections of the cascades suddenly vanished, as if in a dream. The blinding light and dazzling sparks were succeeded by a kind of yellow-tinted twilight. The torrid head was succeeded without transition by relative coolness.

Paul opened his eyes. "Lolla!" he stammered. "Lolla!"

Then, sensing the young woman's body in his arms, he remembered, recovered his presence of mind, and stammered: "Where are we?"

"Saved!" said Ahmed Bey.

"The blasts...the yellow Mercurians...the battle...oh!"

"All that's far behind us. When I saw you fall unconscious, drawn more rapidly by the current of the river, my mind was illuminated by the thought that we were conclusively saved. I dropped Lolla and knocked Brad and Francisco down. I lay down myself, and we passed safe and sound through the empty space providentially contrived between the projecting of burning wind and the surface of the river. The current immediately dragged us into a narrow tunnel, where we are now..."

"Shall we remain lying down?" Paul asked.

"No, let's get up, in order to be more easily able to use our arms and hands."

All four of them stiffened and get to their feet. The Doctor picked up Lolla's body again. She was still in the same condition of mysterious coma. Huddling close together, they could see the black walls of the narrow tunnel speeding by.

Gradually, the rumbling and howling decreased in intensity, and were soon no longer audible. The calm after the din was so strange and profound that for a minute or two the Terrans doubted the reality of the Mercurian battle, an episode to which they had been witness and to which they had almost fallen victim. Their senses had been too greatly affected, however, for them to be able to believe that it had been a collective hallucination or nightmare. The memory of it alone caused them to tremble.

"Let's think about the future, not the past," said the Doctor, who noticed that impression and even experienced it himself. "We'll surely find ourselves among the Mercurians again, for the current of this little river is diminishing in its rapidity, which leads me to believe that we'll soon emerge from the mountain on to a plain..."

"There are four of us now," said Paul. "We'll be able to escape the monsters if they attack us again...always provided that we're dealing with black Mercurians, not the yellow ones..."

"Oh," said the Doctor, "how I'd love to fathom the mysteries of this disconcerting planet! But we'll come back later! We'll come back, and it won't be dangerous then!" He paused for a moment, thoughtfully, and then said: "Monsieur de Civrac, I'm so much more hopeful of saving us that I only ask for a quarter of an hour's respite to disincarnate Lolla, and all of us immediately thereafter..."

"What are you going o do?" Paul asked. "You mentioned a terrible means."

"Terrible, yes, and hazardous; it offers us one chance of success and ninety-nine of failure, but it's the only one we have left. And in our situation, a one per cent chance isn't to be neglected..."

"But what is this means? What does it involve?"

"You'll know soon enough." The tone in which Ahmed Bey pronounced those words made Paul understand that it would be futile to insist.

A quarter of an hour went by. The golden river because less and less rapid. Suddenly, the Terrans saw the luminous orifice of the tunnel in the distance. A few minutes later, they emerged into bright light, in the middle of a vast plain, unlimited on three sides. To their left, however, mountains rose up in the far distance.

"The plain will be fatal to us," Paul said. "The heat and light are too intense there, and the tortures of thirst will soon be added. Let's abandon the river and try to reach those mountains over there. We can climb them, and from the top, we might be able to see which way the twilight zone lies. There we'll be safe from the Mercurians as well as the heat and light. Perhaps we'll have a chance of rainfall, if we stay there long enough.

"I approve of the idea of reaching the mountains," Ahmed Bey replied, "but there's no reason to fear thirst. I only ask for a quarter of an hour of immobility—and, above all, of shade. Yes, shade, in order that disincarnated souls will be visible to me. In the intense light of the plain, the pale sparks that souls are would remain invisible. In the shadow of the twilight zone, or simply some grotto, I'd be able to see them, and to do what's necessary to capture them."

"Let's quit the river, then."

"Yes."

The order was communicated to Brad and Francisco, and a few diagonal bounds too the Terrans to the river-bank. Ahmed Bey was still carrying the inanimate Lolla. Paul wanted to take her.

"No," said the Doctor. "You're still weak because of your injured foot and the fall in the cataract. I have Francisco's muscular legs and supple torso. I'll keep Lolla Mendès…and let's head for the mountains, as quickly as possible."

During the journey, Paul de Civrac looked at Lolla's watch—which he was still carrying in his belt— several times. Every time, though, he saw the crazed hands rotating around the dial with somersaults and rapid surges, like the needle of a broken compass. Another inexplicable effect of the planet Mercury!

They were leaping through fields of russet grass of wearing monotony. There was not a single breath of wind, not a single tree or animal; it was a desert, in an extraordinary light and heat. Fortunately, there were no Mercurians. The fugitives took very little rest, so over-excited were their nerves. They knew that, according to what Ahmed Bey said, their miraculous return to Earth was imminent. It was necessary to reach either a shady grotto or the twilight zone of the Mercurian globe—and immediately afterwards, there would be salvation!

Such thoughts gave the Terrans wings; even though they had one leg fewer than Paul and Ahmed Bey, Brad and Francisco made such good use of their Mercurian bodies that they were traveling and bounding just as rapidly as the column's leaders.

When they arrived at the base of the mountain, however, they saw that it rose up sheerly, presenting a smooth wall for more than three hundred meters.

"Let's go along the cliff," said Ahmed Bey. "We'll find a ravine, gorge or cavern eventually."

He turned to the right. For two mortal hours the fugitives followed the abrupt wall. Above them the eternal clods were traveling heavily through the sky, driven by winds they could not feel and passing over the mountains, the top of the cliff not reaching their height.

Thanks to their Mercurian bodies, Brad and Francisco were indefatigable, but Ahmed Bey, laden with Lolla's weight, and Paul de Civrac, weakened by his recent adventures, and both more sensitive to the murderous climate of the strange planet, began to pant heavily. They understood that they would soon be utterly exhausted.

"Will this cliff never end?" said Ahmed Bey, petulantly.

"I can't do any more," Paul stammered.

At that moment, however, the cliff had an abrupt bend, and the fugitives stopped, astonished by the spectacle.

In truth, the Mercurian world was one of continual surprises. Before the Terrans' eyes a cavern of colossal dimensions opened in the mountain. So far as Ahmed Bey and Paul could judge, it must have measured at least five hundred meters in depth, a kilometer in breadth and two hundred meters in height. And on the floor of the fantastic grotto, an agglomeration of some forty huts was located.

At the appearance of the two Terrans, followed by the two false Mercurians, a few monopods that happened to be outside the huts started uttering whistles and disappearing behind the pyramids.

"We're your prisoners, Francisco!" Paul de Civrac shouted. "We'll go into a hut, where you'll seem to be imprisoning us. Brad will go in with us. You're a chief; so, silent and dignified, you can stop anyone else coming in."

With a movement of his trunk, Francisco made it known that he understood, and would play his part. With Ahmed Bey still carrying Lolla, Paul behind him, Brad mounting guard over his pretended prisoners, and Francisco taking the lead, the group advanced toward the nearest hut. At the same time, a hundred monopods surged from all directions, filling the air with furious whistles.

"Look!" said Paul. "These have red skins!"

"That's true," said Ahmed Bey. "Another Mercurian race, undoubtedly. And look, their trunks are shorter and their eyes black."

"But they're running at us, as enemies!" Paul exclaimed. "They're yet another race, different from the ones with the machines."

"Damn! Fortunately, all I need is a quarter of an hour of tranquility."

Meanwhile, the red monopods stopped short, having arrived within twenty paces of the group in a fury. Their arms pointed at Paul and Ahmed Bey. Their eyes were incontestably expressing extreme amazement, and they were no longer whistling. The new Mercurians were obviously as brutal as the black ones, because they bore no resemblance to the intelligent monopods who manipulated the marvelous and terrible machines in the underworld.

"They're cutting off our route to the hut," said Paul.

"Let's try to go through the middle of them. Keep going, Francisco..."

But before Francisco could make another leap, twenty red monopods had leapt on him and he fell. Brad raced to his aid.

"I don't understand..." said Paul.

"The red race is the enemy of the black," hissed the Doctor. "To the hut! To the hut! Brad and Francisco will get out of it."

Veering to the right, Paul and Ahmed Bey started running toward one of the pyramidal cabins. They had just reached it when a black body bounded over the hut and, landing at their feet, swiftly opened the door.

"Bravo, Francisco!" Paul exclaimed.

Following Ahmed Bey, who plunged in first through the low doorway, with Lolla, Paul went in.

Francisco and Brad hastened after them. The slab of slate that closed the door from within was raised again, and Brad and Francisco braced themselves against it.

Thousand of furious whistles resounded outside.

Ahmed Bey had immediately deposited Lolla on the ground in the middle of the hut. He knelt down at her feet, facing her.

"Monsieur de Civrac," he said, "kneel down to Mademoiselle's left. Now close your ears to the noises from outside. Don't think about the dangers that might still threaten us, but from which we're separated by the thickness of the door, which Brad and Francisco are supporting. The moment is critical—listen to me."

In the gloomy interior of the hut, which only a little light entered through a hole contrived at the summit, Brad and Francisco, solidly braced against the door, watched the Doctor with their red eyes. Paul, kneeling by Lolla's side, waited, his soul suddenly tortured by an inexplicable anguish. Lying there, Lolla seemed to be dead, her eyes closed, her lips bloodless, her cheeks white and her forehead as icy as marble. Kneeling at her feet, facing her, the Doctor reflected momentarily, with his head bowed.

The silence was absolute. Outside, the whistles had ceased; doubtless the red Mercurians were holding a discussion before agitating any further.

Ahmed Bey raised his head, and spoke in a grave and insistent voice. "Monsieur de Civrac, I've told you that the only means of returning to Earth is a new disincarnation of our souls. That's easy for you and me, and easy for Brad and Francisco. I only have to make a few gestures, pronounce a few words, and all four of us, pure souls in the form of sparks, will be on Earth in a quarter of a second. But it's not the same for Lolla

Mendès. The rare state of catalepsy that she's in renders her soul incapable of obeying me and quitting her body on my command. On the other hand, we can't take her with her body; even in the realms of the marvelous there are material impossibilities."

The Doctor paused, paled slightly, and continued: "There is, however, one means—and one alone." He paused again, and his voice was tremulous when he continued: "Monsieur de Civrac, that means is terrible, and although I hope it will succeed, I can be certain of it...."

"Speak, Doctor," said Paul. "What is this means?"

"You have mastery of all your courage?"

"Yes."

"Well, then..." The Doctor hesitated. He looked at Paul with an affectionate pity.

"Speak, I beg you!" moaned the young man.

"Monsieur de Civrac," said Ahmed Bey, in a solemn voice, "it's necessary to kill Lolla Mendès."

Paul's entire body convulsed; a cold sweat pearled on his forehead, and he looked at the doctor with wild eyes.

"Yes," Ahmed Bey continued, energetically, "it's necessary to kill Lola, coldly and cleanly, with an infallible blow. Her soul will escape her body, and it's then that I'll try to capture it. Monsieur de Civrac, do you have the courage to kill the woman you love?"

"Me! Me?" stammered Paul, even paler than Lolla.

"Yes, because neither of our companions can act with the promptitude and skill that human hands provide. As for me, I need to have the freedom of action, the eye, the voice and the presence of mind to be able to seize the precise moment that Lolla's soul quits her mortal envelope. Yes, you must kill this body; it's the only means of returning her soul to Earth."

While the Doctor was speaking, a prompt change had overtaken the appearance of Paul de Civrac. The young man's mind must have comprehended the necessity of the unusual action. His expression was fixed; his eyes were flashing with energetic determination. His weary torso stiffened. It was evident, however, that a terrible combat was taking place within him. He sighed, and his hands were trembling.

"Doctor," he said, in a faint voice, "is there no other way?"

"No."

"And if even this one doesn't succeed?"

"The soul of Lola Mendès will take flight for the other world, to mingle with the infinity of Nature."

A terrible silence hung over the young woman's immobile body. Paul studied her—and gradually, his hands ceased trembling. He raised his head, the energy of his eyes became more emphatic, and he looked at the thaumaturge.

"Doctor," he said, in a resolute voice, "I'm ready to kill Lolla's body. Tell me how I have to do it, in order that her death will be instantaneous and absolute. But before that, I have a favor to ask you."

"Speak!"

"If Lola's soul escapes, you must kill my body in the same way that I've killed hers, and you must let my soul fly away to rejoin hers, mingling, like her, with infinity. If everything is finished for her, it will all be finished for me too. Give me your word."

The Doctor did not hesitate. "Monsieur de Civrac, if I can't bring back the soul of Lolla Mendès, I swear to you that I won't bring yours back. You'll depart together for the future life. But nothing will be finished for the two of you, for nothing that is can cease to be. You will be fused in the great All together."

"In that case, Doctor, I'm ready. Command!"

He had a twinge of pain, however, at the thought of losing forever the sight of the charming body that had been the first cause of his love for Lolla.

The Doctor understood that hidden impression.

"I'll give her another more beautiful than this," he whispered.

His only response was a sigh.

And before the fearful eyes of Brad and Francisco, the marvelous and terrifying attempt was made.

The Doctor had taken off the iron buckle from the belt of his trousers—or, rather, Francisco's trousers. The tongue was long and sharp. "Take this in your right hand," he said to Paul, and hold the buckle with the tongue forward, very firmly.

"It's done," said Paul.

"With your left hand, lift Lolla's head up as far as you can. Good! Support it on your knee, sideways. Now, can you see the vertebrae of the spine, starting at the nape of the neck?"

"Yes, quite clearly."

"Count four of them, from top to bottom."

"One, two, three, four."

"Now apply the point of the tongue directly to the vertebral column, between the fourth and fifth vertebrae, in the center. Your hand isn't trembling?"

"No," Paul replied, his pallor that of death.

"Listen," said the Doctor. "I'm going to pronounce the sacred words. At one point, I'm going to pronounce the word *Siva* three times. When I pronounce it the first time, you'll call upon all the strength of your mind and your muscles, and when the syllable *Si* emerges from my lips for a second time, you'll drive in the tongue. A clean, straight thrust. Is that understood?"

"Understood."

"May the Force be with you![11] Death will be instantaneous...provided that your hand doesn't tremble."

And without waiting any longer, Ahmed Bey commenced the magnetic passes and sacred incantations.

Motionless, eyes fixed, Brad and Francisco resembled caryatids of black stone. As white as a phantom's shroud, Paul de Civrac waited. With his left hand, he supported Lolla's head against his knee; with his right, he placed the shiny steel tongue of the buckle against her neck.

Suddenly, the voice of Ahmed Bey swelled in volume. "Brahma, Vishnu..." he pronounced. Then, slowly: "Siva..."

Paul shivered and stiffened.

"Si..."

An abrupt movement. The tongue sank in.

Ahmed Bey's voice was as powerful and imperious as thunder, and Paul, stricken, saw a spark spring from Lolla's parted lips and rise, scintillating to the tip of the thaumaturge's raised index-finger.

"Brahma be praised!" murmured the Doctor, in a low voice. The soul of Lola Mendès is ours."

But Paul's emotion was so intense that he uttered a vibrant cry and fell backwards.

Brad and Francisco had got up.

---

[11] The original has "*La Force soit avec vous!*" This is the only mention of "the Force" in question in La Hire's text, and it remains a trifle enigmatic, but it is obviously the same one subsequently featured, evidently coincidentally, in *Star Wars*.

"Lie down beside Monsieur de Civrac!" ordered the Doctor, in a dry tone.

The two false monopods obeyed.

Still holding up his left index finger, with the scintillating soul of Lolla Mendès floating above it, Ahmed Bey lay down beside Francisco. With his extended right arm, he touched the three motionless bodies—and in a powerful voice, he recommenced the incantations.

Outside, whistles suddenly resounded. The slate slab sealing the doorway of the hut fell inwards under external pressure—and the red Mercurians hurled themselves through the gap.

In the blink of an eye, the five supine bodies were lifted up, dislocated and torn into a thousand bloody shreds by the powerful talons, and the multitude of monsters fought for their possession, while avid trunks searched the quivering flesh, swelling up with human blood.

PART SIX
ON EARTH

Chapter One
In which Monsieur Torpène Moves from Amazement to Amazement

A man was standing in the middle of Dr. Ahmed Bey's laboratory in the basement of the house overlooking the Parc Monceau, with his arms folded, in front of a marble slab on which a human body was lying, swathed in bandages like a mummy.

Coifed in a small turban embroidered with silver and gold, and dressed in a short braided jacket and a yellow silk skirt tightened at the waist with a dazzling cashmere shawl ornamented with gold, the man in question was the Indian, Ra-Cobrah, Dr. Ahmed Bey's steward.

After having considered the material envelope of his master, Ra-Cobrah sat down on the divan, lit a hookah, and began smoking, grave and meditative, in the faint and confused light spread by the sole minuscule electric lamp that was illuminated in the vast laboratory, masked on the side of the marble slab by a black silk screen.

Since Dr. Ahmed Bey had disincarnated himself in the presence of his friends, the five scientists, in order to travel to the planet Mercury, Ra-Cobrah had been living in the laboratory, eating and sleeping on the large soft divan, his eyes lost in a vague reverie or fixed on his master's body, which was prevented from corruption by an injection of a special liquid, three times a day.

A servant brought the watchman's meals, and the latter, with the natural calm of the race that had produced the Brahmins and the Stylites,[12] awaited the return of the absent soul.

That day passed like all the others, in silence, reverie and immobility, only troubled by the footstep of the servant bringing nourishment, and the gestures necessary to eating, drinking and smoking.

The silent clock suspended in a corner of the laboratory, immediately underneath the electric lamp serving as a night-light, marked nine-twenty, and Ra-Cobrah was getting ready to lie down and go to sleep when an unaccustomed noise caused him to straighten up with a start.

There had been a crackling sound, rapidly repeated five times.

Scarcely was he upright than the Indian saw five sparks streaking the darkness of the laboratory. They headed straight for the marble slabs and stopped, floating two meters above the one supporting the body of Ahmed Bey.

"It's the master!" said Ra-Cobrah, excitedly. And he knelt down on the floor and bowed down, his head between his extended arms. Then he got up, marched to the marble slab and began carefully unwinding the im-

---

[12] The orthodox opinion is that the original Stylites were Christian mystics in the eastern remnant of the Roman Empire, but it would not be surprising of travelers' tales of Indian fakirs brought back in the days of the Raj had credited them with similar exploits, or had at least inspired scholarly fantasists to do so during the occult revival.

maculate bandages with which the limbs, torso, neck and head of the soulless body were wrapped.

When the body, which appeared to have been struck by a sudden and calm death a minute before was laid entirely bare, Ra-Cobrah gently opened the mouth and took three steps back.

Then one of the five sparks detached itself from the marvelous group and, like a dart, penetrated into the open mouth. Almost immediately, the white body took on the colors of life. The mouth closed, the eyes opened, one of the arms stirred, and suddenly, moving slowly, the resuscitated body stood up at the foot of the marble slab in front of Ra-Cobrah, who prostrated himself again.

"Get up, faithful servant!" said Ahmed Bey, gravely.

"Master! May Vishnu and Siva be glorified!"

Without another word, Ra-Cobrah stood up, unrolled a packet of fabrics that had been placed on the second slab, and draped his master in a vast robe of virgin linen. He secured it at the waist with a broad belt of mauve silk embroidered with gold, and put red leather sandals on the feet, retained at the ankles by silk ribbons.

"That's fine, Ra-Cobrah," said Ahmed Bey. "I'm hungry..."

The steward rapped on a gong. Two minutes later, eight black servants appeared, carrying a square table that was already laden with food.

Ahmed Bey had already at down on a divan; the table was set before him and, served by two domestics supervised by Ra-Cobrah the Doctor began eating.

His appetite was, indeed, considerable. An odorous soup, an asparagus omelet, a gilded carp, a copious skylark salmi, gorgonzola, a peach, grapes and a cup of Turkish coffee made up the dinner menu.

For as long as the table was in front of him, Ahmed Bey did not say a word, but when, at a gesture from the steward, the table was picked up and carried away by the servants, and the master had washed his hands in a silver bowl presented to him by a kneeling slave, he said: "Switch off the chandeliers, Ra-Cobrah."

The order was immediately carried out, and only the electric lamp serving as a night-light remained illuminated.

"Good! Now sit down beside me on this divan, and forget that I'm your master, only remembering that I've judged you worthy of being my friend. Let's talk as we have done several times before."

Impassive, but his eyes shining with evident joy, Ra-Cobrah sat down on the same divan as Ahmed Bey and, like him, took between his lips one of the amber mouthpieces at the end of one of the tubes of the hookah, which the slave had brought out last of all and lit before disappearing.

"Have you read the newspapers, Cobrah?" asked the Doctor.

"Yes, Ahmed."

"So you know who the humans lost among the stars were?"

"On Venus," said Cobra, there were two Americans, Arthur Brad and Jonathan Bild. On Mercury there were the Frenchman Paul de Civrac and the Spanish woman Lolla Mendès, with her valet Francisco."

"Good! Well, Cobrah, do you see those four sparks?"

"I saw them at the same time as I saw you, Ahmed."

"Count them from left to right; they're the souls of Lolla Mendès, Paul de Civrac, Arthur Brad and Francisco/"

"You saved them, Ahmed!" said Ra-Cobrah, in a tone of triumphant pride.

"I saved them. Only the soul of Jonathan Bild is missing. That man, as stubborn as a Hispano-American, refused to allow himself to be disincarnated, under the pretext that he liked his body too much to abandon it, and swearing to the great gods that he would return to Earth, thanks to the science of the Venusians, in the flesh, with his own height and his own thinness. Furthermore, Brad and I have brought back in our memories the elements necessary for the construction of a machine that will put us in communication with a similar machine installed by Bild on the planet Venus. But that's for the future; let's think about the present. My task isn't complete. In sum, what I've done presented very little difficulty, but Cobrah, it's now that my task becomes thorny and delicate..."

"What!" said Ra-Cobrah, visibly astonished that anything in the world could be thorny and delicate in its execution, when the Doctor was involved therein.

"Well, yes," said the thaumaturge. "For each of these four souls, it's necessary that I provide a body. Do you understand, Cobrah? The body in question has to be appropriate to the character of each soul, and to be as close as possible in its resemblance to the one that each of these souls left behind in the stars. Well, Cobrah— where are we going to find bodies that will please Lolla Mendès, Paul de Civrac, Brad and Francisco, when the pure souls that they are now are reincarnated?"

Ra-Cobrah was visibly embarrassed. His gaze went from the Doctor's impassive face to the four sparks immobile in mid-air in the laboratory, two meters above the marble slab.

"Indeed," he said, "that is delicate..."

"First we have to find four suitable cadavers, one of them a woman..."

"Yes."

"It's necessary that the cadavers don't have relatives among the living."

"Yes," said Ra-Cobrah. "A family would create complications..."

"And many other things are necessary too."

The doctor stopped talking, and silence was abruptly established between the two men. It lasted for some time. From each amber nozzle terminated one of the tubes of the hookah, Ahmed Bey and Ra-Cobrah drew puffs of odorous smoke, which they expelled gravely toward the high ceiling of the laboratory.

Suddenly, Ra-Cobrah dropped the amber tip at his feet, raised his eyes to the heavens, and said: "Oh, Master! Why haven't you thought of it first?"

"Of what, Cobrah?"

"Androplasty, Master."

At that word, Ahmed Bey was dumbstruck with astonishment. "That true," he murmured. "It's quite simple! Androplasty! Indeed, you're right, Cobrah. Why didn't I think of it?"

"Ahmed! Your soul is still overwhelmed by its extraordinary adventure, Master. It hasn't yet found its ordinary lucidity, its genius." And by means of a tone of affectionate submission, Ra-Cobrah tried to attenuate the audacious semblance of his words.

Ahmed Bey stood up and took the hands of his steward. "Bravo, Cobrah!" he said. "You're well worthy of my confidence and friendship." Then he changed his tone. "It's obvious that androplasty will get rid of any serious difficulty. Now it's only a matter of finding four bodies, one of them female, that are physically well-proportioned, healthy, free of defects, whose organs are intact. Deaths by asphyxiation would be the most appropriate for a satisfactory reincarnation." In his imperious voice, he added: "What time is it, Cobrah?"

"Seven o'clock in the evening, Master."

"Have all the evening newspapers brought to me in the library. Send the secretary to Monsieur Torpène, the Prefect of Police, with this message, written by your own hand: 'The master has returned; he is waiting for you, alone, right away. Can you come?' As soon as Monsieur Torpène arrives, bring him to me yourself. Go!"

Then the Doctor went to stand before the marble table above which the four sparks were still floating. He raised his arms toward them, and pronounced a few mysterious syllables.

The sparks rose up to the ceiling in a flash, and remained there, like motionless diamonds attached by an invisible thread.

The steward bowed his head and went out. Afterwards, the Doctor went into the dressing-room annexed to the laboratory and put on the modern clothes that he had been wearing on the day of his disincarnation.

When he went up the broad marble staircase leading to the ground floor of the house, Ahmed Bey had lost the quasi-transfigured face of a thaumaturge, no longer possessing anything but the cold, impassive and slightly strange features with which his friends were familiar.

Dr. Ahmed Bey's library was a vast room overlooking the Parc Monceau through an immense window extending from the floor to the ceiling. The walls were lined with shelves laden with richly-bound books. In the middle stood an enormous terrestrial globe surrounded by a gallery, which was accessed by four staircases with guard-rails. Divans and profound armchairs were disposed all round the room, some of which had work-tables in front of them equipped with writing equipment and blank paper.

It was in one of those armchairs that Ahmed Bey waited for the Prefect, meditatively. As soon as a servant brought him the evening newspapers, he unfolded hem swiftly and began reading the miscellaneous events section. He marked certain items with a tick, in blue pencil.

He had just completed this enigmatic task when the door opened and Ra-Cobrah appeared.

"The Prefect of Police is here," he announced.

"Send him in."

The Doctor got to his feet.

Monsieur Torpène appeared, seemingly very emotional, holding out his hands eagerly.

"My dear Doctor! You're back! Here you are, in the flesh!"

"Yes, Monsieur, I'm back."

"Alone?"

"No, four of the human souls of which I went in search are in my laboratory, submissive to my will."

"Is it possible?"

"It is! Please sit down here, I beg you, next to me."

"Four souls, you said, my dear Doctor. Wasn't it five human beings that the Fiery Wheel abducted?"

"Indeed." And the Doctor told him about the singular stubbornness of Jonathan Bild, in waning to remain on Venus."

"At any rate," he concluded, "that stubbornness will be profitable for human science, since we'll have a means of communicating with Bild *viva voce*."

"You're joking, Doctor!"

"Not at all. But if you'll permit, we won't talk about that this evening. Sit down, I beg you."

When the two men were both sitting in armchairs, facto face, the Doctor said: "My dear Monsieur, it's not the knowledgeable spiritist Torpène that I wanted to see this evening, but Torpène the Prefect of Police."

"To tell me…?"

"I'll tell you about my voyage when all our friends are gathered here. Today I want to ask you to help me in concluding the task that I've undertaken…"

"And it's the Prefect of Police that you need?" said Torpène, with a smile.

"The Prefect of Police, indeed. This is it: I need four human bodies recently struck by a particular mode of death that has not destroyed any of their essential organs. Death by asphyxia or drowning, without remaining long in the water, would meet the necessary conditions. Now, in the miscellaneous news items published by the evening papers, I've just found a number of cases of death that occurred today in the requisite forms. Would you care to cast an eye over the articles marked in blue pencil? Here, there's a young woman—very beautiful, it's said, and an orphan—who asphyxiated herself with carbon monoxide after her lover's marriage. I need that body, in order to reincarnate the soul of Lolla Mendès…"

"Right!" murmured Monsieur Torpène, a trifle disconcerted.

"Here," the Doctor continued, imperturbably, "we see a young man, unidentified, drowned while rowing on the Seine at Saint-Cloud. He was fished out almost im-

mediately and his cadaver is waiting until it can by iden-
tified in a riverside tavern. No papers were found in his
clothing. I need that cadaver to reincarnate the soul of
Paul de Civrac..."

"That's possible, quite possible," said Torpène, in a
low voice.

"Pick up the other paper," the Doctor said, with a
slightly sardonic smile. "Look there! An Italian laborer,
with no family in France, overwhelmed by misery, took
a room in a furnished hotel in the Rue Planchat yesterday and committed suicide in a bizarre fashion. He was
found this morning hanging from a nail in the ceiling, in
a corridor, with his teeth clenching the extremity of the
gas jet that lights the corridor. The doctor who was immediately summoned concluded, after his examination,
that death was not due to hanging but asphyxia by light-
ing gas. The body has been taken to the Hôpital Bichat,
where it will not be autopsied until tomorrow. I think it
might be exactly what I need to reincarnate the soul of
Francisco."

"Indeed," said Torpène, trying to master himself.
"An Italian...Francisco is Spanish. He would do very
well, very adequately..."

"Thank you," said the Doctor, with comical gravity.
"Now I only need something to house the soul of Arthur
Brad. I think I've also found something appropriate for
him. I've just read the details of a strange affair that has
been exciting Paris for several days in one of my papers..."

"The Hôtel Fulton business?"

"Yes. Will you permit me to summarize what I've
read about it?"

"I'm intimately familiar with it," said the Prefect of
Police, "but I wouldn't be sorry to hear your summary."

"Good. Six days ago, at seven o'clock in the evening, a short, stout Englishman—excellent for Brad, is he not, my dear Monsieur…?"

"Why?" said the Prefect.

"Because Brad is short and stout."

"Oh!"

"I'll start again. Six days ago, at seven o'clock in the evening, an Englishman arrived in a carriage at a hotel in the Rue de Paix. He asked for a large room and had the five large suitcases piled up in his carriage sent up. The hotel staff remarked that the traveler had a heavy watch-chain with a beautiful gold watch, enormous diamond rings on his fingers, and a very expensive tie-pin. He dined simply on a copious meal washed down with expensive champagne and sent for a box of luxurious cigars for a particular shop near the Opéra. To pay for it he handed a thousand-franc bill to the bell-boy, who brought the change back and received a louis as a tip. In brief, the Englishman appeared to the staff to be colossally rich and, moved by curiosity, all the bell-boys examined his identity papers, on which the Englishman had inscribed: Edward Penting, Pretoria. Is that right?"

"Exactly."

"Now, the following morning, Mr. Penting was not seen to emerge from his room. He still had not appeared at noon. At four o'clock in the afternoon, people became anxious. At five o'clock the manager knocked on the door of the room in vain. At quarter past five, in the presence of a Commissaire of Police, the door was broken down. The Englishman was found lying on his bed in a nightshirt, dead. A doctor who was summoned diagnoses death by chloroform. The watch-chain and the chronometer, the jewels, and the wallet—probably stuffed with banknotes—had all disappeared. The suitcases had been opened out on to the carpet, the clothes and underclothes in disorderly piles. Finally, the window of the room overlooking the Rue de la Paix was wide open, and it was observed that the edge of the sill was eroded, as if by the friction of a strong rope. That's all!"

"That is, indeed, all that we know," said Torpène. "The investigation hasn't turned up anything. Replies to the telegrams sent to Pretoria say that no Edward Penting has ever been resident in the city. The suitcases bore labels from Le Havre, but the employee who registered that luggage for Paris hasn't been found. That's all."

"Good," said the Doctor. "Now, listen carefully."

"I'm listening!" said Monsieur Torpène, intrigued.

"The criminal case doesn't concern me. I suspect, in any case, that you'll never find the murderer, who is also the mysterious thief, because you don't have any clues. But that's not the issue. What interests me in the story is that the cadaver of Edward Penting will suit Arthur Brad perfectly. Give me that cadaver, Monsieur Torpène!"

"Damn!" exclaimed the Prefect of Police, staring. "But it doesn't belong to me!"

"I know that."

"It's in the Morgue, where it's being conserved intact, protected from corruption, until the affair can be clarified or the file is closed."

"Obviously."

"It's quite impossible for me to get the cadaver out of the Morgue."

"All right."

"I'm very sorry. My dear Doctor."

"Don't be. When I said: 'Give me that cadaver,' I expressed myself badly. What I meant was: 'Let me obtain it...'"

"What?"

"Yes, let me obtain it."

"How will you do that?"

"That's my concern."

"You'll risk..."

"Nothing! And my intervention will have two excellent consequences."

"What consequences?"

"Firstly, giving a suitable body to Brad."

"And?"

"Secondly, a great service rendered to the French police. The newspapers are mocking you, Monsieur Torpène. Well, I'll shut them up."

"How?"

"Oh, in a very simple manner. Edward Penting, resuscitated, will declare that he was only asleep—people will be obliged to believe him—and that the entire affair was merely an attempted scientific experiment. He'll make his excuses to the French police for the inconvenience caused, and donate twenty thousand francs to the poor of Paris."

"But that's insane!"

"No! People will be obliged to bow to the evidence, since it will be the supposed dead man himself that is talking. So, will you give me *carte blanche*?"

"I don't know whether..."

"You're afraid..."

"Of nothing!" said Monsieur Torpène, curtly. "Do as you wish, since your actions, won't do anyone any harm..."

"Perfect!" exclaimed the Doctor. He got to his feet. "My dear Monsieur Torpène, I ask you to do what is necessary for the body of the asphyxiated seamstress, the drowned young man and the hanged Italian to be transported tonight to the Hôpital de la Pitié, from which I'll take responsibility for bringing them here."

"Agreed. I've made the necessary notes."

"And to thank you," the Doctor continued, "I'll invite you to Brad's reincarnation on your own."

"When?"

"Tomorrow, at noon.

"Where?"

"At the Morgue, of course!"

"I'll be there."

"As for the reincarnation of Lolla Mendès, Paul de Civrac and Francisco, I'll perform the operation on the following night, with you and our usual friends present."

"Good! I'll leave you now, Doctor." Torpène stood up. "Until tomorrow, at the Morgue."

"Agreed."

The Prefect of Police headed for the door, followed by the Doctor. Suddenly, however, he turned round and put his hand on Ahmed Bey's shoulder. "Permit me, however, to raise one objection, Doctor."

"By all means."

These souls that you are going to reincarnate—Lolla Mendès, Francisco, Paul de Civrac and Brad..."

"Well?"

"They have families, friends, interests. They'll have changed bodies, faces...no one will be able to recognize them..."

"You're forgetting androplasty," said the Doctor, placidly.

"Androplasty?" Torpène repeated, uncertainly.

"Yes. Have you heard of rhinoplasty?"

"Of course," said the Prefect, smiling. "It's a surgical operation that has the purpose of rebuilding a nose when that organ has been destroyed."

"Exactly—and the word comes from the Greek: *rhis, rhinos*, nose, and *plastos*, form. Well, analyze the word androplasty; you'll find that it also comes from the Greek: *aner, andros*, man, and *plastos*, form. Androplasty is, therefore a surgical operation whose purpose is to rebuild a face—since the face is the man—when the face has been destroyed, or when, more simply, one wants to modify the expression of an already-existent face..."

"And androplasty..." stammered Torpène, a trifle alarmed.

"I have practiced it, my dear Monsieur. It was taught to me in the secret and mysterious temples of India, where bodies are modeled, just as souls are kneaded there. You understand that it will be easy for me to obtain photographs of Lolla Mendès, Paul de Civrac, Arthur Brad and Francisco. I shall model each one, on their new body, a face similar to the old one, that's all. It's a matter of skill, patience and time. It's agreed, then...I can assume that my three cadavers will be at the Pitié at midnight..."

"Yes, yes…obviously."

"And you'll be at the Morgue tomorrow, at noon."

"Of course. The Morgue, at noon."

And the Prefect of Police, utterly amazed, went out of Dr. Ahmed Bey's house.

Chapter Two
Which relates the alarming event of which the Morgue was the theater

It was ten minutes before noon when Monsieur Torpène passed under the peristyle of the Morgue. The attendant on duty recognized the well-known features of the Prefect of Police, whom he immediately escorted to an office adjacent to the room where the cadavers were exhibited.

"At noon," said Monsieur Torpène, who was familiar with Ahmed Bey's meticulous punctuality, "a gentleman will arrive at the peristyle. He's tall, thin and dark-haired, with neither moustache nor beard. Bring him here immediately."

The attendant bowed, made a military salute and turned on his heels. He went to take up his post at the entrance to the Morgue. The first stroke of midday was resounding on a nearby clock when the attendant saw a large automobile stop in front of him and a man got out, whose appearance tallied with the succinct description given by Monsieur Torpène.

Two minutes later, Dr. Ahmed Bey was shaking the hand of the Prefect of Police.

"Well," said the senior functionary, "have last night's three cadavers been taken to your house? Are you satisfied?"

"Quite satisfied," the Doctor replied. "The young seamstress is very pretty, and her body is one of the finest I've ever seen; the soul of Lola Mendès will lose nothing by the exchange. The rower is a sturdy fellow, well-muscled but slim; Paul de Civrac will be delighted by it. As for the Italian, he has a diagonal scar on his face that disfigures it slightly, but Francisco will gain considerably in being reincarnated, for, if I remember correctly, his corporeal appearance lacked grace. Are we alone?"

"Yes."

"This office communicates with the public exhibition hall?"

"We have only to open that door," Torpène replied, his hand indicating a small door painted pale brown.

"Good! With your permission, I'll close the window, in order that we only receive a little light through that door, which we'll open."

"Go ahead."

The Doctor closed the window—the shutter as well as the pane—and also drew the curtain. In the obscurity that immediately reigned in the room, Torpène saw a spark floating five centimeters above Ahmed Bey's head.

"You're looking at Arthur Brad's soul?" said the latter.

"Yes, Doctor."

"I'll leave you alone with it momentarily. I'm going to take a look at Edward Penting's cadaver."

The thaumaturge pronounced two mysterious words, and then walked to the door through which he had entered. The spark did not accompany him. It stayed where it was, motionless and scintillating, in the middle of the room.

Monsieur Torpène, confounded by admiration, murmured: "What terrible power Ahmed Bey possesses! If he wanted to, he could turn the world upside-down!

Humankind can congratulate itself on the fact that the man wasn't born with criminal instincts."

Meanwhile, the doctor had arrived in the public corridor, from which a glazed screen, protected at a distance by a barrier, separates the room in which anonymous or mysterious cadavers are arranged on a vast inclined slab, kept frozen by refrigerant apparatus in order to ensure their conservation.

At that hour, when people habitually leave work for the midday meal, there was a compact crowd circulating in the public corridor. It was composed of working men and women, clerks and vagabonds, primarily attracted by curiosity, eager to see the enigmatic Englishman whose incomprehensible story had been filing newspaper columns for six days.

Patiently, the Doctor joined the queue, and eventually arrived at the window. There were five cadavers on the slab. The doctor cast a distracted glance over the first two, but paused at the third and leaned forward over the balustrade.

Edward Penting's body looked as if it were simply asleep. Short and stout, with a bulging abdomen, the legs straight and strong, the feet enormous, dressed in a gray suit with pale green checks, a shirt with the unstarched collar turned down, secured by a red cravat with a regatta knot, his face was placid and benevolent. The mouth and eyes were closed in a normal fashion, and without the characteristic pallor of death that marbled the forehead and cheeks, and the particular pinch of the nose, the face would have seemed to be alive.

Around the motionless Doctor, men and women were exchanging stupid, simple or ludicrous remarks, making quips about the paunchy cadaver, or the others, more hideous, with little nervous giggles or murmurs of horror—all of which made up the continuous noise of a crowd talking in hushed voices, pushing, tramping and passing by.

"It's perfect!" said the Doctor, in a low voice.

And, darting one last glance at the cadaver, and a coldly ironic smile at the crowd, Ahmed Bey went back to Monsieur Torpène.

In the exact spot that the Doctor had just abandoned, a young man and a young woman leaned forward, without paying any attention to the murmurs of the people following them, whom they were preventing from seeing the famous cadaver with sufficient convenience. Their arms were linked, and they had the particular expression of joy that animates the faces of a student and a seamstress in the early days of an amorous liaison.

"Hey, Fernand!" said the young woman, who had a pretty pink face aureoled with fine blonde hair, on which a round hat ornamented with enormous cherries was set at a slant. "Is that the one who was killed by chloroform?"

"Yes, my sweet," replied the young man, smiling.

"It's funny!" the young woman went on. "You wouldn't know he's dead! He doesn't look to have suffered. See how tranquil his expression is. It's a nice way to go, chloroform, don't you think?"

"Yes, yes…you uncork the bottle under your nose…or you pour it on to a handkerchief that you attach like a gag…and off you go..."

"When you don't love me anymore," said the little fool, laughing, "I'll buy some chloroform..."

"They won't sell it to you..."

"You think not!" And with a shrug of her shoulders, the girl turned to her lover. "Oh!" she exclaimed. "Did you see that?"

"What?"

"Like an electric spark that flew past, there, over the American's head."

"Nonsense!"

"It did, I tell you."

"Indeed, Monsieur," said an earnest man standing beside the student. "I saw a spark too."

"Where? Where?" The crowd stopped, people pausing forward and interrogating one another. At the balustrade, the student, the seamstress and the earnest gentleman resisted the pressure and gazed at the Englishman's cadaver.

Suddenly, the seamstress uttered a shrill screech and extended her arm, howling in a distressed voice: "His mouth! His mouth! Look! There! There!"

"Eh! What? It's true..."

"The eyes now! The eyes!"

Pale and trembling, the young woman stood up straight, nailed to the balustrade by surprise and terror. Behind her, the crowd swelled; cries emerged from it, and oaths...

"They're open," said the earnest gentleman. Turning round, he tried to flee, but the crowd crushed him against the balustrade.

"Ah! Ah!" howled the young woman, in a heartrending tone. "He's getting up!"

A long cry of horror burst out beneath the vaults of the peristyle. The people who had seen the cadaver open his eyes and slowly sit up were trying to run away, and struggling against those who were arriving from outside and had not seen anything. There were crazed screams, exchanged blows and terrified sobs. The young woman collapsed on to the floor in a faint and was trampled, while the crush carried her frightened lover away. As if broken in two, the earnest gentleman, paralyzed by horror, his eyes wide, felt the balustrade digging into his midriff. There was a panicked stampede of people trying to get away, clashing with those who wanted to see.

And the curiosity-seekers who had not turned their backs of the window were obliged not to miss any detail of the terrifying spectacle.

The cadaver of the Englishman, before whom all the people of Paris had filed, who had been ion the icy slab in the Morgue for six days, had suddenly moved his lips, opened his eyes and gently agitated his limbs. Now he was getting up, slowly, as if stiffened by his long immobility.

He sat on the edge of the slab and looked around, fearfully. With his right hand he touched the body lying next to him. Again his gaze described a semicircle. Then, his eyes, widened by astonishment and an inexpressible emotion, came to rest on the crowd behind the glass, displaying faces contracted and discolored by horror, bodies convulsed by the struggle, legs, arms and heads mingled together...

The resuscitated cadaver was staring at all that when an imperious voice behind him called out: "Arthur Brad!"

A sudden resolution animated him then. He leapt down to the ground, turned his back on the frightened crowd, went around the slab and walked toward an open door. When he had gone through it, the door closed again, shut by Dr. Ahmed Bey.

"Monsieur Torpène," said Ahmed Bey, "may I introduce Arthur Brad, in his new mortal coil."

Pale and extremely emotional, the Prefect of Police bowed.

"Monsieur Brad, I'm Dr. Ahmed Bey, whom you have known on Venus and Mercury in the various forms that he was obliged to take on."

"Delighted to make your acquaintance thus," Brad replied, with a pronounced English accent.

"How do you feel?"

"Well enough in myself," said Brad, looking down at himself, "but I'm very cold, and I'm hungry."

"That doesn't surprise me," said Torpène, who had recovered his presence of mind. "You've been under the influence of the refrigeration apparatus for six days—obviously, you've had nothing to eat during that time."

"Where are Paul de Civrac, Lolla Mendès and Francisco?"

"In my house," said the Doctor. "They're not yet re-incarnated. You'll witness..."

"Good, good!" Arthur Brad interrupted. A wrinkle of anxiety striped his forehead. He looked around and opened his mouth to say something, but hesitated.

"What's the matter?" asked Torpène.

"You might think it childish," stammered Brad, "but I'd like to see my face. It's quite important...you'll understand...is there a mirror here?"

"You'll find one at my house, Monsieur Brad," said the Doctor, laughing. "But don't let your face worry you. I'll modify it for you in such a way that it will be similar in every respect to the one you had before your disincarnation—assuming that you want to resemble your previous form..."

"No, it's all the same to me. I don't have any family, and I don't care whether my friends think I've changed...but I don't want to be too ugly, you see!"

The three men burst out laughing.

"Are you going to come with us, Monsieur Torpène?" asked the Doctor.

"No—I have to stay here, to carry out certain formalities necessitated by the unexpected resurrection of Edward Penting..."

"Edward Penting?" said Arthur Brad, raising his eyebrows.

"Yes, that's the name of the body you're presently using, Monsieur Brad. The Doctor will tell you all about it. When the formalities are completed, I'll come to your house, Doctor, in order to get you and Brad to sign formal statements. And we'll draft a note to give to the journalists. Don't let anyone interview you!"

"Don't worry, my dear friend," the Doctor replied. "My automobile is just outside, and my chauffeur is skilful. We'll avoid the reporters, if any have already arrived."

"Until later, then!"

"Monsieur Brad," said Ahmed Bey, "let's go to lunch."

"With pleasure, Doctor."

After shaking Monsieur Torpène's hand, the two men went out of the office. They were stopped under the peristyle by a policeman accompanied by several town sergeants. The public corridor had been cleared and the crowd was massed outside on the sidewalk. At the sight of Edward Penting, the attendant, who was beside the policeman, leapt backwards shouting: "That's him! That's him!"

"The Prefect of Police is waiting for you inside, Officer," said the Doctor, immediately. "Will you lend me four men to clear the way for my automobile—we're in a hurry." That was said in a voice of such imposing authority that the officer did not hesitate for a moment to obey. He gave his orders to a brigadier and disappeared into the building. Accompanied by four men, the brigadier went to clear the road in front of the automobile, and, when the crowd had parted, the vehicle moved off, soon disappearing around the corner of the quay.

Chapter Three
In which Dr. Ahmed Bey keeps his fantastic promises

Four hours after the extraordinary scene at the Morgue, the evening edition of the *Universel*, Parisian section, was being hawked all over the city by noisy vendors. Its front page bore the following headline:

MYSTERY OF THE HÔTEL FULTON
Exciting Developments

Edward Penting resuscitated! He was only asleep! "It was a simple experiment," he says. He knows where his jewels and valuables are. He is giving 20,000 francs to the poor of Paris. "The file is closed," concludes the Prefect of Police.

There followed a long article recounting the story of the resurrection in detail, but in the manner that Dr. Ahmed Bey had decided that it should be told. And in the stop press, the following item relating to "the mystery of the Hôtel Fulton" could be read:

We are assured that Edward Penting, the individual mysteriously resuscitated, in a friend of Dr. Ahmed Bey, whose extraordinary science and competence in the field of seemingly-supernatural events are known throughout the world. That explains a great many things!
On leaving the Morgue, Monsieur Ahmed Bey, who had witnessed the "resurrection," returned to his house

at the Parc Monceau in company with Edward Penting.
The eminent doctor and the mysterious resuscitee have
refused to give any interview. Nevertheless, Dr. Ahmed
Bey has promised us that, in a matter of weeks, he will
personally explain the entire mystery, in order that the
press can communicate that explanation to the entire
world.

There is, in consequence, nothing to do but wait.
We shall wait.

The front-page article and the stop press item were
reproduced by all the evening papers in Paris, and, the
following morning, by all the newspapers in the world.
During the night, the currents of all the telephonic, telegraphic and transatlantic wires flowed without interruption, and the wireless telegraphy stations of both hemi-
spheres remained on the alert. And it was during that
night that what was perhaps the most moving scene of
the entire adventure was enacted in Dr. Ahmed Bey's
house.

At midnight, the five people who had witnessed the
disincarnation of Dr. Ahmed Bey—to wit, Monsieur
Torpène, the astronomer Constant Brularion, Abbé
Normat, Dr. Payen and Professor Martial—were sitting
on the divans in the laboratory. They had been escorted
there by Ra-Cobrah, who left them there after telling
them that his master would not be long in coming.

They waited impatiently, for, with the exception of
Monsieur Torpène, none of them had seen the Doctor.
They had only been made aware of his return to Earth by
the allusions made by the evening newspapers to the
presence of Ahmed Bey at the scene of the resurrection
in the Morgue. The impatience and emotion of the five

individuals was such that none of them was able to speak.

In front of them, beneath the bright light of the chandeliers, three bodies were laid out on marble slabs. One of them, alone on an isolated slab, was the corpse of a young woman, clad in a luxurious white silk peignoir; her feet were shod in red leather slippers; she had a beautiful coral necklace around her neck, and her beautiful black hair was elegantly combed.

The second slab supported two male bodies; the costume of one was finished off by a smoking jacket, the other with a blue waistcoat; they had both been carefully shaved, but the former wore a moustache while the second had none.

Suddenly, one of the laboratory doors opened and Ahmed Bey's voice was heard.

"Come in, Captain, and don't be astonished by anything."

"Very well, Monsieur—I've seen so many extraordinary things..."

The "Captain" who had pronounced those words with a strong Spanish accent immediately appeared in the glare of the laboratory. Ahmed Bey followed him, taking him by the arm in a familiar fashion and bringing him to meet the five guests, who had all risen to their feet.

"Messieurs," he said, "I have the honor of presenting to you Captain José Mendès, the father of Mademoiselle Lolla, whose soul I have brought back from the planet Mercury!"

And the Doctor introduced each of the five scientists to the Captain. Then, he added: "Yesterday evening I telephoned the military headquarters in Barcelona, where the Captain is in service. I was able to speak to him. I only said a few words, but they were sufficient for the Captain to take the train immediately. He arrived two hours ago. I've brought him up to date with my operations and my actions, past and imminent. That's why I'm late in coming to met you, Messieurs..."

Everyone bowed, and then sat down again, and the Captain, whose hands were tremulous with emotion and who was paler than the corpses lying on the slabs, took his place beside Monsieur Torpène.

Only then did Professor Martial, Abbé Normat and Dr. Payen feel able to speak. They all began to do so simultaneously.

"But Doctor..."

Realizing that they were all speaking at the same time, however, they said no more.

"Don't interrogate me, Messieurs!" said Ahmed Bey, smiling. "I'll tell you about my adventures later. You've seen my soul quit my body, so you have, I'm sure, observed its cadaverous condition following my departure. Now, you can see that same body alive before you. Be satisfied for the moment, I beg you, with regard to myself, and observe in silence the prodigies that will be accomplished before your eyes. You shall be their witnesses and guarantors, and your testimony will be precious when I judge that the time has come for me to reveal my power and my actions to the public."

The five men nodded their heads.

"Captain," Ahmed Bey went on, in a graver tone, "will you suppress the natural emotion that is agitating you, and consider closely the cadaver of this young woman..."

José Mendès got up, and, his features drawn, but firm and composed, he went to the slab. He gazed down at the marmoreal face and said: "This is the body into which you're going to put my Lolla's soul?"

"Yes."

"If I silence my paternal preferences," the Captain continued, "I recognize that she's a beautiful young woman…certainly more beautiful than my daughter was, although her beauty was famous in Barcelona. But those eyes, which must be dark, will they have my Lolla's gaze?"

"They will, Monsieur, for the gaze is merely the expression of the soul."

"Will those lips have her smile?"

"You'll be able to judge for yourself," said the Doctor. "In any case, you know that by means of androplasty, whose effects I've explained to you. I can model the face to the point of rendering it exactly similar to the one in which you represent your daughter. But it's a long and delicate operation, which isn't without pain for the patient. I'll only carry it out if Lola's soul, speaking through that mouth, expresses the desire and you give me the formal instruction…"

"Whatever Lolla wants," the Captain replied, simply, "I want…"

As José Mendès went to sit down again, a door opened and a stout silhouette appeared in the doorway.

"Messieurs," said Ahmed Bey, "I present to you Arthur Brad, under the auspices of Edward Penting."

At these words, an ardent curiosity caused Brularion, Martial, Abbé Normat and Dr. Payen to stand up abruptly. Only Torpène remained seated.

Arthur Brad advanced tranquilly, and the eyes of the four scientists, with those of José Mendès, studied intently the man who had been abducted by the Fiery Wheel, whose original body was mummified on the planet Venus and whose present body had, a few hours earlier, been the cadaver of a mysteriously-murdered Englishman. Such associations of ideas would have rendered many men mad, but the scientists were not among those who would allow their minds to be upset by facts or ideas. As one, they offered their hands to Arthur Brad, who took them one by one and shook them vigorously. As for the Captain, he had sat down again; he was thinking about his daughter.

"And now, Messieurs," said Ahmed Bey, when everyone had resumed their places on the divans facing the marble slabs, I ask you to observe, and not to speak.

He went into the dressing-room and came out again shortly afterwards wearing a long linen robe. As he went past a column he flicked a switch, and the chandeliers went out. Only one small electric lamp above the slabs, fitted with green glass, remained alight.

Ahmed Bey raised his arms toward the ceiling— and three white sparks were now visible, which were seen to descend in a flash and stop a meter above the three cadavers.

Rigid with emotion, Captain Mendès had got to his feet. He had taken a step forward, and he was standing motionless, his eyes fixed on the spark floating above the young woman.

Ahmed Bey had commenced his incantations and sacred gestures, however. His voice swelled, rising until it stopped dead with a long, harrowing cry—and then the spark shone more brightly, swiftly changed position, hovered momentarily over the lips of the dead woman, and suddenly disappeared.

Immediately, the Doctor murmured incomprehensible words in a low voice, and his hands made magnetic passes over the young woman's head.

Holding their breath, all the spectators had risen to their feet. They saw the pale young face take on a pink tint, and saw the throat gently rise and fall.

"Lolla!" Ahmed Bey suddenly cried. "Lolla Mendès, can you hear me?"

"I can hear you," sighed the resuscitated young woman.

"Do you remember the planet Mercury, Lolla?" the Doctor went on.

"I remember…oh, what horror!" An expression of suffering, contracted the lovely features.

"Lolla!" said the Doctor, again. "I willed that your soul be brought back to Earth."

"Is that possible?" moaned the sleeper.

"It is! You're asleep now, but you're going to wake up. Although you'll have a face and body different from those you had before…"

"Ah!" sighed the young woman. "How can that be?"

"Everything will be explained. But listen carefully…"

"I'm listening!"

"You'll see before you, when you wake up, Captain José Mendès…"

"My father!" A stifled sob resounded in the solemn silence that followed the young woman's exclamation. Captain José Mendès was weeping.

"Yes," said Ahmed Bey, "your father." Then, after a further pause, he went on: "Now, Lolla, I enjoin you to remember everything that I've just told you."

"I'll remember!"

"That's good. I'm going to wake you up!" And he added, in a softer tone, turning toward the spectators:

"Now, I'm certain that the emotions that will strike her when she wakes up won't do her any harm..."

With his arms extended, he made magnetic passes, and Lolla Mendès opened her eyes—widened, frightened eyes, still full of the mysteries of the beyond.

"Get up, Lolla!" Ahmed Bey ordered, quietly.

The young woman sat up on the edge of the slab, and looked around indecisively.

"Lolla! Lolla!" cried the Captain—and he came forward, arms extended.

The resuscitated woman leapt on to the floor and hurled herself into her father's arms, in tears.

And while they embraced, recklessly, Ahmed Bey pushed them gently toward the door to the broad marble staircase. There, Ra-Cobrah and two servants were waiting. In accordance with the master's orders, they escorted the father and daughter respectfully up the staircase and showed them into a small drawing-room. They left them alone there, in order that the Captain, instructed by Ahmed Bey, could inform his daughter gradually as to the miracles in consequence of which she found herself back on Earth, in a body that was not her own.

Chapter Four
Which concludes, without androplasty, with the anticipated betrothal

Meanwhile, the initial emotion having passed, and in response to a gesture from the Doctor, Monsieur Torpène and his friends, along with Arthur Brad, had sat down on the divans again.

Immediately, Ahmed Bey reincarnated the soul of Paul de Civrac in the body dressed in a smoking-jacket, and simultaneously reincarnated Francisco's soul in the body deseed in a valet's costume.

The spectators of the astounding scene were in an indescribable state of mind. Their reason refused to believe in a reality that their senses would not, however, allow them to doubt. But their reason had to bow to the evidence when Paul de Civrac and Francisco began to speak.

A few minutes sufficed for Paul and Francisco to take account of what had happened to them. Their mental faculties recalled their disincarnation on the planet Mercury, and they were entirely at their ease as soon as Ahmed Bey, having made the introductions, had acquainted them briefly with the origins of their present bodies, that of Arthur Brad, and the moving reincarnation of Lolla.

He concluded by saying: "I've chosen your current 'outfit' as best I could, Monsieur de Civrac, and yours too, Francisco. Nevertheless, if your new faces don't please you, I can remodel them in the resemblance of your previous ones."

"How?" asked Paul de Civrac.

The Doctor explained the operation of androplasty.

"Well, no," said Paul. "I've had enough of extraordinary things. I want to resume my simple human life like anyone else, without delay. My entire family consists of a brother and a sister; I'll explain the unprecedented adventure to them, and they'll love me in my new appearance as much as in the old one. However, there's someone who'll make the final decision—if my face doesn't please her, it will be necessary to resort to the androplasty, Doctor. Have you a mirror here? I wouldn't be displeased to make my own acquaintance...before asking you to introduce me to Mademoiselle Mendès..."

Smiling, Ahmed Bey took Paul to the dressing-room and left him there.

"What about you, Francisco?" he said, when he came back.

"Me, Monsieur? I was so ugly that I can only have gained by the change. I'll keep my new face, whatever it might be. As for the body, I can see that it's better than the one my poor mother gave me. Perhaps the muscles aren't as solid, but good food and exercise will take care of that. It only remains, Doctor, for me to thank you, Mercury isn't a place for a Spaniard or a Christian. Without giving you orders, though, I'd be very glad to see the Captain and the Señorita again. Is she, at least, as beautiful as she was before?"

"I think so, Francisco. You'll be able to judge for yourself..." He turned to Paul, who was coming back from the dressing-room. "Well, Monsieur de Civrac, does your portrait suit you?"

"It suits me, Doctor, and I thank you. But I'll shave off my moustache and change my hairstyle."

"No androplasty, then?"

"No, no androplasty."

"Francisco doesn't want any either."

"He's right! He looks good in his new skin. The best of all of us is Arthur Brad."

"It's a pity that Bild isn't here," said Brad. "He wouldn't be annoyed. But Doctor, although I had a good lunch and dinner, I'm hungry."

"Me too!" said Paul.

"And me!" Francisco sighed.

"It's four o'clock in the morning, Messieurs," said Ahmed Bey, "but one can still have supper at that time."

On these words, a door opened and Ra-Cobrah's voice announced: "The Master is served!"

"What did I tell you, Messieurs? Monsieur de Civrac, Brad, would you care to follow me? You too, Francisco. Today, you're not Captain Mendès' orderly, but my guest. As for you, Messieurs"—the Doctor turned to the group formed by Torpène, Brularion and their friends—"you know the way to the dining room. It's around the table that we'll talk about science, astronomy and adventures!"

And they went up the staircase. At the op, Monsieur Torpène and his friends went one way while Ahmed Bey took Civrac, Brad and Francisco into the small room to which the Captain and his daughter had been taken.

At the appearance of the four men, Lola Mendès and her father got up from the sofa on which they had been sitting. Ahmed Bey took hold of Lolla's hand, and Paul's, and without saying a word, brought the two young people face to face, in the full light of the chandelier.

There was a minute of silence, passionate observation, hectic joy and controlled emotion. Lolla wept; Paul tried in vain to stem the tears that we misting his own eyes—and suddenly, grasping the young woman's hands, the young man took a step forward and deposited, on the pure forehead that was raised toward him, the most ardent and chaste of kisses...

Through the gaze of their corporeal eyes, the immortal souls had recognized one another.

"Captain Mendès," said Paul de Civrac, in a tremulous voice, turning to Lolla's father, "I have the honor of asking you for your daughter's hand!"

"Father," said Lola, "I beg you to grant me Monsieur Paul de Civrac as a husband."

The Captain, his eyes moist with tears, advanced toward the fiancés and hugged both of them. "God has truly united you in Heaven," he said. "On Earth you will be my two children."

"*Viva el Señor Capitan!*" cried a stentorian voice. Everyone turned to the door, where a tall fellow was standing, his mouth open with the proffered cry.

"Francisco!" said the Captain.

"The very same, Señor, although somewhat changed, to his advantage. But the Señorita will decide whether she still wants me to serve her in future."

"Of course I want that, Francisco!"

Then Arthur Brad emerged from the corner in which he had put himself during the familial effusions. A stout figure—even stouter than the Fiery Wheel—he advanced and bowed to Lolla Mendès, to the extent that his rotundity permitted.

"Mademoiselle," he said, "let me present my good wishes...and my congratulations to you, my dear de Civrac..."

"But it's Arthur Brad!" Lolla exclaimed. Impishly, she offered her cheek, on which the American placed a paternal kiss.

"It's a pity," he said, "that that stubborn old fool Jonathan Bild isn't here..."

"We'll talk about it at table, Monsieur Brad," said the Doctor. He offered his arm to Lolla Mendès—and a few minutes later, all of Ahmed Bey's guests, himself included, were gathered around a table presided over by the beautiful Lolla.

There was little conversation during the first courses. Then the Doctor, who was less emotional than his guests, related his adventures succinctly. Paul de Civrac recounted his, as did Brad and Francisco. The stories connected and linked up with one another easily.

"As for purely scientific observations," the Doctor said, "they'll be the subject of an article that the scientific supplement of the *Universel* will soon publish, and which Monsieur de Civrac and Monsieur Brad will write with me. Our work won't conclude there, however. Tomorrow, with Monsieur Brad and some skilled technicians, I shall begin the construction of a machine that will put us in communication with Jonathan Bild, resident on the planet Venus. I shall be happy, Messieurs, for you to monitor our work as closely as possible. I repeat once again that that science has even more need than we do of your testimony."

"A machine, you say?" said Brularion.

"Yes, a machine similar in every respect to the one with which Bild is equipped on Venus. Once our apparatus is established, we shall be able to communicate with Bild, as, for instance, the wireless telegraph station in the Eiffel Tower communicates with the one at Bizerte."

"But the Earth and Venus are between eleven million and sixteen million leagues apart, in the periods when we're best placed to observe the planet."

"That's of no importance," the Doctor replied, "and the name that Bild and the Venusians have given their machine will be sufficient in itself to reassure you..."

"What do they call it, then?"

"The interplanetary radiotelephonograph."

"I understand the meaning of the word," said Brularion, "but I don't understand the machine at all..."

"Why bother building the machine?" said Francisco. "By means of disincarnation, Doctor, you can go to Venus and come back..."

"That's true," Ahmed Bey replied. "Along with the people I would like to accompany me—but that isn't sufficient for science, for the goal of science is to serve all of humankind equally. That's why I'm building the machine. Since I can't surrender the secret of the disincarnation and reincarnation of souls, we ought, in accordance with the desires of Bild and the Venusians, to give whoever wishes to do so the scientific, if not the material, means to construct a machine similar to ours. And that will only be one step. Bild and the Venusians are fully prepared to find a means of coming to Earth—that's why Bild didn't want to allow himself to be disincarnated."

"The Académie des Sciences has some fine sessions in prospect!" said Abbé Normat.

"And Paris," said Ahmed Bey, looking at Paul and Lolla, silently isolated in absolute bliss, "has an admirable marriage on the horizon!"

That was the final word. The scientists got up and took their leave, taking away secrets of which they were only to speak when Ahmed Bey had revealed them publicly himself. Lolla Mendès, the Captain, Civrac and Francisco were taken to the rooms that their host had prepared for them on the first floor of the house.

It was not until the next day that work began on the radiotelephonograph that would put the Earth in communication with the world of Venus and Jonathan Bild.

PART SEVEN
THE INTERPLANETARY
RADIOTELEPHONOGRAPH

Chapter One
In which prodigious realities are witnessed

It took exactly thirty-eight days to construct the radiotelephonograph; Dr. Ahmed Bey had left no stone unturned in order to bring the work to a rapid conclusion. His immense fortune permitted him to hire a hundred technicians selected from among the very best, and ensured that the factory at Creusot responsible for the delivery of the metal components for assembly carried out in twelve days an assignment whose magnitude would have required twenty times as long for any ordinary client.

It was on the Gravelle plateau, in a large area of open land, that the tower with the mobile cupola that was to contain the machine was constructed. The components brought from Creusot were assembled in a neighboring hangar. To the right of the tower stood three metallic masts 120 meters high; they supported antennae similar in appearance to those of a wireless telegraphy station, but these antennae were made of an alloy of copper, gold and silver; they had a large surface area and formed an inverted pyramid of wires.

As soon as the installation of the machine in the tower was complete, Ahmed Bey and Arthur Brad put their signatures to an invitation conceived as follows:

M.... is invited to come, on Thursday next, at nine o'clock in the evening, to the laboratory on the Gravelle plateau, to witness the first experimental trial of the interplanetary radiotelephonograph and the transmission of the first messages between Earth and the planet Venus. At that time, Venus, the evening star, will be close to its inferior conjunction, and, in consequence near to the Earth, which will favor the communication.

This note was sent to Monsieur Torpène, Monsieur Brularion, Abbé Normat, Dr. Payen and Monsieur Martial, and, in addition, to the presidents of the five Académies and the two Chambres, and, finally, to the Parisian editor of the *Universel.*

These thirteen individuals arrived almost at the same time, whether by automobile or horse-drawn vehicle, at the entrance to the tower. They were met by Francisco and introduced into a workroom that occupied the whole ground floor of the tower, where Lolla and Paul de Civrac—who were to be married a fortnight hence—and Captain Mendès were already assembled. Monsieur Torpène made the introductions. Almost immediately thereafter, Ahmed Bey and Arthur Brad appeared, both dressed in workmen's overalls. They had come down from the machine room installed above the work-room.

"Would you care to follow me, Messieurs," said the Doctor. He opened the door through which he had come and began to climb a spiral stairway, followed by Brad.

Two minutes later, the nineteen individuals, including Francisco, were in an immense round room with an extremely high domed ceiling, brightly lit by four electric globes.

On one side of the room seventeen armchairs had been set out against the wall, in a singular semicircular row.

"Please sit down, Messieurs," said Ahmed Bey, gesturing toward the armchairs with his hand.

Monsieur Torpène had already placed Paul and Lolla in the two central armchairs; the others at down to either side without paying any attention to precedence. Only Ahmed Bey and Arthur Brad remained standing.

"This is the interplanetary radiotelephonograph," said the Doctor, simply.

His extended hand pointed to an enormous, shiny and fantastic object in the middle of the room. The machine was divided into two parts, clearly separated by an empty space two meters wide. It was mounted on a white marble podium with three steps to either side.

The right-hand section of the machine was composed, firstly, of a large container set on top of an ebony box resting directly on the marble, from the upper face of which emerged yellow-tinted metallic wires extending upward on porcelain stalks embedded in the edges of the upper casing. These wires, twisted in a helix were then wound around other porcelain stems fixed in an ebony plate, and disappeared. From the middle of that ebony plate rose a copper column ten meters high, terminated at the tip by two enormous electromagnetic coils. Next to the column there was an ebony gibbet five meters high from which a kind of copper peg was suspended, from which an insulated metal wire emerged that vanished into the wall of the room. Finally, there was a telephone transmitter underneath the peg.

Even for a knowledgeable technologist, the machine was incomprehensible. That was the conclusion expressed after five minutes of silent examination by

Monsieur Brularion and endorsed by the grave nodding of the head of the venerable president of the Académie des Science.

Ahmed Bey smiled.

"And yet," he said, "this machine is justly reminiscent of the Ducretet wireless telegraph transmitting apparatus.[13] It's the enormity of the proportions that has misled you. You should also add to it this telephonic transmitter.

"This is, then, the transmitter of the machine for suppressing distance, if I might put it like that?" said Monsieur Martial.

"Yes," replied the Doctor. "And this is the receiver." He indicated the machine to the left.

It was simpler and not as huge: porcelain pillars on an ebony box, with electromagnetic coils, commutators and, finally, a complete telephonic receiving apparatus, next top which an enormous phonograph funnel expanded.

"If I'm not mistaken," said Monsieur Torpène, "it's a complete apparatus, enlarged and improved, for wireless telegraphy, combined with a telephone apparatus and a phonograph."

"Exactly," said Ahmed Bey. "All that is terrestrial, but what is Venusian is these metallic wires, composed of an alloy of gold and platinum for which Jonathan Bild gave me the formula on Venus, and whose composition I shall reveal in my paper for the Académie des Sciences. I haven't invited you here today to give you a lecture,

---

[13] Eugène Ducretet (1844-1915) was the leading French pioneer of wireless telegraphy; he transmitted the first wireless telegraphy signal in Paris, between the Eiffel Tower and the Panthéon, in 1898.

but simply for you to witness the first communication between Earth and the planet Venus."

He paused momentarily, and then went on: "In much the same fashion as wireless telegraphy, we shall send waves—not Hertzian waves but luminous ones—from the solar light storied in this machine by the Venusian method. We shall send those waves to Jonathan Bild, and he will send us others in reply. The method of transmission and reception is quite simple. I shall speak into the telephonic transmitter and the vibrations of my voice will produce forces inside the machine that will liberate the stored solar light. It will be liberated with varying intensity in accordance with the intensity of the vibrations, and those luminous waves will travel, via these wires here and the antennae outside, all the way to the Venusian apparatus, where Bild will receive them, as we shall receive those he will send to us. And the waves that Bild will send us by speaking into his machine we will receive here, via the external antennae. In the receptive section of our machine, they will be transformed into vibrations that will operate the mechanisms of this telephone, which, in its turn, will influence this phonograph—from which, Messieurs, the voice of Jonathan Bild will emerge loud and clear."

As the doctor spoke, his own voice had become grave and vibrant. It concluded on a triumphant note.

The guests were suddenly invaded by an intense emotion, at the common thought of the miracle to be realized: the words of two human beings exchanged across millions of leagues of interplanetary space.

There was a long and profound silence.

"Messieurs," Ahmed Bey sudden resumed, in a calmer tone, "Arthur Brad is going to speak to Jonathan Bild."

The Doctor pressed a button; the electric globes went out simultaneously and the dome of the tower disappeared with a sound of metallic friction. The nocturnal sky—filled with stars on the beautiful summer night—appeared to the guests, who had raised their heads.

"Look up," said the Doctor, "and you'll see the luminous waves flying through the firmament."

Meanwhile, Arthur Brad had gone to stand in front of the telephonic transmitter in the right-hand section of the machine.

"Send the call signal, Doctor," he said.

Ahmed Bey's hand was on a porcelain lever. He pulled it downwards. There was a shrill hiss inside the machine. Crackling parks striped the obscurity of the immense round room, and suddenly, up above in the sky, a blinding luminous zigzag appeared, shone, paled and went out.

Beneath the light of a small electric lamp suspended in the middle of a semicircular screen, Ahmed Bey looked at the second hand of his watch and counted aloud: "Ten... twenty... thirty. One! Ten... twenty... thirty. Two! Ten... twenty... thirty. Three! Ten... twenty... thirty. Four! Messieurs, Jonathan Bild is alerted. Within five minutes, we shall be notified..."

In the silence that followed these words, the voice of Constant Brularion was heard, saying: "But what if Jonathan Bild is dead?"

"He isn't," replied the Doctor, coldly.

"How do you know?"

There was a moment's silence, and then Ahmed Bey replied, in the same cold voice: "I disincarnated yesterday and my soul has been to visit Jonathan Bild on the planet Venus."

A kind of frisson passed through the shoulders of the spectators drowned in the shadows, No one dared say anything more.

As Ahmed Bey gestured toward the sky, everyone raised their heads—and suddenly, a luminous zigzag, still vague, appeared in the night. Immediately, it became more distinct, passed in a flash and disappeared. At the same instant, sparks crackled and an electric bell resounded in the left-hand section of the machine.

"Bild is ready," said the Doctor. "Speak, Brad!"

And without a whisper coming from the row of armchairs, in the silence of the tower, before the machines that resembled, in the darkness, crouching apocalyptic monsters, Arthur Brad slowly pronounced words that were about to resound, ten million leagues away, through the void of interplanetary space, in the ears of Jonathan Bild and the Venusians.

The portion of the sky circumscribed up above by the circle of the tower was striped continuously by luminous zigzags of different breadth and intensity.

Suddenly, Brad stopped speaking.

There were five minutes of a silence more profound than the silence of death.

Then other zigzags appeared, coming from space. Sparks crackled in the tower and words emerged resoundingly from the phonograph funnel.

"Jonathan Bild and thirty Venusian scientists, to Señorita Lolla Mendès and all of you, greetings!"

Chapter Two
In which there is an anxious wait

There was an amazement throughout the entire world that far surpassed the panic caused by the Fiery Wheel and the astonishment produced by the projected message that had arrived a few days afterwards.

On the morning after the extraordinary night, the *Universel* was the first to publish, beneath the signature of the astronomer Constant Brularion, an account of the meeting at the Gravelle laboratory, as well as the full text of the conversation between the Terran Arthur Brad and the Venusian Jonathan Bild.

All the great newspapers of the world produced a second edition on the same day reproducing the *Universel*'s prodigious news, which had been cabled, telegraphed and telephoned from everywhere to everywhere else during the morning.

Observatories, Academies and scientific societies were excited. National conferences were organized, and then, with surprising rapidity, a worldwide scientific congress, which would be held in Paris in the great hall of the Trocadero.

Polemics were, however, launched in the newspapers. The majority of the world's great periodicals, all the French newspapers, the New York *Herald*, the *Daily News*, the *Times*, the *Novoye Vremya* and the *Neue Freie Presse*, sided with the *Universel* in accepting without discussion the veracity of the interplanetary communication. *Cosmos*, the *Daily Telegraph*, the *Revue des Deux*

Mondes,[14] the *Daily Mail*, the *Gazette de Francfort* and almost all the German newspapers denied the facts and talked about American hoaxes, French frivolity and English credulity. In these peevish periodicals Ahmed Bey was treated as a "mad spiritist," Brad, Paul and Francisco as charlatans and Lolla as a woman "of dubious character," and so far as they were concerned, Bild had never existed. As for Brularion, he was called, with the well-known finesse of Teutonic wit, an "astronomer of the hairdressing salon" and Monsieur Torpène became a "policeman escaped from Charenton."

The *Universel*, however, was not put off by such trivia. Until the eleventh of July, the date when Venus would pass directly between the Earth and the sun and when, for astronomical reasons, the communications would have to be interrupted, the *Universel* published a daily account, in full, of the interplanetary communications.

Bild had no adventures to recount. The planet Venus was populated by a single race of beings forming a unique nation divided into two classes: the class of intellectual workers and the class of manual workers. There were no artists. On Venus, art had been replaced by science. Any worker of the inferior class could pass into the superior class by inventing a machine or apparatus capable either of facilitating Venusian life or hastening the

---

[14] In its early days, when edited by François Buloz from 1831 to 1877 the *Revue des Deux Mondes* had been prominent in promoting the Romantic Movement, but since it had been taken over by Ferdinand Brunetière in 1893 it had reflected that editor's strong commitment to Naturalism and a hatred of Symbolism that extended to a fervent disapproval of all imagination in literature; the animosity was mutual.

solution of the principal problem of science that would enable communication with the inhabitants of other planets. In such a society, whose government was composed of a council of ten members made up of equal number of the two classes, elected by regional assemblies, Jonathan Bild was receiving generous hospitality.

The Venusians bore little resemblance to human beings. Their body was a bony frame solely designed to support an assemblage of muscles and nerves; they had no legs, but immense wings, which could be lowered and held rigid in parallel to rest on the ground. Their form and stature were those of an immense bird, but they had two arms, or, rather, two tentacles, garnished with thousands of long and powerful suckers; they made use of these as multiple hands, with a prodigious dexterity and rapidity.

Their head was, properly speaking, merely a lantern: a bony spherical case, half of which opened as an immense eye and the other half containing, speaking in human terms, a brain, a seat of intelligence. They had neither speech nor hearing as we understand them. They "spoke" by means of the eye, whose enormous pupil varied in form, color and luminous intensity in accordance with the modulations of thought. In addition to that visual language, however, they had a written language composed of signs analogous to those of terrestrial Morse telegraphy, which they traced on golden tablets with a colorant punch made of unbreakable matter. The fundamental symbols numbered fourteen, but they had thousands of variations scarcely evident to the human eye, and a single sign often expressed a thought that a human could only have rendered in several sentences.

Bild had learned fairly rapidly to understand the visual language and assimilate the graphic alphabet. The

Venusians talked to him with their eyes and he replied by means of a punch and gold tablets.

With Jonathan Bild's radiotelegrams, therefore, the *Universel* compounded the most extraordinary and exciting serial that the paper had ever published.

On the evening of the tenth of July, that serial came to an end—but at the World Scientific Conference that opened the same day at the Trocadero Dr. Ahmed Bey read his paper, entirely devoted to the machine for suppressing distance. He only mentioned the disincarnation of souls briefly, limiting himself on that subject to calling upon the testimony of Monsieur Torpène, Monsieur Brularion, Abbé Normat, Dr. Payen and Professor Martial. In the scientific world, those gentlemen enjoyed such a reputation for intelligence, probity, wisdom and common sense that no doubt was raised, even among the scientific delegates from Germany.

From the day after the opening of the Conference onwards, the opposing newspapers ceased their polemics and finally conceded the truth. A book was published, under the auspices of a financial and scientific committee. It contained Ahmed Bey's paper in full, countersigned by Arthur Brad and Paul de Civrac, the record of the first session of the Conference, a description of the plans of the rediotelephonograph and the complete text of Bild and Brad's interplanetary conversations. The work had a print run in the millions, was translated into twenty-three languages, and was distributed throughout the world.

Its conclusion was this:

In his last telephonogram, Jonathan Bild announced that, at the exact moment of the inferior conjunction of the Earth and Venus, he will embark with six

Venusians in a traveling apparatus that the Venusian scientists have just completed. In terrestrial terms, that will be at nine p.m. on the eleventh of July. The distance from Earth to Venus being then about eleven million leagues, and the Venusian apparatus traveling at ten thousand leagues an hour on average, Bild expects to arrive on Earth forty-five days and twenty hours after his departure from Venus. It will, therefore, be on the twenty-sixth of August at approximately five p.m. that the Venusian apparatus will touch down on terrestrial soil. The people who have read these lines are requested to notify the nearest telegraph office of anything in the sky or on the ground that seems out of the ordinary on or around the date of August twenty-sixth.

That was signed by Arthur Brad, Ahmed Bey and Paul de Civrac, and countersigned by thirty of the most celebrated scientists in the world, including Monsieur Torpène.

The book in question, entitled *The Earth and Venus*, was published simultaneously in all the capitals of the world on the fifteenth of July. It was distributed profusely, gratuitously. The newspapers advertised it on a daily basis and also reprinted the conclusion.

And the entire Earth waited.

Meanwhile, in Paris, in the midst of an enormous affluence in which all aristocracies mingled with enthusiastic democracy, the marriage of Lolla Mendès and Paul de Civrac was celebrated. Arthur Brad and Ahmed Bey were Lolla's witnesses, Monsieur Torpène and Francisco were Paul's. The immense crowd was finally able to contemplate the young woman and the young man who had left their original bodies on the planet Mercury—for the full story of the successive

279

disincarnations and reincarnations had been published the day before in the newspapers under the signature of Ahmed Bey, with the official authorization of Monsieur Torpène and the formal ratification of the French government.

Ahmed Bey, Arthur Brad and Francisco were no les admired and acclaimed—and in the mind of the multitude, confounded in the same unique thought, the certainly was implanted from then on that anything as possible; humankind was beginning to sense that it was godlike.

It was in a private apartment in Ahmed Bey's house that the newlyweds lived while awaiting the construction of a villa in the grounds of the interplanetary laboratory at Gravelle. The day after his marriage, Paul de Civrac was appointed director of the laboratory by the French government, to which Ahmed Bey had made a gift of it. Arthur Brad accepted the position of chief of interplanetary communications; Captain José Mendès requested the liquidation of his retirement pension and Francisco became the new family's steward. As for Bild, he was to be entrusted with the foundation and direction of a laboratory similar to the one in Paris, which the United States government intended to build, along with a radiotelephonograph, in the vicinity of New York.

During the night of the twenty-fifth and twenty-sixth of August, few civilized people on Earth were asleep, and on the day of the twenty-sixth, normal work was abandoned. In the cities and rural areas, on the roofs and terraces of houses, in public squares and streets, in the midst of fields and on the summits of mountains, people watched, directing reflecting and refracting astronomical instruments, naval telescopes and simple binoculars at all points of the sky.

All the telegraphic and telephonic offices in the entire world were at the ready; senior functionaries of the postal, telephonic and telegraphic services of every nation were permanently stationed in their offices.

That feverish expectation was not entirely due to curiosity. In fact, before separating, the governmental delegates to the World Scientific Conference had voted a prize of ten million francs to be divided between the first person to indicate the Venusian vessel to a post office, the employees of that office and the people in charge of the line at the posts relaying the message. All telegrams were to be transmitted immediately by the most direct route to the central office in Paris, and sent from there to the telegraph station installed at the Gravelle laboratory.

In the laboratory itself, along with Ahmed Bey, Arthur Brad, Paul and Lolla de Civrac, José Mendès and Francisco, delegates of all the great scientific societies in the world were stationed, one from each society. There were also representatives of governments, newspaper editors, and a host of reporters. Everyone was eating and lodging in houses near the grounds of the laboratory; the present tenants were sub-letting apartments, outbuildings and individual rooms at crazy prices. A company selling collapsible houses erected a kind of vast caravanserai in a field, containing two thousand places—which were filled in three hours.

The first telegram arrived at two o'clock in the morning on the twenty-fifth of August. It read: *Honolulu. Venusian machine visible in sky. David Glenko.*

"We need to wait for confirmation of the news and a description of the machine," said Ahmed Bey. "Optical illusions will be innumerable."

Indeed, from one minute to the next, further telegrams arrived. Soon, the hundred receivers that had been installed did not pause for a second. The operators worked in one hour shifts and the telegrams were brought to the work-room where Ahmed Bey, Brad and Civrac were stationed, with fifty interpreters. The Venusian apparatus was appearing at all points of the globe. It was seen everywhere. It was about to land everywhere.

The hours passed in feverish activity.

"It's necessary to wait for one of these thousand of correspondents to confirm the preceding one, to specify the point at which the apparatus will land and to give a succinct description of the apparatus itself. Until then, illusions, optical illusions…"

The night and day of the twenty-fifth and the night of the twenty-sixth brought nothing conclusive. By nine a.m. on the twenty-sixth, 16,895 telegrams had been received, but no correspondent, having sent one, had sent a second…

During the day on the twenty-sixth, the flood of telegrams abated.

"Daylight isn't as propitious as daylight for imaginative illusions," said the smiling Ahmed Bey. "Besides which, it's not until after five o'clock in the afternoon according to Bild's notification and out calculations, that the thing ought to arrive."

The day went by without any confirmation of a prior telegram.

From seven p.m. onwards, the number of dispatches increased by the minute.

"Is the projector ready?" Ahmed Bey asked Brad.

"Yes."

"The phonographs?"

"Them too."

At the summit of the tower an electric beacon had been set up which would light up as soon as the arrival of the Venusian apparatus was indubitable, and four phonographs, one of enormous power, would hurl to the four points of the compass the words announcing the time and place of the marvelous landing.

The entire evening and night of the twenty-sixth and twenty-seventh went by without the coppery voice of the phonographs ringing out.

On the twenty-seventh, at eight a.m., Ahmed Bey, Brad and Paul de Civrac lay down on mattresses in the workroom and feel profoundly asleep. They had not slept for forty-eight hours. Francisco, stationed nearby, had orders to wake them as soon as the checkers who were numbering and classifying the telegrams received one duplicating a signature already seen.

At nine a.m., Lolla and her father arrived. They sat down in the workroom and chatted to Francisco near the three sleepers, waiting...

But the entire day went by: nothing.

By six p.m., the number of telegrams received had reached 359,000, but they all bore different signatures. There was not a single confirmation.

Having slept, eaten and taken a few minutes' physical exercise in the courtyard surrounded by the laboratory buildings, at nine p.m. on the twenty-seventh, Ahmed Bey, Brad and Paul de Civrac sat down in the workroom again.

Ten o'clock chimed, then eleven, and then midnight...

"As long as Bild and the Venusians haven't made a mistake in their calculations, said Paul. "The slightest error might have sent them into the infinity of interplanetary space."

283

"Yes," said Brad, "if their apparatus isn't steerable once launched. But if it is steerable, they could repair any error of direction while *en route...*"

"Unless unknown laws of attraction have sent them off course," murmured the Doctor, scanning the four hundred and twenty-second-thousandth telegram with his eyes. Almost immediately, however, he uttered a stifled exclamation and said: "Listen!" And with the sudden emotion that his exclamation had provoked, he read: "Astronomical Observatory Gaurisankar, Himalaya, 27 August, 3 a.m. Incandescent bolide arrived over Earth, from direction of Venus. Telegrams will follow at fifteen minute intervals. Archibald Simpson."

"This time," said Arthur Brad, "I think it really is Jonathan Bild. I knew Archibald Simpson in Boston. He's the coolest and most circumspect astronomer in the entire world."

"I know," said Ahmed Bey. "That's why the telegram caught my attention."

"Let's wait," Paul concluded.

And fifteen minutes later, another telegram from Arthur Simpson arrived.

27 August. 3-15. Bolide increasing in size.

At quarter past three, astronomically, counting from the conventional midnight, it must be night-time at Gaurisankar," said Paul.

"And daylight here," said Brad.

Immediately, however, further telegrams from the far side of the world confirmed Archibald Simpson's information. The later concluded with a final telegram:

Bolide no longer over my horizon.

But then, by means of new telegrams that were arriving, they would be able to track the progress of the bolide relative to the movement of the Earth.

Suddenly, Ahmed Bey rose to his feet. "Stop everything!" he shouted.

Every apparatus ceased functioning.

"Light the projector!" Ahmed Bey ordered, in the absolute silence he had provoked.

Brad pushed an electric button on the table. "It's done," he said.

Then Ahmed Bey, in a strong and vibrant voice, read the following telegram:

"Observatoire de Verrières, 28 August, 4-35. Apparatus landed Carrefour de l'Obélisque, Verrières wood. Going there immediately. Brularion."

Five minutes later, while the phonographs, multiplying the Doctor's voice a hundredfold, each repeated the long-awaited news three times, to the south, the north, the west and the east, two automobiles set off at top speed, heading for the Carrefour de l'Obélisque in Verrières wood near Paris, carrying Ahmed Bey, Brad and Monsieur Torpène, Paul de Civrac, Lolla, her father and Francisco. Ten minutes later, the Gravelle plateau was deserted; automobiles, horse-drawn vehicles and bicycles were flying along the roads at top speed, carrying the curious crowd, breathless with excitement.

Chapter Three
In which destiny closes the door of mystery
by means of a catastrophe

From his station in his Observatory at Verrières, Constant Brularion noticed an abnormal phenomenon in the sky early on the night of the twenty-seventh and twenty-eighth of August. It was a luminous dot growing imperceptibly in size, approaching the Earth rapidly. Brularion did not was to compromise his renown by a premature announcement of the Venusian apparatus; he would rather not win the prize and not sent a telegram until the matter was certain. Without communicating his discovery to the astronomers around him, he tracked the progress of the phenomenon across the sky.

At four o'clock in the morning the scientist had no further doubt, but he took pride in only sending one tele-gram to Gravelle, which would be definitive. It was only when the seemingly-incandescent object fell at a definite point in Verrières wood that Brularion turned to the as-tronomers and said, in a calm voice: "Messieurs, the Ve-nusian apparatus has arrived."

There was a tumultuous din. People wanted infor-mation about the form of the apparatus and the exact spot where it had landed, but Brularion went down to the Observatory's telegraph post and sent the famous tele-gram to Ahmed Bey Then he sent another telegram to General Durland, who was in command of the troops based in Verrières, in anticipation of military protection having to be placed around the Venusian apparatus. All the garrisons in the world were on the alert, because it could not be known in advance where the landing would take place.

Then he climbed into his automobile and, followed by all his colleagues in other vehicles, Brularion set off for the Carrefour de l'Obélisque. The journey took three minutes.

Aided by the drivers of the cars, the astronomers established a barrier of strong ropes around the clearing, guarded by a few soldiers brought from the Observatory, where a detachment had been posted. In the clearing, for meters from the large trees that marked its center, a monstrous object was lying, somewhat reminiscent of a broken gas-holder with its framework twisted. The earth had been torn up all around it, forming mounds. The machine was radiating a terrible heat, preventing anyone from getting any closer to it than fifteen paces.

"I have a strong suspicion," said Brularion, "that we won't find anything inside but crushed and burned bodies." The astronomers, backed up against the rope nodded their heads anxiously.

Meanwhile, outside the cordon, an incessantly-growing crowd was gathering, and a great murmurous conversation began in low voices. People for two or three kilometers around had seen the object fall.

Suddenly, horns resounded. The crowd parted and Dr. Ahmed Bey, followed by his friends, leapt into the enclosure. Almost immediately, cavalrymen arrived, and then a battalion of infantrymen riding on the backs of armored vehicles, commanded by General Durand himself. The soldiers took up their positions and the enormous crowd was obliged to stand motionless outside the cordon, while the scientists and officials gathered within. In the first row, as close as possible to the Venusian machine, was a distinct group comprised by Ahmed Bey,

Arthur Brad, Paul and Lolla, Francisco, Brularion, General Durland and Monsieur Torpène. All their hearts were beating with intense emotion.

"We have to wait for the mass of metal, heated by its passage through the atmosphere, to cool down completely," said Ahmed Bey.

And they waited, studying the disconcerting object, fearful that they would find nothing inside it but death.

After an hour, Ahmed Bey was finally able to get close enough to the disorderly mass of metal to reach out and touch it.

"General," he said, "would you be kind enough to bring the engineers forward."

An order was shouted and fifteen soldiers from the Engineer Corps, commanded by a young captain, formed a chain around the machine. Advised by Ahmed Bey, the general and the captain directed the operation.

First of all, the mounds of earth were cleared; then the broken and twisted metal beams surrounding the central canister were removed to the extent that it was possible. That core, made of a gray metal that was recognized as platinum, was finally freed. It was enormous, embedded in the earth at an angle, deeply dented in places but intact in others.

At a word from Ahmed Bey, the crowd was ordered to maintain the most absolute silence—and everyone listened. No sound was coming from inside the shell. Seizing a soldier's pick-axe, Ahmed Bey rapped on the metal, striking rhythmic blows similar to the signals employed by coal-miners, but there was no response.

The Doctor allowed five minutes to go by, and then rapped again—in vain.

"Messieurs," he said then, in a loud voice, "this shell must have a door, presently closed. We have to find it, and open it."

"It might be located in the part of the cylinder buried in the ground," said Arthur Brad.

"In that case, we need to break through the shell itself."

They set to work. Ropes were thrown over the shell and secured to pickets, and the soldiers, Ahmed Bey, Arthur Brad and Paul de Civrac, hanging on to the ropes, scaled the cylinder on all sides, examining it meticulously.

Everywhere, however, the continuity of the shell was seamless, with no bolted plates, equally smooth over the entire visible surface, like an iron cannonball.

They were returning to the ground, discouraged, when someone shouted: "A hole! There! A hole!" And one of the military engineers, covered in earth and brandishing his pick-axe, emerged from a ditch that he had excavated along the wall of the cylinder. Then ran to indicated spot, and Ahmed Bey did, indeed, see a hole, disengaged by the soldier from the earth obstructing it. It was perfectly circular, some forty centimeters in diameter. It allowed them to perceive that the walls of the shell were twenty centimeters thick.

"Bring an automobile headlight!" shouted the doctor, and swiftly took off his jacket and his shoes. The captain of the engineers brought the headlight.

"Pass it to me once I'm inside," said Ahmed Bey.

With his arms forward, to either side of his head, Ahmed Bey wriggled through the hole. He was seen to disappear entirely; then one of his hands reappeared, grabbed the headlight and bore it away.

The general had to demand silence again. Not seeing anything, and not hearing anything, the enormous crowd of spectators became restless. The soldiers were barely able to hold them back. Then the captain climbed on to the shell to shout news of what was happening.

"Now," he concluded, "shut up and don't move. We'll keep you informed."

The multitude applauded, and the captain slid back down a taut rope to the ground.

Meanwhile, the group around the mysterious hole—Arthur Brad, Paul, Lolla, Francisco, Brularion, Torpène and the other scientists and officials, waited in ardent anxiety. The sun, rising above the trees, inundated the clearing with cheerful light. The shell shone, enormous, deformed and still incomprehensible: an extraterrestrial monster seemingly bound to the earth by the taut ropes.

A quarter of an hour went by.

Suddenly, Ahmed Bey's head appeared, framed in the circular opening.

"Send me eight strong men," he said, simply, "each carrying a torch, an adjustable wrench, a hammer and a chisel. Monsieur de Civrac, Brad, will you please accompany them—and you too, Monsieur Torpène and Monsieur Brularion, if you don't mind the gymnastics."

"Have you seen them?" asked the general.

"No. The cylinder is only a carcass—the true Venusian apparatus is in the center, linked to the shell by buttresses. The apparatus is a perfect cube, furnished with portholes, or so it seems to me, and a door, but it's hermetically sealed. Come in!"

Ahmed Bey's head disappeared and Arthur Brad slid into the hole, followed by Paul de Civrac, Brularion, Torpène and then eight of the engineers. The last of them passed the headlights to the other seven, and was engulfed in his turn.

Then, the people who remained outside, in front of the hole, heard hammer-blows and grating sounds from within, sonorous impacts that reverberated in the air.

Then silence fell.

An anguish now passed through the groups of officials and scientists, through the cordon of troops and through the entire crowd. The sound of the breeze in the trees was audible. But that solemn absence of all human sound did not last long; soon, a murmur rose up in the densely-packed crowd, and that murmur increased, punctuated by vocal outbursts and cries.

The captain was about to scale the cylinder again in order to demand silence for a second time when Ahmed Bey's head appeared in the circular opening. Ordinarily pale, that face was white, with eyes widened by emotion.

"General," said the Doctor, in a blank voice, "send in a dozen men with blankets. They'll find some in the automobiles. Quickly!"

There was a sudden panic.

"What is it? What's happened?"

"Are they all dead?"

"What about Jonathan Bild?"

"Are there Venusians? How many?"

"What are they like, exactly?"

"But what about Jonathan Bild? Jonathan Bild?"

Ahmed Bey was opening his mouth to speak when a dozen soldiers arrived, laden with all the blankets, traveling rugs and cloaks they had been able to find."

"Pass them all in!" the Doctor ordered, and disappeared.

Methodically, the soldiers passed all the rugs and cloaks through the hole; then, forming a line, they waited, while the captain, standing on top of the shell, harangued, informed and tried to calm down the crowd, which was becoming tempestuous.

Suddenly, it fell silent and immobilized of its own accord, as if those thousands of brains had sensed the presence of death and mystery.

Dr. Ahmed Bey was the first to emerge from the shell. He made a sign to the soldiers, who received and removed a long mass wrapped in a blanket. The mass was immediately placed on the ground. Ahmed Bey knelt down beside it and uncovered it. The body of a tall, thin man became visible, his face pale and his eyes closed.

"Jonathan Bild!" murmured Lola, her eyes welling with tears.

"He isn't dead," said the Doctor. He took a minuscule bottle from his waistcoat pocket, took out the stopper, poured its contents on to a handkerchief, and applied the damp cloth to Jonathan Bild's mouth and nostrils.

Then he rose to his feet. "General," he said, "I hope to save him. Please clear the road leading to Monsieur Brularion's observatory. Captain—my automobile!"

"What should we do then?" asked the general.

"Receive the bodies wrapped in the rugs and pass them to these soldiers. Don't unwrap them, and have them transported to the Observatory immediately. Then, have the crossroads guarded in such a manner that no one can approach the machine."

"But tell us..." Professor Martial risked.

"Later, later! Read tomorrow's *Universel. Au revoir*, General. Soon, Messieurs! Madame, you come with me. Paul will join us in a quarter of an hour, with Brad and Francisco."

Preceded by four soldiers carrying Jonathan Bild, inanimate on the taut blanket, Ahmed Bey gave his hand to Lolla, and marched to his automobile, followed by the General. Having emerged from the shell, Brularion joined them The captain had cleared the road to the Observatory. And between two ranks of the noisy crowd, the automobile sped away.

The next day, on its first page, the *Universel* published the following brief bulletin:

JONATHAN BILD AND THE VENUSIANS
YESTERDAY'S EVENTS

In yesterday's evening edition we reported the arrival of the Venusian machine and the events that occurred prior to two p.m. At that moment, the machine was guarded by an entire infantry regiment deployed in a series of cordons, between which mounted officers and men of the Republican guard were circulating. We shall give a description of the machine, furnished by Dr. Ahmed Bey himself, further on.

At that time, too, Jonathan Bild was still in a worrying state of unconsciousness. Let us say right away that Jonathan Bild, thanks to the care of Dr. Ahmed Bey and Professor Martial, eventually recovered consciousness at four twenty-five. He opened his eyes, stammered a few incomprehensible words and then went to sleep, under the influence of a cordial injected into him with that purpose. His sleep is still continuing at the moment when these lines are being written, but the general condition of his organs and their resumption of normal functioning gives reason to hope that when he wakes up, at around midday today, he will be able to get up, eat and talk. He has not sustained any serious injury, and is not thought to have any internal damage. Everyone is looking forward impatiently to his awakening, for only Jonathan Bild can give the world the desired enlightenment regarding the planet Venus, the Venusian apparatus and the Venusians themselves.

In fact, the Venusians are all dead. There were six in the machine with Jonathan Bild. The corporeal form of the Venusians is known by virtue of our previous reports. How did they die, and when? Was it during the voyage from Venus to Earth? Was it during the landing, or subsequent to it? Dr. Ahmed Bey does not know; perhaps only Jonathan Bild will be able to inform us on that subject.

But of what did the Venusians die? That too is a mystery. Their bodies—covered not with avian feathers, as some of our colleague have written without justification, but with a rough white hairless skin devoid of hair, feathers of down—decayed within an hour into formless gelatinous masses. Their bones and organs have dissolved; one can scarcely distinguish the form and framework of wings reminiscent of the wings of our bats. As for the eyes—the immense Venusian eye—they were the first to decompose; they no longer form, along with the brain, anything but a small lump of greasy and corrupt matter within the softened cranium.

It is in vain that Dr. Ahmed Bey, with the aid of Oriental liquids of which he has the secret, has tried, by means of repeated injections, to arrest that extraordinary decomposition. As we write these lines, the six Venusians who came to our planet are nothing more than a single mass of putrescence.

Let us now pass on to the machine.

We are obliged to limit ourselves to giving a description without seeking to explain the dispositions and
the mechanism. Our most knowledgeable mechanical
engineers, including Monsieur Louis Delaforge, the
technical director of the École Nationale de Mécanique
et d'Électricité, has examined it carefully and admitted
that he does not understand it at all.

The Venusian machine is composed of two distinct
parts. The first is an enormous cylindrical shell, similar
to our gas-holders, twenty meters tall, ten meters in diameter and twenty centimeters thick. It was surrounded
by stanchions and an external framework of metal,
which was broken and completely dislocated during the
fall. The shell, the stanchions and the framework are
made of pure platinum—which is to say that from the
terrestrial viewpoint, they are immensely valuable, since
for us, platinum is a more precious metal than gold.

The second part, enclosed in the center of the shell,
in which it is sustained by elastic buttresses made of a
red metal whose composition is as yet unknown to us,
consists of a cubic platinum box five meters square; it is
perforated by five hermetically sealed portholes without
windows and an arched doorway, similarly sealed,
providing an opening for each side of the box. The interior is softly padded with a metal more elastic than rub-
ber. There are instruments and apparatus bolted to the
walls, whose functioning can only be explained by Jonathan Bild. One of the items of apparatus has, however,
been recognized as being intended to produce oxygen
and to absorb atmospheric nitrogen. A provision of bis-
cuits was discovered in a storage-locker, which appear
to be concentrated meat, but of what animal, again, only
Jonathan Bild can tell us. It was doubtless on these bis-
cuits that Bild was nourished, since we know that the

Venusians live uniquely by absorbing a kind of gas, which the manufacture on their planet.

Today, the construction of a hangar has begun around and above the Venusian machine. It is not transportable; the scientists will continue to examine it on the spot.

That is all that we know for the moment.
Our evening edition will give further details.

The article was certified as exact by four signatures: Ahmed Bey, Arthur Brad, Brularion and Torpène.

In its evening edition, the *Universel* merely announced that Jonathan Bild had woken up, was well, but somewhat exhausted, and that he was inside the Venusian machine, giving explanations to Ahmed Bey, Arthur Brad, Brularion, Torpène and Delaforge, who were examining the enormous apparatus with a few other scientists.

The newspaper report concluded:

We shall give these sensational explanations tomorrow.

The next day's *Universel* was, indeed, sensational, but not in the way the public expected. The front page headline displayed the disturbing line:

FRIGHTFUL CATASTROPHE

Yesterday, at nine forty-five p.m., the Venusian machine blew up, destroying itself, shattering the hangar that surrounded it and ravaging Verrières wood around the Carrefour de l'Obélisque. Thirty-four soldiers are dead and twenty-two wounded.

Ahmed Bey, Jonathan Bild, Arthur Brad and Mes-
sieurs Torpène and Brularion have been killed.

The cause of the catastrophe remains a mystery. It
has, however, been attributed to the special gases with
which the Venusians nourish themselves. These gases
were, it appears, stored in containers under formidable
pressure. There is no way of knowing how and by what
the explosion was provoked.

More details this evening.

The promised details, however, contained no new information. The only interplanetary voyagers to have escaped the tragedy were Paul de Civrac, Lolla and Francisco. Fortunately for them, they had remained at the Gravelle laboratory during the first day of the investigation; they were only due to go to the machine the following day.

It was impossible to recover the bodies of the victims, celebrated or unknown. The formless and bloody fragments of human flesh and limbs that were collected throughout the extent of the wood were not identifiable. All those who had disappeared were reported dead—and it was an irreparable loss for human science. All the irritating questions that the world was asking with regard to facts and events were to remain unanswered.

Of the Fiery Wheel itself and its supposed destruction on Venus, nothing was known, Brad having said nothing about it before being authorized by Bild. All the fine projects of interplanetary communication were abandoned. In fact, Paul attempted to send messages to Venus by means of the radiotelephonograph at Gravelle, but he did not receive any, even though the astronomical positions of the two planets were favorable, perhaps because none of the Venusian scientists of the mysterious planet had any knowledge of human forms of the expression of thought. Bild was no longer on Venus to listen and reply, nor were the six Venusian scientists who had worked with him on the radiotelephonograph.

After several months of discussion in scientific societies and journals, silence gradually fell on the extraordinary adventure of the Fiery Wheel was the point of departure and Ahmed Bey the most extraordinary hero.

Impenetrable mystery enveloped everything: the Fiery Wheel, the disincarnation of souls, Venusian life. There was only scant discussion of a book in which Paul de Civrac recounted his adventures and those of his companions, in the Fiery Wheel and on the planet Mercury. And in the abandoned Gravelle laboratory, the useless radiotelephonograph gradually rusted.

In any case, sometime after Paul de Civrac's book appeared, the world was distracted from interplanetary preoccupations. A frightful war erupted between the people of the white race and those of the yellow race, which lasted for ten years. No definitive victory was won by either side, but the political geography of the world was changed dramatically. A United States of Europe was established, in opposition to a Asiatic Confederation. South and North America formed a single nation, mistrustful and abrasive, positioned between Europe and Asia, and while Asia gradually completed the conquest of Oceania and Europe annexed Africa, America, immense and isolated, strove to augment its power and internal wealth, in a terrible egotism of which it was eventually to perish.

Paul de Civrac and Lolla witnessed that transformation of the Earth, but took no part in it. They were living on a remote island in the Indian Ocean, where the last sages of Benares and Calcutta had taken refuge.

They were uniquely occupied in researching, from the mouths of Brahmins and in the sacred books of the temples, the secret of the disincarnation and reincarnation of souls, which had been lost with Ahmed Bey. Captain José Mendès and Francisco had died, in quick succession, soon after they had taken up residence on the island.

Nothing any longer attached Paul and Lolla to the Earth. Indifferent to the agitations of their fellows, they devoted themselves entirely to researching the marvelous secret that would permit them to return to Mercury, to go to Venus, and to voyage without peril in the interplanetary realm where they had suffered so much but for which, by virtue of a very human contradiction, they were now nostalgic. Perhaps that was because it was a long way from Earth that they had begun to love one another. A prisoner who has fallen in love in prison forgets the horrors of captivity, only recalling the felicities of love.

In fact, Paul and Lolla died without having found the secret of the disincarnation of souls, but at least they had acquired, by means of their research, the wisdom of the ancient Brahmins, which taught them this precept, within which their material existence was conformed:

The Earth is, for human beings, a point of transition between two infinities.

Ill. Georges Vallée, Ferenczi, 1922

Afterword
Which consists of a few brief notes
on Alien Physiology and Ecology
as imagined in *La Roue fulgurante*

It was always common practice for writers of *feuil-leton* serials to make them up as they went along—a method that could easily lead to narrative difficulties, even in sentimental and historical melodramas in which ready-made pieces of plot could be slotted together jig-saw-fashion to maintain dramatic tension and provide denouements. In a serial whose entire *raison d'être* was to feature the unprecedented, the astounding and the mind-boggling, however, it was a strategy that was, in essence asking for trouble. It is a great deal easier to im-agine spectacular events and bizarre circumstances than it is to produce rational explanations for their occurrence and appearances. In an ideal world, of course, a writer of *roman scientifique* would work out the possible explana-tions before making up the events, but in reality, things are rarely done that way, even nowadays, and it would have been almost unimaginable in the world of popular *feuilletons*.

Inevitably, therefore, writers of imaginative *feuille-ton* serials often found themselves, as their works pro-gressed, accumulating an increasing burden of exotic puzzles for which solutions had to be vaguely promised, even though they could not ultimately be delivered. If one adds to that problem the conventional assumption that stories set in the "imminent present" will, in the end, leave the world more-or-less unchanged, so that it can

301

tacitly continue to masquerade as the world in which its readers are actually living in (give or take a nine-day-wonder or two), it is easy to understand why the temptation for writers to cut through their self-created Gordian knots simply by blowing everything to kingdom come, as La Hire did at the end of *La Roue fulgurante*, often became irresistible. In all honesty, what practicable alternative did La Hire have? He was, of course, chickening out on his artistic responsibilities, but any modern reader, long accustomed to the kinds of idiocies that an overly prompt imagination is inclined to commit when stretched, will appreciate only too well that so much imaginative clutter had accumulated in the plot of *La Roue fulgurante*, most of which makes no sense whatsoever, that any attempt at pretended explanation would only have served to increase its manifest absurdity.

On the other hand, there is a sense in which some of the seeming paradoxes contained in the plot of the novel might be able to serve as useful stimuli to further imagination and ingenuity, by prompting attempts to explain the seemingly-inexplicable. It is also worth noting that some of the ideas tentatively expressed in the early chapters of the novel, before La Hire ran out of inspiration and began freewheeling on an empty imagination-tank, were ideas that proved to have a lot of mileage in the melodramatic currency of what eventually became known as "science fiction," and in the curious modern mythology of "flying saucers." Some of those ideas might, therefore, warrant a little further thought and attention.

It should also be emphasized that the author's attempt to wrap the plot up and put it away with a bang is—like all such attempts—a blatant fudge. The ending of a story based in speculative science can never leave

302

the world unchanged, because any invention credited to the scientific method can always be replicated by that method, even if the invention and its inventor have both been blown to smithereens. We might not have discovered exactly what the Fiery Wheel was within the narrative as it is written, but in the world within the text, that information would have been bound to come out eventually, because it is a stone cold certainty that, even if the one featured in the story was the only one in existence at the time, its clones would undoubtedly follow eventually where it had led.

With the aid of the wisdom cultivated by a hundred years of science fiction writing and reading, we now know perfectly well why the Fiery Wheel abducted five people from the surface of the Earth: scientific curiosity. The Saturnians, individuals made of exotic matter and living in a vaporous environment, had become intensely interested in the bizarre nature of the Earth's ecosphere, in which the role of gases and vapors is so extensively supplemented by liquids and solids, and wanted to try to figure out what could possibly be going on inside those weird squidgy things running around on the surface. Unfortunately, their relative ignorance of the highly esoteric science of solid state physics had left them ignorant of the likely effects of people shooting bullets aboard their nifty spacecraft—which, although as shatterproof as the Saturnians themselves, was obviously not immune to high-velocity-solid disruption.

Will the curious Saturnian scientists in the world of the text allow the loss of their prototype Wheel to put them off further exploration? No way. They will be back, not necessarily tomorrow, but some day, more eager than ever, but taking more precautions. They will come back to Earth, to Mercury, and to Venus, not just for a second time but again and again, until they find out what there is to know. Throughout the solar system, things will never be the same again—and our piddling little world wars are of little or no consequence in *that* ongoing story, any more than the Mercurians' strange internecine conflicts or the Venusians' mysterious breathing difficulties.

It is, inevitably, difficult for us to deduce very much about the ecology of Saturn and the ethnology of the Saturnians on the basis of the observations made by the five humans abducted aboard the alien craft, and the feeble attempts they made at self-education before losing their heads completely and starting shooting (thus proving the essential insanity of human nature to their inquisitive hosts) soon ran into contradictions that even they could see. Nevertheless, the speculations in question have since sprung to a lot of other human minds, with the result that the notion of creatures of "pure energy" or "pure mind" eventually became a sciencefictional cliché, partly because of its paradoxical echoing of the traditional notion of the human "soul" as a kind of detachable entity, possibly resembling a quasi-electrical spark in its "pure" state.

We must, of necessity, follow the example of the skeptics in the novel in bowing to the manifest evidence and accepting that, whatever the case might be in our world, human beings really do have detachable *personas* in the world within the text, which really are capable of independent superluminal space travel and serial incarnation, in the fashion previously mapped out by Louis-Sébastien Mercier and Camille Flammarion. Although the issue does not come up explicitly within the novel, we must also accept, logically, that the same is true of the Mercurians, who must have the vacatable "slots" into which such entities may fit, or Ahmed Bey and Arthur Brad would not have been able to reincarnate themselves on Mercury. The principle of mediocrity encourages us to believe that the same is probably true of the Venusians and Saturnians as well.

Even within the scant discussion that the kidnap-victims conduct aboard the Wheel, the point is made that the Saturnians cannot possibly be "pure souls," because they would not need a spacecraft if they were, but the description of their quasi-electrical character does suggest, strongly, that the state of matter in which their natural bodies exist is more closely akin to the quasi-material state of detachable "souls" than it is to the vulgar lumpen envelopes in which terrestrial and Mercurial souls are clumsily wrapped. The Venusians, although solid, also must partake of an exotic material state, or they would not have decayed so spectacularly on exposure to Earth's atmosphere, so the possibilities of organic organization are obviously far more complicated and prolific than our limited knowledge of the narrow range of terrestrial organic chemistry has led us to conceive.

In fact, that is the most obvious inference to be taken from the novel viewed as a spectrum of ideas; without it, the account of Mercurian ecology could not possibly make sense. Ahmed Bey must, in fact, have been having a really bad day, intellectually speaking, when he accepted, even provisionally, that the only food the monopods consumed was each other. It does not require a genius to see the problems that notion produces with regard to the law of conservation of mass-energy. If the only substance the Mercurians consume is each other, how on Mercury could they possibly leave cadavers behind when they die, even temporarily, without suffering a drastic reduction in numbers over time? Given that they are, as La Hire puts it, "pullulating," something else is obviously happening. Indeed, something akin to that something else might well be happening to the humans too, given that they sweat copiously in the intense Mercurian heat, while Paul and Francisco only consume a cupful of water each and Lolla does not consume any at all. (As a lady, of course, she only "glows" rather than perspiring, let alone sweating, but that does not solve the problem.)

Clearly, the Mercurians can only obtain a small fraction of their body-building nourishment from ocular vampiric cannibalism—perhaps something more like a vitamin supplement than staple alimentation—and the rest must come from somewhere else. Where? Photosynthesis might seem an attractive hypothesis, given the proximity of Mercury to the sun and the alleged density of its atmosphere, but the monopods, even though they are scared of the planet's sinister night-side, do not seem to be particularly photophilic, building their cities in the shade and underground and being able to see in the dark; it is, therefore, at least worth considering other possibilities,

As a big fan of Camille Flammarion, La Hire would have been familiar with the fascination Flammarion had with the idea of aliens beings for whom respiration and nutrition were the same process: aliens living in dense atmospheres who aspire their nourishment along with their oxygen, much as aquatic filter-feeders take in their food along with the water that simultaneously supplies their respiratory needs. Perhaps, therefore, the Mercurians derive the bulk of their nourishment from the atmosphere, with or without the assistance of photosynthetic fixation. That hypothesis becomes more plausible, of course, when one bears in mind that we are explicitly told that the Venusians derive their nourishment by some such means, and it seems a natural assumption that Saturnians, who live in a gas giant and fly vaporous spacecraft, do too.

That is not the only other possible explanation, however, and it might be with considering at least one more, given that Ahmed Bey, during his brief stroll around Monopodville, is not only puzzled by the problem of monopod postmortal decay but the problem of monopod reproduction. He sees no evidence of sexual differentiation, let alone of pregnancy and childbirth. (The fact that I have elected to refer to the monopods as "it" rather than "he" when not possessed of a human soul was a judgment call, as French pronouns do not work in the same discriminatory fashion as English ones; it does not necessarily imply that they are sexless.) Perhaps, therefore, the monopods do not actually reproduce themselves, but are instead produced by a process of spontaneous generation, perhaps as the end phase of a chain of mutations that convert inorganic substance into a sequence of organic forms. If so, that might help to account for the remarkable apparent dearth of organic species on Mercury, which would be difficult to explain by means of any orthodox evolutionary theory.

We cannot know which of these hypotheses is true, or even which of them might be true within the fundamental physics and chemistry pertaining in the world of the text—which obviously differs from ours in some salient respects—but it is worth bearing in mind that whatever is happening on Mercury to sustain the indigenous organisms is probably also applicable to some degree to the human visitors, who can obtain some benefit from eating the local flowers and drink the local blood but obviously need some further assistance, of which they are not consciously aware, in order to be getting by there. Whatever the trick is, it is presumably unknown to the Saturnians, who do not appear to have made any provision aboard their pioneering spacecraft for the care and feeding of captive specimens, but will surely know better once they have had a chance to study squishy-but-solid beings of various kinds at their leisure, and have cultivated a certain expertise in alien husbandry.

Perhaps these hypotheses are not really alternatives in the sense that they are mutually exclusive. Indeed, there is a certain attractiveness in the possibility of running them together, and suggesting that the kinds of atmospheric nutrition that the Saturnians and Venusians routinely practice are not as similar to our processes of nutrition as we might readily assume, but involve a more subtle alchemy of the flesh more akin to that implied by such concepts as "spontaneous generation" or serial mutation. After all, the nature of the Fiery Wheel, the feeding habits of the Venusians and the puzzling ecology of Mercury all suggest that matter in general is more mutable than it seems to be within the limited range of human terrestrial experience. Perhaps we are the odd ones out in the solar system's family—and perhaps, in that case, the peculiarly crude relationship that our bodies enjoy with their sparklike passengers is, if not an exception to a more general rule, at least only one kind of liaison within a complex spectrum. Perhaps the secret of disincarnation and reincarnation that Ahmed Bey and his Brahmin predecessors were so churlishly intent on keeping to themselves is only the starting point of an entire new theoretical and practical science, a mere finger-exercise in a potential orchestration of manipulations of the mind-matter relationship that would *really* boggle the mind, instead of just giving it a little tickle.

All that is, of course, pure speculation, which goes far beyond the teasing hints casually thrown out by *La Roue fulgurante*, almost certainly by accident—but that is, after all, the real point of *La Roue fulgurante*, and of speculative fiction in general.

Brian Stableford

Ill. ??, Ferenczi, 1929

Ill. P. Santini, Tallandier, 1938

Ill. René Brantonne, Jaeger d'Hauteville, 1954

Ill. Moebius, J.-C. Lattès, 1973

SF & FANTASY

Alphonse Allais. *The Adventures of Captain Cap*
Henri Allorge. *The Great Cataclysm*
Guy d'Armen. *Doc Ardan: The City of Gold and Lepers*
G.-J. Arnaud. *The Ice Company*
Charles Asselineau. *The Double Life*
Cyprien Bérard. *The Vampire Lord Ruthwen*
Aloysius Bertrand. *Gaspard de la Nuit*
Richard Bessière. *The Gardens of the Apocalypse*
Albert Bleunard. *Ever Smaller*
Félix Bodin. *The Novel of the Future*
Louis Boussenard. *Monsieur Synthesis*
Alphonse Brown. *City of Glass; The Conquest of the Air*
Emile Calvet. *In a Thousand Years*
André Caroff. *The Terror of Madame Atomos; Miss Atomos; The Return of Madame Atomos; The Mistake of Madame Atomos; The Monsters of Madame Atomos; The Revenge of Madame Atomos; The Resurrection of Madame Atomos*
Félicien Champsaur. *The Human Arrow; Ouha, King of the Apes; Pharaoh's Wife*
Didier de Chousy. *Ignis*
Jules Clarétie. *Obsession*
Michel Corday. *The Eternal Flame*
Captain Danrit. *Undersea Odyssey*
C. I. Defontenay. *Star (Psi Cassiopeia)*
Charles Derennes. *The People of the Pole*
Georges Dodds (anthologist). *The Missing Link*
Harry Dickson. *The Heir of Dracula*
Jules Dornay. *Lord Ruthven Begins*
Alfred Driou. *The Adventures of a Parisian Aeronaut*
Sâr Dubnotal *vs. Jack the Ripper*
Alexandre Dumas. *The Return of Lord Ruthven*
Renée Dunan. *Baal*
J.-C. Dunyach. *The Night Orchid; The Thieves of Silence*
Henri Duvernois. *The Man Who Found Himself*
Achille Eyraud. *Voyage to Venus*
Henri Falk. *The Age of Lead*
Paul Féval. *Anne of the Isles; Knightshade; Revenants; Vampire City; The Vampire Countess; The Wandering Jew's Daughter*
Paul Féval, *fils. Felifax, the Tiger-Man*

C. Nodier, A. Beraud & Toussaint-Merle. *Frankenstein*
Henri de Parville. *An Inhabitant of the Planet Mars*
Gaston de Pawlowski. *Journey to the Land of the 4th Dimension*
Georges Pellerin. *The World in 2000 Years*
Ernest Pérochon. *The Frenetic People*
Pierre Pelot. *The Child Who Walked on the Sky*
J. Polidori, C. Nodier, E. Scribe. *Lord Ruthven the Vampire*
P.-A. Ponson du Terrail. *The Vampire and the Devil's Son; The Immortal Woman*
Edgar Quinet. *Ahasuerus*
Henri de Régnier. *A Surfeit of Mirrors*
Maurice Renard. *The Blue Peril; Doctor Lerne; The Doctored Man; A Man Among the Microbes; The Master of Light*
Jean Richepin. *The Wing; The Crazy Corner*
Albert Robida. *The Adventures of Saturnin Farandoul; The Clock of the Centuries; Chalet in the Sky; The Electric Life*
J.-H. Rosny Aîné. *Helgvor of the Blue River; The Givreuse Enigma; The Mysterious Force; The Navigators of Space; Vamireh; The World of the Variants; The Young Vampire*
Marcel Rouff. *Journey to the Inverted World*
Han Ryner. *The Superhumans*
Brian Stableford. *The New Faust at the Tragicomique;The Empire of the Necromancers (The Shadow of Frankenstein; Frankenstein and the Vampire Countess; Frankenstein in London); Sherlock Holmes & The Vampires of Eternity; The Stones of Camelot; The Wayward Muse.* (anthologist) *The Germans on Venus; News from the Moon; The Supreme Progress; The World Above the World; Nemoville; Investigations of the Future*
Jacques Spitz. *The Eye of Purgatory*
Kurt Steiner. *Ortog*
Eugène Thébault. *Radio-Terror*
C.-F. Tiphaigne de La Roche. *Amilec*
Théo Varlet. *The Golden Rock. The Xenobiotic Invasion; The Castaways of Eros; Timeslip Troopers* (w/André Blandin); *The Martian Epic* (w/Octave Joncquel)
Paul Vibert. *The Mysterious Fluid*
Villiers de l'Isle-Adam. *The Scaffold; The Vampire Soul*
Philippe Ward. *Artahe*
Philippe Ward & Sylvie Miller. *The Song of Montségur*

MYSTERIES & THRILLERS

M. Allain & P. Souvestre. *The Daughter of Fantômas*

A. Anicet-Bourgeois, Lucien Dabril. *Rocambole*

A. Bernède. *Belphegor*; *Judex* (w/Louis Feuillade); *The Return of Judex* (w/Louis Feuillade); *The Shadow of Judex*

A. Bisson & G. Livet. *Nick Carter vs. Fantômas*

V. Darlay & H. de Gorsse. *Arsène Lupin vs. Sherlock Holmes: The Stage Play*

Séamas Duffy. *Sherlock Holmes in Paris*

Paul Féval. *Gentlemen of the Night; John Devil; The Black Coats ('Salem Street; The Invisible Weapon; The Parisian Jungle; The Companions of the Treasure; Heart of Steel; The Cadet Gang; The Sword-Swallower)*

Emile Gaboriau. *Monsieur Lecoq*

Goron & Emile Gautier. *Spawn of the Penitentiary*

Rick Lai. *Shadows of the Opera: Retribution in Blood; Sisters of the Shadows: The Curse of Cagliostro*

Steve Leadley. *Sherlock Holmes: The Circle of Blood*

Maurice Leblanc. *Arsène Lupin vs. Countess Cagliostro; Arsène Lupin vs. Sherlock Holmes (The Blonde Phantom; The Hollow Needle); The Many Faces of Arsène Lupin*

Gaston Leroux. *Chéri-Bibi; The Phantom of the Opera; Rouletabille & the Mystery of the Yellow Room; Rouletabille at Krupp's*

Richard Marsh. *The Complete Adventures of Judith Lee*

William Patrick Maynard. *The Terror of Fu Manchu; The Destiny of Fu Manchu*

Frank J. Morlock. *Sherlock Holmes: The Grand Horizontals; Sherlock Holmes vs Jack the Ripper*

Antonin Reschal. *The Adventures of Miss Boston*

P. de Wattyne & Y. Walter. *Sherlock Holmes vs. Fantômas*

David White. *Fantômas in America*

Pierre Yrondy. *The Adventures of Thérèse Arnaud*

SCREENPLAYS

Mike Baron. *The Iron Triangle*

Emma Bull & Will Shetterly. *Nightspeeder; War for the Oaks*

Gerry Conway & Roy Thomas. *Doc Dynamo*

Steve Englehart. *Majorca*

James Hudnall. *The Devastator*

Jean-Marc & Randy Lofficier. *Royal Flush*
J.-M. & R. Lofficier & Marc Agapit. *Despair*
J.-M. & R. Lofficier & Joël Houssin. *City*
Andrew Paquette. *Peripheral Vision*
Robert L. Robinson, Jr. *Judex*
R. Thomas, J. Hendler & L. Sprague de Camp. *Rivers of Time*

NON-FICTION

Stephen R. Bissette. *Blur 1-5. Green Mountain Cinema 1; Teen Angels*
Win Scott Eckert. *Crossovers* (2 vols.)
Jean-Marc & Randy Lofficier. *Shadowmen* (2 vols.)
Randy Lofficier. *Over Here*

ART BOOKS

J.-M. Lofficier & D. Taylor. *Tongue*Lash*
Jean-Pierre Normand. *Science Fiction Illustrations*
Raven Okeefe. *Raven's L'il Critters; Rave's Faves*
Randy Lofficier & Raven Okeefe. *If Your Possum Go Daylight...*
Daniele Serra. *Illusions*

HEXAGON COMICS

Franco Frescura & Luciano Bernasconi. *Wampus*
Franco Frescura & Giorgio Trevisan. *CLASH*
L. Bernasconi, J.-M. Lofficier & Juan Roncagliolo Berger. *Phenix*
Claude Legrand, J.-M. Lofficier & L. Bernasconi. *Kabur*
Franco Oneta. *Zembla*
L. Buffolente, Lofficier & J.-J. Dzialowski. *Strangers: Homicron*
Danilo Grossi. *Strangers: Jaydee*
Claude Legrand & Luciano Bernasconi. *Strangers: Starlock*